6.00

TO BLOODY SAMAR

in the Philippines they sent Captain Morrow after the Spanish-American War. They picked him because he was mature, courageous, humane. And because there was serious trouble on that dangerous and savagely beautiful island.

Morrow went there to put down warring guerrillas, but he also went to help the Filipinos stand on their own feet—to prove that the Americans were different from the Spaniards whom they had defeated. There were long and hazardous patrols by Morrow's command into the mountains; but there was also the hatred and suspicion of the native population to overcome. Both the fights, Morrow knew, would take patience and faith; and courage.

There on Samar Morrow met Lucy Leslie, the young schoolteacher, who had made the perilous journey to help the Filipino children. There, too, he met young Lieutenant Palmer, in love with Lucy but a man with a secret. These three play out a private drama set excitingly in the midst of insurrection and murder.

The searing heat of the jungle, the strength of brave men and women, the birth of a great idea, are all caught in this sweeping and compelling story.

This is an original novel—not a reprint—published by BALLANTINE BOOKS, INC. A hardbound edition of this book, priced at $2.00, is available at your local bookstore.

THE FAR COMMAND

BY

ELINOR
CHAMBERLAIN

BALLANTINE BOOKS—NEW YORK

A condensed version of this novel was published
in *The Star Weekly*, Toronto, Canada, January
12, 1952, under the title *The Bamboo Plow*.

COPYRIGHT, 1952 AND 1953, BY
ELINOR CHAMBERLAIN
LIBRARY OF CONGRESS CATALOG CARD NO. 53-9111
PRINTED IN THE UNITED STATES OF AMERICA

BALLANTINE BOOKS
404 Fifth Avenue · New York 18, N. Y.

THE FAR
COMMAND

PART ONE

1

THE Dos Picos massacre, destined to take Morrow from Manila to "Bloody" Samar Island, occurred in May of 1902 near the coastal town of Magtalisay. In the Philippines at that time such an event was almost commonplace. The Treaty of Paris had ended the war in 1898, but worse fighting had followed under the name of insurrection; and now that the insurrection was officially over, battles and skirmishes went on under the name of pacification. Men were still killed as in war, and war's cold acceptance of violent death still numbed men's hearts. More compassionate than most, Morrow heard the story with pity, but he heard it casually. It was one of many. And he had no reason, when the story first reached his ears, to think it might ever have any special meaning for him.

To Harry Palmer, Inspector Second Class, and to Justin Lloyd, Inspector Third Class, Philippine Constabulary, both with the courtesy title of lieutenant, the massacre was at once a matter of significance. Their commanding officer was one of the victims. When a man brought them the terrible news, less than a day after the ambush had done its work, the first shock and the first new responsibility were theirs. They set out at once to recover the bodies. Accompanied by six Filipinos who were Constabulary soldiers, and guided by the ragged and wary man of the mountain forest who had brought the information, they

1

went up the Sumpitan River in a large dugout and landed at the point nearest Dos Picos mountain.

Very likely the route their guide chose was the one followed by the party that had walked into the ambush. It was a path that had been roughly cleared to the river within recent weeks for hauling down a banca, a dugout like their own, from the place where it had once stood as a giant tree. In spite of the jungle's swift new growth, the opening remained less forbidding than the rest of the river wall; it seemed to invite ascent.

It was not, however, an easy climb. It was steep, even precipitous in places, and rocky. As always in these mountain forests, everything was wet. Clambering, clinging, slipping, the men clutched at roots and vines. Though the height of the first rise was not more than six or seven hundred feet, it seemed like six or seven thousand to them before they reached a shelf of level ground where they could rest.

It was already the middle of the afternoon, the hottest part of the day, and wherever their gray Constabulary uniforms could be seen through the plastering of mud that had just been acquired, they were dark with sweat. The two American officers sat in silence near the edge of the drop, letting heart and lungs recover normal rhythm. The six soldados, less tired, squatted near, uneasily silent, their brown faces immobile, their eyes restless. Their scarlet blanket rolls were brilliant and startling against the varied but monotonous greens of the jungle. The guide had started up the next ascent; he waited, looking back, obedient but with impatience in every line of his body.

Palmer stood up. "Well, let's get going."

The montesino was off at once, with officers and soldiers hurrying to keep up. But the going was somewhat easier and they could move faster without much difficulty. The soldados murmured to each other, with wary eyes on the thick foliage on either side, but Palmer and Lloyd watched only the guide and the track, with more thought of what was waiting for them ahead than for what might be lurking near. Once the guide stopped and pointed, and they looked out and up through an opening in the jungle to see

2

their destination, the saddle between the double summits of Dos Picos.

It took an hour more for them to reach it. They rounded a slight curve and knew they were there, and saw that their foreknowledge, their preparation, had not and could not have diminished the shock of that scene.

Here the giant tree had been felled, killing many smaller trees in its own death and making its own clearing. Here it had been shaped and hollowed into a boat; the chips still lay about in bright heaps, not yet changed or hidden by weather and jungle growth. At the far end of the open space stood the stump, a dozen feet high, perhaps six feet through, buttressed by enormous, wide-spreading flanges. Between two of these buttresses, facing Palmer and Lloyd, drawing their attention not only by its own horror but also by its position at center stage in this unnatural theater, hung, head down, the crucified body of a man. Palmer and Lloyd saw the red hair and knew it was their captain, Inspector Pearson.

Without a pause, without a word, Palmer walked toward the stump. Lloyd, who had been momentarily stopped in his tracks and whose legs were shorter, had to run to catch up. He muttered and swore as he moved. "By God, we'll get the devils! Murdering, filthy apes!" The Filipinos now hung back.

When Palmer and Lloyd reached the stump, they could see the body of Horton, the schoolteacher, and beyond him lay the body of John Boult. Horton had been a friend. Boult, a traveler and wild-game hunter, who had arrived wholly by chance in their town of Magtalisay, had been merely a new acquaintance. But he, too, was an American. They felt the same sense of outrage for him as for the others.

Rain, sun, insects, some bird or beast, had already begun the work of returning the bodies to the elements of which they had been formed, and part of the story of their death was undecipherable. But enough of the story remained. Pearson's abdomen had been ripped open with a bolo so that his intestines hung down in his face. Horton had

3

been spread-eagled on the ground and tied there by a score of rattan lines binding him to bamboo pegs driven into the earth. It seemed certain that his face had been smeared with something sweet to attract ants, and it seemed likely that he had lived like this for some time. As for Boult, evidence indicated that he might have been killed quickly, in the early moments of the attack, and that the mutilations had come after death. One detail, in fact no worse than the others, yet had an effect of peculiar and haunting ghastliness. His eyes had been removed and two stones had been placed in the sockets.

Lloyd began to swear again.

"Save that for later," Palmer said curtly. "No time for it. Got to get them down to the river before dark. Got to find Johnstone, too."

"Yes, what about Johnstone? Think he was captured? Where's that *montesino*?"

But when they looked around for the guide, he had vanished. They glanced at each other with no need to speak their thoughts. The fellow had not been paid. Why had he disappeared? Had they followed him into another ambush?

Palmer shrugged and turned to the waiting soldados, ordering them with gestures and in broken words of their dialect to get the bodies of Horton and Boult ready for carrying. With Lloyd's help, he himself cut down the captain. Then the two of them got their backs to the stump and stood on guard, watching the green wall that encircled the clearing.

The air was heavy and very still. No insects sang. Two of the men had gone for bamboo carrying-poles, and now, unexpectedly, the sharp, noisy hacking of their bolos could be heard. Palmer's revolver was drawn before he understood the sound. But no real alarm came. The work went on. The two men returned with strong lengths of bamboo. Palmer, relaxing slightly, noticed that the men kept glancing at something on the stump above his head. He craned his neck, but could see nothing.

One of the soldados volunteered an explanation. "*La señal, teniente. La señal del papa Faustino.*"

4

Palmer scowled at him. They were obsessed by that name. Pope Faustino! An outlaw calling himself a pope, scaring them out of what wits they had! By stepping away from the stump, he could see a rectangle from which the bark had been removed directly over the spot where Pearson had been crucified. There was a crude carving in the yellow wood, of a hand, perhaps, or a claw, with four sharp, curving talons. Pope Faustino's mark! And these fools of Constabulary soldiers looked at it with more fear than they had shown at the sight of the men massacred there, as if the mark of el papa made the scene more terrifying than his deed.

A sudden wind fell on the clearing with a roar, ceased, and then returned, bringing the still louder rain. For a few seconds the sun continued to shine on them oppressively, and then there was nothing about them but the cold gray downpour. Since the jungle was hostile, they stayed in the open, the men proceeding with their task as well as they could. When the heaviest part of the shower had passed, they were ready to descend the mountain.

It was the soldados who heard the cry for help and found Johnstone not far from the track. He shook violently with the chill of a malaria attack, but managed to tell them that he had fallen with a sprained ankle before his companions walked into the trap. He had been hiding in fear and pain ever since. "G-g-g-get me home!" he begged. No; he had seen nothing, nothing. "G-g-get me home!"

Daylight had nearly ended by the time they reached the river, and they still had to make a raft for the bodies. Before they were done, night was about them, and they finished the task in the wavering flare of torchlight. But they were not attacked.

At last they began their swift passage downstream. The torches accompanied them, the burning knots of resin, reflected in the black water, marking the two forward corners of the raft as it glided behind the dugout. They moved at first in the silence proper to a funeral procession, hearing only the gurgling of the current in an occasional eddy at the side of the river, but as Johnstone passed into the fever stage of his illness his delirious voice, rising now and then to a hoarse scream, provided an eerie accompaniment to their journey.

2

TWO months after the Dos Picos ambush, about one month after Morrow had heard the story and had half forgotten it, he was called to the office of the Executive in Manila. It was a suffocating day, with the clouds that would end the dry season blackening the sky in promise, but not yet cooling the air. As he crossed the street to enter the Ayuntamiento, the first drops of rain fell in what seemed a futile effort, each one raising a small puff of dust in which it was then lost. But suddenly a gust of shrieking wind lifted a cloud of dirt and whirled it away. Morrow ran for the doorway and reached it just in time. A gray, roaring wall of water advanced down the street. At once the wonderful smell of damp earth rose from the ground and it was cool and a man could breathe again.

Inside the office, the Executive, rising to shake Morrow's hand and then ponderously lowering himself again into his chair, had to deepen his voice to outmatch the noise of the rain. "I'll make it short," he said. "I'm a busy man, but if you agree to do what I hope you will, you're going to be even busier." He sensed Morrow's indifference and asked, making it sound like a challenge, "Know the island of Samar?"

"I've never been there."

"On the west coast there's a town called Magtalisay. On San Pedro Bay, opposite Tacloban. Know Tacloban?"

"I was there once for a few hours. I can't say I know it."

"Samar must be about the only one of the islands you haven't visited. You see, I've been making inquiries. However, whether or not you know Samar, you must've heard

6

what happened there in April. Constabulary captain named Pearson was killed; sounded at first like an accident. But the details have been coming in, at last. Pearson fell into a trap. Outlaws. It's an ugly story."

"I heard about it in Cebu, sir. Same sort of thing happened there."

"This affair's worse, Morrow." He lifted a handful of papers. "I'm going to give you these to read in a minute. Correspondence about the affair. But think of it first. See it. Samar's nothing but mountains. Wonderful spot for outlaws. Different hiding place for every day of the year. Like some of the other outlaw bands—you're right, there's a similarity to what's been going on in Cebu, and Albay, Cavite, Oriental Negros—this one has a sort of religious leader. Pope Faustino, he calls himself. He and his *pulajanes* made a specially devilish job of killing Pearson—it's all in these letters. But I see you're still thinking you've heard all this before, and what has it got to do with you."

"Yes, sir. I am."

"I'm getting there. Pearson's second in command stepped into his shoes. Young fellow named Palmer. Maybe if the District Inspector had known it was ambush and not accident, that would not have happened. Maybe young Palmer handled his report so he'd get a chance to run things. I don't know. Looks like it. Can't condemn him too much. Ambition, courage, that sort of thing. Dare-devils anyhow, a lot of 'em. They have to be. Anyhow, he set out to capture Faustino and a lot of glory. And he's learned it's a lot easier to get a fishhook in than it is to get it out. On his first expedition into the mountains after the so-called pope, his guides deserted him and his party was lost for two days. On his second trip his soldados, the total enlisted men in his Constabulary company, deserted. Now, I don't need to tell you how serious that is, do I?"

He waited until Morrow nodded, and then went on. "So here are Palmer's reports, along with a request for some American soldiers to clean things up. And a letter from the mayor of Magtalisay begging us not to send the Army back there. Take them. Read them. Then I'll finish

7

what I have to say." He held the papers out to Morrow. "The mayor's letter is in Spanish, but I'm told you read and speak Spanish as well as you do English. Go over these carefully. All the time you want." His shrewd eyes watched Morrow closely as he read.

Unaware of, or indifferent to this scrutiny, Morrow went through the papers swiftly. Short and firmly built, with a square face, deeply lined and leathery, he looked chunky as he sat there, even heavy, without the power that his body showed in motion. He was, the Executive judged, in his middle thirties. With his eyes turned down, his face was stolid; it gave nothing away. His mouth was controlled and secret. But when his eyes were seen, they lent force and expression to the other features, and his face showed then a restless energy and some feeling the Executive tried to name but could not. Neither sadness nor bitterness, though it seemed to hold some relationship to both.

Having finished the others, Morrow read once through the letter from the presidente, the mayor, of Magtalisay, looked out the window at the gray curtain of rain, and then read that letter through again. That done, he returned all the papers to the desk.

"Well, Morrow?" the Executive asked eagerly. "You must've guessed what we want. Will you go?"

"No." He paused as if that was all, but as the Executive shifted in his chair, getting ready to argue or persuade, he went on. "I'm a photographer, sir. My rank as captain in the Army meant nothing. I've never commanded men. Possibly you don't know that during the war I got into difficulties with General Otis and narrowly missed a court-martial, or whatever it is that happens. And if all this wasn't reason enough, earlier this week—"

The Executive interrupted. "Sit down again, Morrow. You seem to think we're through talking, but I don't agree. All right, go ahead. Earlier this week?"

"I booked passage to Saigon. I've been in the Philippines too long. Nine or ten years. I'm leaving. I'm going to photograph the ruins at Angkor Thom and Angkor Wat in Cambodia. The only work ever done there has

8

been done by Frenchmen, and there's never been a photographer of any kind near the place. That, sir, is the sort of work I'm fit for. And there must be a hundred men within a mile of this building who could do a good job in Magtalisay."

The Executive leaned forward with a smile. It seemed to him that Morrow was trying to convince himself more than the Executive that he was the wrong man to go to Samar. "Morrow," he said, "I'm going to take the liberty of contradicting you a few times. Your Army life has nothing to do with this. This is the Constabulary. A horse of a different color. What if you haven't commanded Americans? Constabulary privates are Filipinos. Filipinos, I might remind you, from the very district they're policing, which is something that has never been done before in the history of the world in pacifying a native people. The British may have native police in India, but they take them from the north to police the south, and vice versa. I tell you it is of the greatest importance for all the future relations between Americans and Filipinos that Filipinos should suppress Filipino disturbances and arrest Filipino outlaws.

"Now, where was I? I get talking about the importance of teaching these people to police themselves and I forget everything else. It's a great thing, Morrow. It's a basic principle of democracy. The world is watching us, you know. Germany, Holland, Great Britain, Russia. Getting ready to laugh and pick up the pieces when we fail. They call us idealistic fools.

"But to get back to you. Between the two of us, disagreement with Otis is no disgrace. And Saigon— Cancel your passage. Time enough for that later.

"Now I'll tell you something else, Morrow. In Washington I looked over some of the war photos you took out here." He glanced up at the grinning portrait of Theodore Roosevelt on the wall. "With the President. His collection of photos. He said he knew you. Said you were a boy trying to be a Wild West cowpuncher in the Dakota Territory when he started his Elkhorn ranch. Well, he doesn't

9

know about this affair. But if he did, he'd say— Do I
need to tell you what he'd say?

"Morrow, your objections aren't worth all my argu-
ments. You know how the natives make things out of
bamboo. They use it for everything. They make houses
of bamboo. Dishes. Ribbon. They pull things on bamboo
sleds, they scratch their backs with bamboo claws, they
probably make clothes out of bamboo. By God, as if the
wooden plows they use aren't bad enough, in some places
they probably break the ground with a bamboo plow.
They use the material they can lay their hands on to do
the work that has to be done. We have to do the same
thing with men.

"So don't tell me you're not the ideal man for the job.
I think you're the best there is available. That's enough
for me." He leaned back in his chair. "Well?"

There was a long silence, which Morrow broke at last.
"What chance is there of arming the Constabulary with
something better than those twelve-gauge Remington
shotguns I've seen them using?" His eyes were now as
shrewd as the Executive's. "Don't misunderstand me. I'm
not making that a condition. I'll go. But some of the outlaws are armed with Krags, and the shotguns are no match.
Nor a single-shot rifle, either. But I've been told there
are some Springfield repeaters coming in."

The Executive had been ready for a longer argument.
He stared for a bewildered moment. Then he smiled.
"This is the time to ask for what you want. Once you're
down in Samar, you'll have a harder time making your
voice heard up here. You'll go?"

"I'll go."

"I'll notify them over at the commissary that you're to
have anything you ask for if they can get it. And they're
to damn well try."

"I want extra ammunition for target practice. Full uniforms for all the men. Musical instruments—"

"Anything you ask for, if they can get it. But what about
yourself? You haven't asked about your rank or your pay.
You'll be Inspector First Class, equivalent to captain. I'd
like to do better for you, but that's the top rank for com-

manding a company. I'm afraid the pay's not very good, but—"

Morrow looked annoyed. "When I said I'd go, I accepted the rank and pay. What matters is the men's equipment and their health. I've seen them on other islands. Their spirit—"

The Executive stopped him. "Take all that up with the commissary. But to go back to your rank. You're to be boss down there. Those desertions worry me. It's the worst we've had of that sort of thing. I want to know why it happened and I want to know it won't happen again. So you have full authority to do whatever has to be done. Maybe Magtalisay does need the Army. And anything you recommend about Palmer and Lloyd will be followed through.

"You know, Morrow, this is a frontier, and on any frontier you get the best and the worst. The men who leave home are either men with vision, with ideals, with big hearts and minds, or they're riff-raff, anything from a drifter to a criminal. Human nature being what it is, we're judged by the worst of us. And the only thing for us to do is to spot the bad ones and get rid of them. I'm not saying that's what you're going to find, you understand. I'm saying that whatever you find, it's up to you. We want the Constabulary in Magtalisay put on a solid footing. Is it all clear?"

"As clear as it will be until I get to Samar." Morrow got up, ready to go.

"Wait. I'd like to ask you a question. You read the letter from the presidente of Magtalisay twice. What did you think of it?"

"Two things. There's what meets the eye, sir. You know what I mean, the hope for peace, the reference to Lincoln, the fear of the trouble if the Army has to be called in. His appeal made me agree to go."

"His appeal moved you more than mine did?"

"To be frank, it did. But there's another side to it. The presidente may be hand-in-glove with the *pulajanes* himself. It wouldn't be the first time the mayor and the out-

11

laws squeezed the people between them. That might be the reason he doesn't want the Army called in."

"Inspector Morrow, you have not disappointed me." He stood up and shook Morrow's hand. "Good-bye and good luck." He was still watching the swinging door through which Morrow had left when his clerk ushered in the next man on his calendar.

"Wasn't that Morrow?" this visitor asked. "I haven't heard anything of him for a couple of years."

"He's been down in Mindanao and now he's just promised to go to Samar."

"Bloody Samar? He must be crazy. I heard that one of those outlaws down there with a price on his head sent in a pig's head and asked for the reward. I don't understand what that meant, but it sort of got under my skin."

"Morrow's a funny fellow. Never asked for a thing for himself. Doesn't talk much. I got the idea he's not used to conversation."

"That's true. He shies away from what we call society out here. What's he going to do in Samar?"

"Clean up some trouble in a spot where we can't afford to make a mistake. Maybe you heard that story about him down in Mindanao earlier this year. He persuaded some particularly wild and dangerous fellows to come in and surrender their arms. They were promised they could return at once to their homes. Instead, some damned bonehead clapped them into jail."

"I know. Morrow let them out."

"Of course. Nobody can prove he did it. Fortunately, or some other bonehead might try to put him in jail for saving the good name of the United States Government. No, I don't think we've made a mistake in sending him down there. I hope he hasn't made a mistake in going."

3

ON the deck of the small steamship, *Nuestra Señora de Esperanza*, Morrow looked over the port rail at the island of Samar. As the *Esperanza* passed through the narrow strait between Samar and Leyte, the mangroves edging the muddy shore seemed almost within reach of an outstretched hand. Slow mile after slow mile slipped by. Islets, sandbars, and confluent streams repeated themselves with variations so slight that there was nothing to mark the *Esperanza's* progress, and her regular chuffing, the steady throb of the turning propeller, only emphasized the monotony.

When she neared the southern end of the strait, all the territory Morrow could see he knew would be his. He looked beyond the mangroves to the green slopes of the mountains, so velvet-smooth to the eye with their rock covered by foliage, and wondered how soon, how well he would know these peaks. The strait widened and a small stream flowed into it, briefly permitting a glance through a channel in the mangrove swamp. Would that brown thatch on a hut almost concealed in a small plantation of coconut palms ever give him shelter? And the men in that parao below him in the strait, would their lives ever touch his more closely? Sail furled, outrigger stretched like spider legs over the water, the small boat waited for the *Esperanza* to pass, and the men in it looking up were as silent and secret as the island behind them.

Unexpected emotion filled him, excitement, eagerness, apprehension, in a confusing mixture. He gripped the rail tensely. Would he never grow too old for that childish feeling that he was on the edge of something tremendous, that he was coming face to face with Opportunity, vague but glorious? His father's voice, unheard for many years, still had the power to reach him with his question: "What are you here for? There's a riddle for you to spend your life on!" The savage and contemptuous tone turned the question, profound but ordinary, into a prediction of unending failure.

Morrow's grip tightened on the rail until he was conscious of the strain. He forced himself to relax then, and turned to walk aft. Excitement and eagerness were not for him. He'd do the best he could, with no emotional decorations. As for apprehension, any fool would know that was justified; there was no disguising the danger of climate, terrain, and outlaws. It was plain, everyday danger, with nothing secret in its menace. What worried him more, he admitted frankly to himself, was the problem the two lieutenants might present. What would alarm him still further would be a large colony of Americans, trying to snare him in their social affairs. But he understood there were no other Americans in Magtalisay.

He came to a halt at the imaginary line on the deck where the third-class passengers who traveled under an awning were separated from the passengers who traveled first class in the Esperanza's filthy cabins. Standing there, he quickly spotted the three non-commissioned officers he had brought with him to train the company he hoped to recruit. About a dozen yards away Sergeant Ramos and Corporals Fermín and Saavedra, in their gray Constabulary uniforms, squatted in the center of a circle of other Filipinos. Ramos was talking.

He would be talking, Morrow thought. In the ten years he had known him, Ramos had talked as often as there were listeners available. And there were usually listeners as willing as those now around him. Even that rather sedate Filipino, a little apart from the others, sitting on a coil of rope, not squatting like the rest, was attentive. Morrow strained his ears, caught a few words, and shrugged. Ramos was recounting the endless and fabulous history of the fighting cock he claimed had once been his. This rooster's achievements in the cockpit had been extraordinary, but his amatory accomplishments were yet more in defiance of natural law, and the descriptions of his monstrous offspring, though never illogical, always brought

14

that look of incredulous and delighted surprise to the listeners' faces.

With satisfaction, Morrow turned away from the racy, indecent flow of dialect. Ramos' inventions would make friends for him in any country of the world; and for this almost as much as for his personal loyalty and other qualities, he had been selected to come to Samar. Like the band instruments in the steamer's hold, the baseball bats, the uniforms complete to American shoes, the bags of rice that would feed the new recruits and were an innovation in Constabulary practice, Ramos' tongue had its part in Morrow's plans.

The strait had changed, and the *Esperanza* was now passing a cleared though muddy shore from which three rickety bamboo docks projected over the shallow water. Beyond them appeared the nipa huts of a small village, surrounded by a straggling palm grove and a few rice paddies. Two naked children on one of the docks were watching the *Esperanza*. Their slowly turning heads were the only moving part of them, while beside them a thin dog scratched himself lazily, yawned, scratched again, and collapsed like an empty skin. Nothing else stirred, and the heat and torpor exhaled by the barrio spread across the water to the boat. Morrow pulled out his handkerchief and wiped his face.

Again the shoreline changed, climbing to a white limestone precipice hung with green vines. The *Esperanza* rounded this cliff and was out of the strait and in a shallow bay. Feeling her way with constant soundings, she crept eastward over the brown water, which rose and fell sluggishly in an oily swell. At last, near a labyrinth of bamboo fishtraps, like fencing surrounding crazy fields of water, she dropped her anchor to the muddy bottom.

She lay more than a mile from shore, and already, in answer to her whistle, a small fleet of boats had begun to come out to her. In a few minutes the quiet of the voyage would end in shrill and clamorous bargaining, with cascos bumping hollowly against her sides, waiting to be loaded with goods, and bancas, carrying produce for sale, circling hopefully about.

Morrow remembered then that there was another first-class passenger for Magtalisay, a schoolteacher who had been kept in her cabin by seasickness ever since they sailed from Manila. He felt a sudden responsibility and also a little shame for having been glad that she had been safely confined; though he hadn't seen her, he was sure that her absence pleased him more than her presence could have done. In compunction, he went to her cabin and knocked.

"This is Magtalisay," he said through the closed door. "You've got about half an hour to get ready to go ashore. I'll see that a good banca is ready for you. If you need anything else, let me know." He got a murmur of thanks in reply and promptly forgot her again.

Before she had appeared, he rode ashore on a casco carrying Constabulary supplies. The day had turned dark and more oppressive, with a solid overcast of clouds suddenly covering the western sky and smothering the light of the afternoon sun but not the heat. The casco, propelled first by a great oar at the stern and then by poles, crawled almost imperceptibly toward the headland, around it, into the estuary, and at last in sight of the town. The first houses, standing unevenly on poles, seemed to stagger out across the water. Behind them the heads of palms separated into fronds, waving and clashing in a breeze that had not yet touched the heavy air in which the casco crept; yet even through this stillness spread the smell of dead fish, rotting seaweed, the salt mud flats, and human filth.

"The perfumed East," Morrow said aloud to himself in English, and was surprised at the glance drawn by his words from the only other passenger on the casco. Morrow stared at the other's face, which was partly turned away again. The man was the solitary Filipino he had noticed earlier, listening to Ramos; a man in the common dress of transparent camisa hanging outside his trousers, but not a common man; a young man with a face strongly lined. He showed no further interest in anything but their destination.

Magtalisay looked much like other towns Morrow knew. On rising ground, beyond the shacks built over mud and water, were nipa palm houses of slightly larger size and

16

better construction. Still farther away the ground swelled higher into a considerable hill, dominating the town and in turn dominated by a much steeper and loftier height. Halfway between shore and hill the upper part of a church façade, gray and austere, rose through the green of trees.

Along the estuary beach, decay and neglect were plain. Four piers extended over the stinking ooze and out into the deeper water, three leading from warehouses and all in a state of dilapidation that told Magtalisay's poverty. Morrow climbed from the lighter to the dangerously sagging boards on which the Constabulary's boxes and bundles and sacks were being unloaded, and surveyed the work going on.

Ramos stood near the shore, directing newly hired cargadores who were already moving the supplies into the town. These cargadores were ill-fed, ragged men who did not look capable of much labor, but under Ramos' orders, with his briskness and humor to inspirit them and with the promise of good pay to renew strength in their arms and legs, they were happily setting to work. Loads on backs or on carrying poles, they made a staggering line through the clusters of curious children, up a clay bank, and so off out of Morrow's sight.

On one of the other piers there was activity too, and Morrow's interest, alive to everything in this town that was to be his home and his responsibility, turned in that direction. A very tall, thin white woman with white hair was supervising the loading of baled hemp onto a casco. She looked up and caught Morrow's glance, and at the same moment, inaudibly in the general commotion, a plank in the pier near where she stood gave way under a laborer and he saved himself from falling by letting the bale he carried drop into the water.

Morrow cupped his hands around his mouth and shouted, "Can I help?" But of course she could not hear, and he started on the trip down one pier and out the other. He saw now that she had only two cargadores, both feeble old men, to load her hemp. When he had at last picked his way to her along the treacherous structure, he had a definite offer of aid ready. "I'm afraid my sergeant

17

has taken all the best *cargadores*, Señora. Shall I send some over to you? Those two you have are surely going to fall into the water."

He had spoken in Spanish, unable to guess her nationality, but she answered in English with an American accent. There was, however, no American warmth in her voice. "These men were good enough for my husband and they're good enough for me. And they're all I can pay for, in case you'd like to know."

Morrow began an astonished apology. "I beg your pardon. I didn't intend—" He went on in explanation, "It's going to rain soon and of course the sooner your hemp is under cover, the better. It's a shame to let good hemp—" His eyes turned to the bales and his words faltered. For this was not good hemp, and it was not worth shipping. It had been badly stripped and not properly dried; the color was poor, much of the pulp clung to the fibers, and there was already, he noticed now, an odor of fermentation. He looked up and saw she knew what he was thinking. Again he said, "I beg your pardon."

She turned her back on him and gave an order to one of the old men as he tottered under a heavy load.

Not daring to risk another offense to her pride, Morrow walked back to the shore, where the sight of Ramos and the activity around him restored his spirits.

Ramos saluted and gave a brief report. "Señor capitán, the two American *tenientes* are coming. It will rain hard soon, so I have sent the rice first. Next the materials for your camera." He spoke the last words with special care, almost with affection; for as only he and Morrow knew, most of the boxes labeled photographic supplies held extra ammunition and Colt revolvers that Morrow had demanded and obtained beyond the customary equipment. "Fermín and Saavedra have gone to the headquarters."

Morrow nodded and went on to climb the bank and make his first survey of Magtalisay from that higher point. Once there, however, his eyes were distracted from the weed-grown, rutted street by the sight of the solitary Filipino. Though the man walked rapidly, he limped, and

Morrow's memory woke. El Cojo, the Lame One! Morrow could not recall his real name, but now he knew who he was: a Filipino revolutionary, a member of the Katipunán, who had been crippled in the revolt against Spain, who had been exiled, and who was now taking advantage of the amnesty to return to his country. El Cojo, the Filipino patriot. Morrow granted him that title ungrudgingly, with no sarcastic overtone, as not all Americans would have done.

But there was no time for speculation concerning what El Cojo's arrival might mean. Turning onto the road from the direction in which the laden *cargadores* were disappearing, were two Americans in Constabulary uniform. One was on crutches, and of necessity came slowly, but it seemed to Morrow that their pace showed reluctance, that they could have come faster if they had wished. When he saw their faces he was sure of it. There was no welcome for him.

They halted and waited for him to approach, the crutches, perhaps, their excuse. The slighter, fair young man saluted; the other, hanging between his clumsy bamboo supports, did not raise his hand. They waited, too, for Morrow to speak, and though this was good military etiquette, it added to the coolness of the meeting. White men at isolated posts in foreign countries do not usually greet newcomers of their own kind with formality.

Morrow answered the salute and asked, "Which is Palmer? Which is Lloyd?"

The fair young man opened his mouth, looked hesitantly at his companion, and then said, "I'm Lloyd, sir."

Palmer's bad temper ended any further attempt at courtesy. "For God's sake," he said, his voice not loud but ugly, and his eyes never quite meeting Morrow's, "why did they send Constabulary! The Army, that's what we need! The Army! Ten American soldiers could clear out the whole lot of filthy murderers, and then I could take care of the place alone. I cabled to them to send the Army. I cabled three times! All we have to do is stand a dozen of these wild men, any men, any dozen, up against a wall and shoot them. That would teach them a lesson.

19

What the hell do we want with more Constabulary? Those two filthy Filipino non-coms now at our headquarters giving orders—" His crutches trembled and he had to interrupt himself to regain his balance.

Morrow gave him no chance to start speaking again "You've said enough, Palmer. Corporal Saavedra and Corporal Fermín are brave officers with good records earned in Negros and Panay." His voice was mild; his intent was to soothe Palmer as well as to check his abuse of the two Filipinos. "We'll forget what you said and start over again. Lloyd, steady him there."

Palmer was not willing to be soothed. He burst out again, "Brave officers! Monkeys in uniform! Lying, thieving, filthy apes. Chase them up the trees where they belong. Let them swing by their tails! No slobbering native-lover is going to come here and tell me—" His eyes caught Morrow's and he was abruptly silent.

This time Morrow spoke in a different voice. "Lloyd, I told you to steady him there. Now turn him around. Take him back!"

"Yes, sir. Did you say that before, sir? I'm having trouble with my hearing." He hurried to substitute his shoulder for one of Palmer's crutches. "Palmer's a sick man, sir. He shouldn't've come down here. I'll be at headquarters, sir."

"Constabulary office and living quarters under the same roof?" Morrow asked.

"Yes, sir. We use one big room for an office. It's a big bamboo house, sir. You'll have Pearson's room, I suppose, sir." He guided Palmer in an about-face, and looked back and saluted as they started off. Palmer did not raise his eyes again.

20

huts on stilts were closed tight against the rain, with no sign of life about them. The piers, in their state of decay, might have been deserted for years. She was alone on the muddy beach, with the tottering buildings, the gray-green tossing palms, the gray-brown river, and the gray sky.

She told herself that this was no place from which everyone had fled for some mysterious reason, but a town full of people trying to keep dry. She must be practical and get under shelter. The warehouses looked forbidding, but there would be houses in the town. The path up the clay bank had gained some of the unlovely qualities of a waterfall, but it was still unmistakably the way to go. She scrambled up and saw a road ahead of her. It led toward more of those peculiar houses, though these were bigger and their stilts were set in the ground, not in the water.

As she came to each house she scrutinized it, wondering if it might be a place to stop, but many were clearly abandoned and falling down, and the rest were blind and uninviting with their closed shutters. She hurried past.

Then she could see trees up the road, not palms but real trees that had a canopy of real leaves. Her feet squelched faster through the mud until she reached their protection and halted in relief. It was not much more than damp there under the branches, for remarkably little rain dripped through the thick foliage. She closed the umbrella and looked around.

She was in the plaza of Magtalisay, the town's public square. In the center was a fountain choked with stones and weeds. On one side of the square, facing her, was the church, and on the other three sides were substantial two-story buildings, of stone below, with iron grilles over the windows, and of timber above. In this second story the sliding windows, made with many tiny panes of translucent shell, were shut. Through a crack, however, interested eyes had seen her, and steps were already being taken to see that she reached a safe and comfortable place.

She put up her hand to straighten her hat, and when she drew it away discovered her fingers were stained with black dye. Then her hair and her face must be streaked! She pulled off the wretched piece of straw and dropped

23

it on the ground, and commenced scrubbing her face with a handkerchief, with the effect at least of coloring that piece of cloth. A survey of the rest of her clothes revealed that she could not have been wetter if she had fallen into the sea, but she would have been a great deal cleaner. Her shoulders were spotted where her hat had dripped. From the mud that soaked the hem of her skirt the discoloration had spread upward, and her skirt was brown almost to her knees. She suspected, but was too modest to investigate and make sure, that her petticoats were in the same state. The weight of water in their ruffles pulled at her belt, and she tried, with little success, to squeeze them dry.

She thought of the plans she had made for her arrival. Wearing this linen suit, she would step down on the wharf. There would be people waiting. Not for her, since no one was expecting her arrival. But among them would be someone who had known Tom Horton, perhaps the officer in the Constabulary who had sent her the cable about Tom's death. She would say that she was Lucy Leslie, poor Tom's fiancée, and she had come, not to help Tom, as they had arranged, but to take his place. She then would ask to see Tom's grave, and she would spend a little time there. Her suit was white; not deep mourning, but appropriate, since she was not a widow. And then she would have found a suitable boarding house where she could rent a room.

For the first time she realized how absurd these plans would have been even in good weather. A boarding house in Magtalisay! But where was she going to live? What was she going to do? If she had not been in such a hurry to leave Manila before the Bureau of Education discovered that she was acting against their advice, she would at least have made inquiries. And then she wouldn't have felt so alone in the world as she felt now.

But she refused to be frightened, and she looked around again. When it stopped raining, she would knock at the doors of those big houses, one after another. But suppose it got dark before it stopped raining? It was late afternoon and it seemed to be getting dark already. Maybe

24

she should go at once. She couldn't, after all, be any wetter than she was already. But she waited a little longer, and then a little longer, until she felt that if she didn't move at once, she'd be too cold and afraid to move at all.

Lucy's normal step was light and impetuous. She forced herself to an imitation of this natural, eager swiftness, and crossed the rough pavement and the mud to an enormous door. It was a very massive barrier, opening down the center, with iron bands for strength and ornament fastened on it by great nails, and with a smaller door cut in one of the leaves. She knocked and listened and knocked again. The rain drowned the sound. Even when she pounded with her fist it seemed doubtful that anyone inside could hear. She pounded once more.

Behind her she heard a sharp noise like a pistol shot. She whirled about and flattened herself against the house. But it was not a shot; it was the crack of a whip. Rolling and bouncing into the plaza came a two-wheeled hooded carriage pulled by a pony whose clattering hoofs she heard now, and driven by an old Filipino on a perch over the dashboard. A waterproof cover hid the inside of the hood and any passengers. But there was someone behind the cover. A long arm reached out and pointed straight at her. The whip cracked again, the pony leaped, and the carriage pulled up in front of her so abruptly that the pony slipped and staggered on the wet stones.

The cochero unfastened the cover and someone Lucy could not see plainly leaned forward and said, "As miserable as a wet cat." It was a woman's voice, an American voice. "Get in, young lady. Aren't you wet enough? Get in!"

Lucy needed the second command, but she didn't wait for a third. Up over the wheel she climbed, and sat down in darkness, for the cochero was already buttoning them in.

"Here's a blanket. Pull it around you," the voice went on as the carriage started with a violent jerk. "It'll keep you warm and keep your wet from soaking into me, I hope. We have to sit close on this narrow seat. Though the Lord knows I'm narrow enough myself, like a scarecrow in good circumstances, and your ruffles and flounces

25

have had most of the starch taken out of them. What's your name?"

"Lucy Leslie."

"It's a good thing I was still down in the town and someone that saw you knew where to find me. I suppose you came in on the *Esperanza*. Where else? But why didn't you come ashore before the rain? I'd've seen you then. I was down loading my hemp. Why didn't somebody meet you? Don't you know anybody here? Why didn't that new Constabulary officer help you get ashore? He seems to like other people's business. What are you doing here anyhow? Who are you?"

There were too many questions to answer all at once, and they sounded more like a scolding than like curiosity. Lucy repeated, "My name is Lucy Leslie."

"You told me that before, but that doesn't say who you are," the woman grumbled.

"I'm the new schoolteacher."

"Well, for heaven's sake! Why do they send a girl to a place like this? It's no place for a woman."

Lucy was dull with weariness; it was stubbornness alone that made her answer. "You're here."

"And that's why I know what I'm talking about. No place for a woman. Are they all fools in Manila to let you come? Well, my name is Emerald Sands. I'm English but I was born American. I'll take you where you'll get dry and warm. And I'm a very respectable woman, in case that's worrying you. But I say you ought not to be here."

"I'm going to take Tom Horton's work and finish it for him. Nobody else wants to come. And he said these children beg to learn. They have to have a teacher."

"Horton. That's the teacher that got killed."

"Did you know him? Tell me—"

"I don't mix with people. I don't stay in Magtalisay much. You ever been here before? No; you haven't. The people that saw you and sent for me told me you were a stranger. How do you know so much about Horton? Why were you hammering on that door?"

"I am a stranger here. I was going to marry Tom."

"You don't know what door that was?"

"No," Lucy said faintly. The spark of life that had made her defend her purpose and ask about Tom seemed gone.

"That's the door of the school. And you pounding on it as if to wake the dead. That's as hard to explain, if you ask me, as anything I've ever seen." The carriage jolted, shaking but not interrupting her words. She kept on talking. Lucy tried to listen, but could not seem to follow. The carriage tilted them against the back of the seat; they were climbing. Lucy let the sentences flow past her, hearing less and less.

"Don't worry about that animal that's pulling us . . . tough as an elephant . . . pulled Arthur and me up this hill many a time . . . tough and de-vilish sly . . . you need a good supper . . . more than lemonade . . . better than the sangwitches the Marchioness made, though I dearly love the Marchioness . . . chicking, that's what you'll have . . . And here we are! Now then, out with you, young lady."

Lucy found herself standing on the ground, looking at everything at once in a blurred confusion. One picture alone remained with her from that moment: the town far below, a cluster of roofs, some of brown thatch, some of glistening galvanized iron, among the shining green crests of the palms; and the white tower she had glimpsed as she left the Esperanza, a tiny thing on a promontory that from this height seemed hardly above the level of the sea. She did not even realize that the rain had ended and the sky was clearing.

"Up steps and into the house."

Lucy felt a hand on her arm, and stumbled toward the veranda. The house was shadowy under wide eaves.

As they reached the top step a long beam of light fell across the gleaming floor of the room within the wide doorway. It was a room like nothing Lucy had ever imagined. There was greenery everywhere, palms and ferns and strange plants, even on the walls and hanging from the ceiling. Bamboo birdcages stood about, and gigantic bamboo chairs cushioned in green. Some flower filled the air with a sweet, rich fragrance. A tiny brown woman,

27

holding the lamp from which the light streamed, moved toward them soundlessly on bare feet.

"Let's have a look at you," Emerald said. She released Lucy's arm and took the lamp, raising it high above their heads, and studied the girl.

Too exhausted for embarrassment, Lucy stared back. She herself was of medium height, but Emerald Sands was at least a head taller. She was extremely thin, as if a person of normal proportions had been stretched and left long and narrow. Her head was covered with short, soft white curls, and she wore a green dress of an unfamiliar shiny cloth made in a fashion that must have been all her own, for it had no trace of what Lucy knew as style. Her eyes were steady and piercing.

Her scrutiny finished, Emerald returned the lamp to the servant. "You have spunk," she said to Lucy with approval. "You're wet, you're tired, you're dirty, you're a stranger. But not a tear. I like that. Tears never yet wound up a clock or worked a steam engine. And you look me straight in the eye. I like that, too. But you're young. And I'm afraid under that dirt you're pretty. You ought not to be here. However, you're here. And you need my help. It's been a long time—but never mind. Come along."

She spoke in a strange language to the servant, and the woman turned and glided away. Urged by Emerald's hand again on her arm, Lucy followed. This was another picture that was to remain strong in her memory: the Filipina as she went before them, her small figure, enigmatic though humble, her graceful carriage, the glimpse of her brown, wrinkled cheek, the knot of her thick black hair, the shadow of her thin shoulder showing through the transparent sleeve of her camisa, her trailing skirt, and the light on the keys jingling at her waist.

They crossed the big sala and went out through another wide doorway to another veranda, where the wind blew gently and a table was elaborately set for a meal. In the center, beside a bouquet of red flowers, sat a fantastic creature with a triangular black face and staring sapphire eyes. "Tigre!" Emerald cried indignantly, and the animal,

28

which Lucy had not thought alive, leaped and ran like a cat, its claws clicking lightly on the polished floor.

In a room where everything was bamboo, even the pipe that made the shower bath, she washed herself and her hair; she put on a kimono of Emerald's, so long that she tripped on it; she ate her supper and learned that the empty third place was laid for Arthur, Emerald's husband who had been dead for ten years. The tawny animal with the black face, which was really a cat sold to Emerald by a Chinese sea-merchant, bit her foot, and Emerald was pleased and cried, "Tigre loves you!" The day ended in a four-poster bed hung with a mosquito net, making an enclosure so large that it was almost a room in itself.

5

IN the same heavy rain through which Lucy came ashore, Morrow supervised the placing of the Constabulary supplies under the house used as a headquarters. Then, after arranging a twenty-four-hour guard that he himself would share with Ramos, Fermín, and Saavedra, he picked up his small case of medical supplies and went upstairs. He found the office, recognizing it by the safe and the desk on which a pile of papers with curling edges represented the business part of Constabulary work, and came finally to a veranda away from the weather, where he found Palmer and Lloyd. The rain had covered the sound of their voices, but he knew they had been talking about him, for at his arrival they broke off and looked at him uneasily. Palmer, his face sullen, lay in a long chair; Lloyd, balanced on the rail, was anxious and wary.

Morrow warned himself not to make too much of their hostility. They had been self-promoted and now they blamed him for their demotion, but their resentment ought not to last. If they saw he was friendly, surely they'd be friendly too. He said to Palmer, "First of all, that leg. What've you been doing for it? Get that bandage off and let me see it. Ulcers can be a lot of trouble."

The need for help made Palmer start to obey, but he had hardly touched the bandage when he stopped. "How in hell do you know it's an ulcer? Who told you? D'you have spies here?"

"Now look here, Palmer," Morrow said tolerantly, "you're a sick man and a sick man can be excused for a little bad temper. But not for refusing help. Of course I know it's an ulcer. Ulcers all smell alike. You may be so used to it that you don't notice any more. In fact, you must be used to smells or you couldn't live in this part of town. Until the rain started it was terrible, and we'll get another place as fast as we can. Now let me see that leg." A muchacho had followed him with a basin of hot water and he began to wash his hands.

"I don't know what good you can do," Palmer said in a surly tone, but he stripped his leg and exposed the ugly yellow sore.

"How long have you had it?"

"I don't know. Two weeks. Three weeks."

"Four weeks ago tomorrow," Lloyd said. "It came from a leech on that last trip into the mountains. Our guide, sir, took us into leech country without warning us."

"One of their goddam filthy Filipino tricks," Palmer growled. "Well, there it is. You wanted to see it. How do you like it?"

"What've you been doing for it?"

"I pour hot water over it and tie it up. It won't heal. Just gets bigger."

Lloyd leaned over and took a long look. "That's bad, Harry. You ought to get to a hospital. You're taking an awful chance. Don't want to lose your leg. What do you say, sir?" He turned to Morrow.

"If he wants to go, we can cable to Tacloban and have the *Esperanza* call here again for him. How about it, Palmer?"

"You'd like to get rid of me, wouldn't you? I'm not leaving Magtalisay till I get Faustino."

Morrow ignored the intended rudeness. "I think we can cure this ourselves. Of course you take a chance, but that's up to you."

30

Palmer hesitated as if suspecting this too might be a plot to get rid of him. Then he said, "I'm staying."

"All right," Morrow said; "then you're under my orders." He took out a new bandage and began, with no other treatment, to wind it around Palmer's leg. "The first order is that this bandage is not to be touched for a week. If it leaks through we put more bandage on, but that's all. The theory is that the discharge is the best dressing for the sore. Is that clear? Disobey orders and we ship you to a hospital the first chance we get. You have to trust me for this, Palmer. And you're to keep off your feet. You're confined to quarters. Got that?"

Without raising his eyes, Palmer nodded.

"But you're allowed to talk," Morrow went on. "And I need information. I read your reports, but I want the rest of the story. Begin with that patrol when you picked up the leech that started this sore. When did you get the leeches? Before the men deserted? Well, Palmer?"

"Let Lloyd tell you."

"Sure, sure," Lloyd said. "But tell him about what?"

"Tell him about that last *patrulla*."

"All about it, Harry?"

"Don't be a fool, Jus. Tell him everything that matters."

"Sure," Lloyd said. "Sure. I don't hear so good lately. It was like this, Captain Morrow. We got the information—you know how it comes, sir, nobody admitting he really knows something, but you put the thing together from what this one says and that one says—well, we sort of got to understand that Pope Faustino and his men went into hiding way across the island after they murdered Pearson and the others. So we waited. They were out of our territory, but we knew they'd be back. We only had eight men then."

"You had more than that once."

"Yes, sir. Ten. Two had deserted."

"Why?"

"Well, sir, I don't know. They weren't much good anyhow. We never had our full company, sir. Pearson was just getting started. Anyhow, so now Faustino made a raid on Sogod. That's a barrio just north across the river.

31

And one of our men brought in a fellow that told us he knew where Faustino and his men were hiding after that raid. He said he'd guide us there. He led us into that leech country. You can't trust one of 'em."

"Is that all? When you met the leeches you turned back?"

"No, sir," Lloyd said, aggrieved. "We've seen plenty of leeches. We don't turn back for leeches, sir. Then this fellow took us to an old empty shack and said Faustino had been there but had gone away. That night all the men deserted."

"Just like that? Why?"

"They didn't wait to tell us. They just disappeared. Maybe they had rice to harvest, like the other two said before they disappeared. How should we know why they left? Even if they told us, we couldn't believe anything they say."

"Men never do things without a reason," Morrow said. "It might not be the reason you'd do something, but it's a reason for them. Can you guess what their reason was? Were they afraid of Faustino? Weren't they satisfied with their pay? Haven't you any idea?"

"Well, sir—"

"How can you read their minds?" Palmer demanded, interrupting Lloyd. "How can you tell what goes on inside their heads? Half dirty monkey and half devil—"

He was stopped by Morrow. "Now wait. That's not getting us anywhere. I want to know why they deserted so that it won't happen again. You haven't heard anything since?" When they were silent, he went on, "Well, what about their guns and uniforms? Are they gone too?"

"Yes, sir. Not very much ammunition, though."

"What guns? How many?"

"Eight of those old Remington shotguns."

"It would be a good loss," Morrow said, "if they weren't in bad hands. I suppose they went straight to Faustino. Have you tried to get them back?"

"No, sir."

"We might try offering a reward. Well, maybe you can

tell me more about something else. What have you learned about Faustino?"

"What do you have to know," Palmer demanded, "except he's a thief and a murderer? 'Damn, damn, damn the Filipino.' That song has the right idea. 'Underneath the starry flag, Civilize 'em with a Krag!' That's all you have to know."

Morrow persisted patiently. "Sometimes it's useful to know more. Does he have a family in Magtalisay or any of the barrios? What's his past history?" He finished fastening the bandage and washed his hands again. "Haven't you heard a thing?"

"His home is hell, and the devil is his father and mother," Palmer muttered. "I guess I ought to thank you for the bandage."

"You needn't," Morrow said dryly. "But you might get out your maps of the town and the district. Or you get them, Lloyd. Palmer can't walk around."

Both lieutenants spoke together. "Maps? What maps?"

"No information and no maps," Morrow said, discarding his patience at last. "I don't know whether this is plain obstruction or pure ignorance. How long have you men been here, anyway? Three months? Four months?"

Neither man answered audibly, but Lloyd hung his head and Palmer made an angry, futile gesture with his clenched fist.

Morrow closed his case and picked it up. "Well, I'll see what use you can be now. Lloyd, you've been supply officer?"

"Yes, sir."

"While Palmer is laid up, he'll take over those duties."

"Excuse me, sir," Lloyd said, his attention on the medicine case. "Do you have any quinine? I don't have much left."

"You have malaria?"

"No, sir, and I'm not going to have it. I take my dose of quinine every day—"

"No wonder you're deaf," Morrow said. "Stop taking it at once. That's an order. If you get malaria, you'll get all the quinine you need. Unless you're so full of it to

33

begin with that it doesn't do any good. So stop taking it now. You'll need to hear. You'll be drilling the men."

"What men?"

"The men I'm going to recruit," Morrow said. "Wait. Here's another thing I want to know. We'll see if you can give me an answer here. What's Faustino been doing in the last two weeks?"

"We don't know, sir," Lloyd replied. "Everything's been quiet."

"I wonder if it's really been quiet," Morrow said. "Or have the people just given up the idea of coming to the Constabulary for help? They're not such fools as you seem to think they are." He stood a moment looking at them, but when both men were silent and avoided his eye, he turned and walked out.

Breaks in the clouds promised the end of the rain. Morrow called Ramos, and before the last drops had fallen they were on their way through the long neglected and now muddy streets to learn what they could, in the short interval of daylight left, about the town of Magtalisay. They crossed the plaza not a quarter of an hour after Lucy had been taken away by Mrs. Sands.

Morrow was saddened by the signs he saw everywhere of poverty and hopelessness, of disease and fear. There was great work for someone to do here. That child there with the swollen belly needed better food, and his mother, who was reaching to snatch him out of sight of the man in uniform, should learn that the Constabulary meant help, not trouble. These empty, tottering houses should be rebuilt and occupied again. The family in that house— he could see them watching him surreptitiously as he went by—should be taught a little about sanitation, for the litter and filth about the ladder that led up to their door was a threat to their health. A drainage ditch would keep this street from getting so muddy and so full of ruts. There was work for a man here, some fortunate and gifted man; there were a thousand things small and large to be done to make Magtalisay a good place to live in.

Ramos' thoughts were on other matters. He was pleased with himself. He'd had a fine day. The dialect on this island was a little different from his own sort of Visayan, but it hadn't handicapped him. It was he who had organized the long train of *cargadores* to carry the supplies from the wharf to headquarters; he had rounded up the loungers and the idle fishermen, and, wise as a turtle, as he had been careful to tell them, he had distributed the various weights according to age and strength. And, as instructed by the señor capitán, he had dropped hints about what the boxes and bales and bundles held: new uniforms for the Constabulary, red blankets for the Constabulary, rice to feed the men who would enlist, shoes for special drills in the plaza before an admiring crowd, and other fascinating things that would be revealed when the suitable moment arrived.

Also, and this was entirely his own idea, he had let fall a word here and a word there about the señor capitán's prowess. The capitán's name, so Ramos had informed his listeners, might be Morrow, which meant *mañana*, but an enemy who waited around for *mañana* to meet the señor capitán Mañana would find he had waited too long. He would find he had been beaten today. Morrow had the strength of the carabao, the guile of the turtle, and, like a python swallowing its prey, an inability to stop before he finished whatever he undertook. Moreover, Ramos said, generously sharing his hoard of knowledge and supposition about this strange *americano*, the capitán wore around his neck on a chain a powerful *anting-anting*, and no bullet or knife could touch him. At this, there were whispers about the *anting-antings* given by Pope Faustino to protect his men, but Ramos swore that Morrow's *anting-anting* was the best of all. He could tell them stories, but he'd let them wait and see. He himself, Ramos, wouldn't give three cucumbers for Faustino's *anting-anting*, and anyone who would was a *bobarrón*, with less sense than a monkey, and if they didn't know yet how little sense monkeys had, he'd tell them of a pet monkey of his that fell in love with a crocodile. And on the spot he had invented the story, and it was long and ribald and good, with the monkey coming to an unfortunate but curious end.

One respectful step behind Morrow, he strutted along, hand touching now and then the smooth hilt of his knife, pistol rubbing comfortably against his hip.

They walked in the direction of the promontory at the edge of the bay. The wet clay sucked at Morrow's shoes and at Ramos' bare feet. The street became no more than a muddy path between long beds of weeds; apparently for many months no sleds or carts had come to this part of the town. Here all the houses were empty and rotting. Fences had grown into tangled hedges. Occasionally a rustling and grunting in the underbrush betrayed the activities of a scavenger pig, and two or three times some craven dog, a slinking skeleton inside a mangy hide, came out to growl at them and then cower back, trying to tuck its upward curling tail between its legs.

The old road crossed a stretch of ground in which no houses stood and ended at the foot of the cliff. Rising diagonally up the side was a flight of steps cut out of the rock. Stones and dirt had fallen from above, making the footing bad, but the steps were sound. Morrow and Ramos climbed to the top.

The level ground was a much wider expanse than Morrow had expected. Roughly rectangular, it extended, he estimated, for some eight hundred feet along the bay, while in the other direction, paralleling the estuary, it was at the widest about half that length. On the northern edge, above Magtalisay, there was a low thick wall, more to keep anyone from falling off than for any other protective purpose, for the place was a natural stronghold. On this side the steps could be easily defended; water and precipitous height were on guard at the south and west; and though on the east a greater hill rose, there was a protective chasm between. The two rusty cannon pointing over the bay were man's silly addition to a fortress made safe by nature.

There were two buildings, the old tower, built for a lookout against Moro raiders, and, not far from the steps, a larger structure, wide but low, which was not visible from the bay or the town.

As Morrow started toward the southwest corner where the tower stood, the clouds over the setting sun parted, and

36

yellow rays struck horizontally across the neighboring island of Leyte. They burnished the black water between the islands and the river's wide mouth; they turned the tower into a squat pillar of gold. The shadows of the two men appeared suddenly on the ground at their left, stretching for an incredible distance, with long spidery legs matching mincing steps with the feet to which they were joined.

The tower was strongly buttressed; built for defense and observation. Inside it was dark, little of the dying day's final brilliance coming through the narrow windows. Yet, though Morrow could see the interior only dimly, there was something about it that suggested it had been lived in not too long ago. The air was less dusty, less moldy, less undisturbed, than in a place unoccupied for years.

"I could live here," Morrow said aloud in English. Ramos looked at him curiously but was silent; English words had no meaning for him. He and Morrow could converse fluently in Spanish and not quite so fluently in dialect, but these other sounds meant that the capitán was talking to himself. "Why that big building isn't in use—" Morrow didn't finish this sentence but walked toward the other structure, with Ramos beside him, their shadows reaching ahead.

A foundation and a single story had been built of stone, but the second story and the roof, if they had ever existed, were gone now. This was the reason the building was invisible from below the cliff. It had surely been intended for a barracks; it was large enough and had been designed in the style the Spaniards used for cuartels to house their garrisons, with a central door and four windows on either side, and iron bars across the windows. Morrow looked through the door and saw debris; doubtless the fallen second story and roof, of bamboo and palm thatch. He shook the bars of the windows and found them strong. Yes, it would do. They could use this place, up high in the sweet air. As he walked along the front of the building, the yellow sunlight shaded into orange and then into red, turning the stone first to the color of fire and then to the color of blood. And then the stone was gray again. The day was over.

At the bottom of the steps it was much darker. The evening was quiet but for the breeze rattling the fronds of the palms, and, with the twilight obscuring the decay and neglect, there was a peacefulness in this deserted part of Magtalisay that Morrow found much to his taste.

Over the street spread the branches of an enormous mango tree that even at midday must have cast a midnight shadow. Morrow entered this blackness, slowing a little to save stumbling in the path. He was conscious of no warning. There might, however, have been a rustling in the leaves. The depths of a tree so large can no more be stirred by a light wind than the depths of the sea, and it was possible that he heard and responded to some sound of which his body only and not his mind took note. All he knew was that something dropped from the tree, his shoulder was gripped in fierce and powerful fingers, and there was a knife that went harmlessly through his sleeve. Before he had realized the threat, he had reacted to it.

The assailant twisted and attacked again.

Ramos knew when the man dropped from the tree, feeling it through the soles of his feet rather than hearing it. He drew his knife, but waited for Morrow's word before he interfered. He could see a writhing nucleus in the cell of blackness that held them, one body indistinguishable from the other. But he watched and listened in confidence. His capitán had learned some strange tricks from a man of the islands of Japón. And then he had also the anting-anting.

The confused sounds of the struggle were cut off clean, and there was a moment of silence. A groan followed, then the sharp thud of some small object falling to the ground, then a much heavier thud and a louder groan.

Morrow's voice said, "Ramos, pick up his knife. It's here, close. Got it? Good. Now help me get him to his feet. He doesn't want to move, but there's nothing wrong with him but a broken arm."

Ramos slipped his own weapon inside the back of his belt and put the other knife beside it; like his own, his quick fingers had learned, it was no work bolo, but something more wicked, a blood brother to the Malay kris. "Sí, señor capitán. Do you think there are any other large mangoes *gusarapientos* hanging on this tree?"

"Who knows? Anyhow, let's not stay to see what they taste like. Get his left arm. Now. *Arriba!*"

They got their first good look at their prisoner by lamplight at headquarters. He was about as tall as Morrow, or above average height for a Filipino, thickly built, muscular, but lean. He wore a pair of short ragged trousers of faded red, and a belt to support them and hold his knife; otherwise he was naked except for the mud that coated most of his bare skin. He refused to answer their questions and kept his eyes turned from theirs.

Morrow sent Ramos for bamboo to make splints. "And get a big *pañuelo* for a sling. And hurry. You must relieve Fermín. He has to go on guard again at midnight."

Alone with his attacker, he waited in silence for the materials he needed. Then, again alone with the man, he cut the splints, set the bone, and bandaged the arm, silent except for one or two brusque commands. But he watched the prisoner every second; he saw that the man was studying the room, saw that the man knew that he, Morrow, was alert in spite of his casual manner, saw the sweat on the man's face when his arm was stretched along the bamboo, felt the passion of enmity that poured from the man's eyes when they chanced for a second to meet his. And on the man's arm, inside the elbow, Morrow noticed a tiny scar where he thought blood had been drawn for signing a *pacto de sangre.*

The bandaging finished, Morrow began again asking questions, this time more methodically. "What is your name? . . . Where is your home? . . .Why did you attack me? . . . Do you live in Magtalisay? . . . Are you of Faustino's men? . . . Did Faustino order you to kill me? . . . Is there someone you want us to bring to see you? Your wife? Children? Father? Mother?"

The prisoner sat without a change of expression and answered nothing.

Morrow was not surprised. Faustino was not the only outlaw leader to borrow a holy title to increase his hold on his followers, and that hold could grip a man's will and spirit and turn him into a fanatic. If, besides, there was a blood brotherhood, the fanaticism would be increased. This Faustino, he thought, can be a clever man as well as a ruthless one. It was even possible, his thoughts went on in a wild supposition as he regarded the muscular body and the controlled face of his captive, that this might be Faustino himself. These leaders were daring and fatalistic, ready to make a gamble like the one this man had made tonight. And if this should be Faustino, here, trapped—

"Señor capitán!" Ramos was back, panting, his rapid Spanish coming in spurts. "I saw this perro hocicudo had no anting-anting. I told myself, Is it to be believed, Ramos, you parapoco, that a dog like this will attack if he does not feel safe? I answered, No, he will not. And therefore he had an anting-anting. When he made his plan, and climbed the tree, and waited, his anting-anting kept him safe. And thus the anting-anting was lost when he jumped. Or when you shook him off as you might a feather that tickled you. And therefore I returned to the tree and made a search. And therefore this!" He held up a broken strand of hemp cord from which hung a tiny case.

The prisoner, forgetting that his feet were bound together, made a leap toward the talisman and fell to the floor. While he righted himself awkwardly, his gaze followed the anting-anting from Ramos' hand into Morrow's with such passionate yearning and apprehension that Morrow felt an impulse to return the object to him.

But of course he must make use of it. Like its owner, it had dropped into his hands and he must not be tempted by sentiment. He began to examine the case with exaggerated care. It was woven of some soft but stout material like malabago bark and was sewed tight shut. With his jackknife he slit the stitches, and emptied the contents into the palm of his hand. There were three small brown bones and a bit of paper covered with writing that proved to be a jumble of letters, meaningless except for the signature, Faustino santísimo. The bones were graduated in size and resembled those in a man's smallest finger, though Morrow thought they might not be human.

He felt the tense expectancy of the outlaw and of Ramos.

40

Both were waiting for what would happen next with this captured charm that was magic to both of them. He would have to do something final, and he must do something dramatic.

He sighed and said to Ramos, "You are right, sargento. This is an anting-anting of Faustino, and a powerful one, because this man has trusted it and it has made him brave. But he has used it for a wicked purpose and therefore eventually it failed. At last wickedness defeats itself. Tell him all that. He will understand you better than me."

Ramos translated Morrow's words.

"Now ask him again who he is."

Ramos obeyed, but there was still no answer, only an upward glance from under scowling brows.

"Why won't he speak? It is an opportunity. He could tell us that he himself is Faustino and how could we say he lies?"

Ramos killed the faint hope that had prompted this suggestion. "He would not dare say he is Faustino, for all know Faustino's strength is of the spirit and not the arm. This man is young and strong."

So already Ramos was accumulating information for him, Morrow thought. But he let that pass for the moment, returning to the matter of the talisman. "Ramos, find a big stone. Then we will show the prisionero what we think of his magic charm."

When Ramos came back, Morrow began his ceremony by burning the woven case that had held bones and paper. Next he tore up the paper and burned it, too. Last, very slowly, with the butt of his revolver he ground the three bones against the stone. They were old and brittle and ready to crumble to dust, and he made a thorough job of it, crushing the fragments and finally shaking the powdery substance that was left out the window, where the night wind caught it and blew it away.

Ramos looked on with awe, trying to conceal the fact that he felt an uneasiness over this defiance of Faustino's power. This would make another story for Ramos to tell, as Morrow knew; he was counting on Ramos to spread the tale far and wide.

41

And the *pulaján*, seeing his charm destroyed while he was still suffering most sharply from the knowledge that it had failed him, could hardly bear to watch as Morrow worked over the bones. When Morrow was done, he hid his face in his hands in an attitude of despair.

6

THE next morning was bright, and the warm sunlight gave the houses and the palms and the bushes and even the weeds so much gaiety and color and life that neglect and squalor could almost be ignored. Red hibiscus blossoms made the tangled hedges brilliant, and the foliage everywhere was thick and richly green.

The captured *pulaján* was on his way to the municipal authorities. He walked beside Ramos, with Morrow and Lloyd following. They in turn were followed by a lengthening parade of naked and half-naked children and a few adults, who kept a careful distance behind and halted, pretending to be interested in something else, if one of the men in uniform turned his head.

This procession went a little out of the way so that the *pulaján* could be shown to Johnstone. Johnstone was the Army Signal Corps sergeant in charge of the cable office, and the sole survivor of the ambush on Dos Picos. If Johnstone could identify the prisoner, another charge would be placed against him.

As they reached the steps they could hear the clicking of the telegraph instrument. Lloyd called, "Phil! Come on out!"

"Why, Jus!" a woman's voice answered, and they saw a tousled head of yellow hair rise above the bamboo railing of the veranda. A yawning face turned toward them. "This sure is early for a call. I can't sleep inside, it's too hot—" She noticed Morrow and her voice changed from complaint to interest. "Well!" Then the complaint returned, but with archness in it. "You might have let me know, sent a *muchacho* or something, Jus. So I'd be dressed." Their upward view accentuated the lines of her face and its sagging flesh.

"We came to see Phil, Gracie."

"Oh, now why do you always come just to see Phil? Don't you know I'm here too?" She stood up and walked over to the door. "Phil, come on out!" She wore a cheap and scanty thin silk Japanese kimono without sleeves, and in spite of what she had said did not seem to mind not being dressed, for she stretched slowly and completely, making it quite evident that she wore nothing but the single garment. Returning to the edge of the veranda, she sat on the rail and, still more revealingly, leaned over them.

"Introduce your friend, Jus."

Johnstone appeared in the doorway and a sudden smile of welcome transformed his bony face. He made a quick gesture to Gracie to pull her kimono together, and then ran down the steps with his hand out. "You're Captain Morrow. I'm Johnstone. Meet my wife. I always say, cap, that I like to shake hands with a new face. Especially here in Magtalisay." Broken, disclored teeth marred his smile, but its sincerity was clear. "Come into the office."

"No time now," Morrow said. "We're taking this—"

"Sure there's time. Always time in Magtalisay. No time like the present, anyhow."

"Thanks," said Morrow. "But another day. This is a business—"

"O.K., O.K. I can take a hint. I wanted to meet your boat, knowing you'd be on it, but yesterday I was down with malaria. It always catches me on the wrong day. Fate, I always say. You believe in fate?"

Morrow seized this opening. "It would be fate if you recognized our prisoner. Look him over. Ever see him before?"

Johnstone looked the man up and down swiftly and shook his head. "Don't think so. What did he do?"

"You never saw him before today? How about up on Dos Picos? See him there?"

43

Now Johnstone's denial was more positive. "No. No. That day I never seen nobody."

"All right, sergeant. We'll go on then. Glad to have met you and Mrs. Johnstone."

Gracie leaned over him, in eager response. "Glad to meet you, too, captain. I hope we'll see a lot of you. It gets lonesome here." She reached down to shake his hand, and her fingers pressed warmly and clung.

Then Johnstone's hand was thrust out again, and Gracie let go. "Say, cap, you don't play chess, do you?"

"I have played."

Now it was Johnstone's hand that clung. "Kismet! A chess player! How about tonight? No? Then tomorrow night? No? Then soon! It's got to be soon."

"Soon," Morrow agreed, and got away.

Meanwhile the procession headed by the Constabulary officers and their prisoners had grown larger. And it was less silent, for Ramos had used this short halt to relate just how the prisoner had been captured and what had happened to his anting-anting. There were murmurs now whenever someone joined the crowd, and the captive's head hung lower. Yet there was no ridicule for him; there were no insults from anyone but Ramos. There was instead an interested neutrality, and it could not have been plainer to Morrow that this was considered merely an opening incident in a long campaign. It was too soon for them to choose sides. Americanos and *pulajanes* could both be dangerous to ordinary people. It wasn't safe to displease either of them by appearing hopeful or disappointed about anything that might occur. They'd wait.

Out of sight of the Johnstone house, Lloyd began to laugh. "Gracie hopes she'll see a lot more of you. She let you see plenty of her, didn't she?" He glanced sideways at Morrow, but, failing to catch any clue to indicate Morrow's reaction to Gracie, he changed to Phil Johnstone as a subject for his remarks. "That's all the respect the regular Army has for the Constabulary, sir. Phil's a sergeant and he called you cap. An Army captain would have him courtmartialed for that, sir. But what can we do? At least we got our names changed so that the initials on our collars are P.

44

C. instead of I. C. The Army always said that I. C. stood for Inspected and Condemned. And you know, sir"—he got more serious, seeing a way to put in a good word for his friend—"that sort of thing is hard for a man to swallow, especially a man like Harry Palmer. Were you in the Army, sir?"

"For a short time."

"Harry and I were in the Volunteers. Together, from the beginning. There were some brave men with us, sir, and some got the Medal of Honor. Some that deserved it didn't get it. Harry is one of those. He swam a river under fire to carry a line across. By God, you never saw anybody so cool! Once he captured ten googoos single-handed. He's a sick man now, sir. You have to remember—I mean, I hope you remember that, sir."

"I know that, Lloyd. And I'll remember he has a loyal friend. It's good luck to make a good friend, but I think it takes more than that." They were at the plaza. "Now then, where's the cárcel—the jail?"

"It's on that street that comes in on the other side of the church. Right across there, sir. You can see it in a minute."

They went quickly past the fountain and the church, and Morrow stepped alone into the entrance of the cárcel. This wide, arched opening was like a dark tunnel through which could be seen the light of a small paved courtyard. An iron gate closing that court was of little use as a barrier, for part of the grille had rusted away and a man might easily have crept through. The whole place looked deserted.

"Oy!" Morrow called. "Carcelero!"

A door in the tunnel wall opened slowly, and in the rectangle of light a man's silhouette appeared, stretching and scratching. A start, a sudden straightening of shoulders, a furtive adjustment of his clothes, showed that he recognized the official nature of this call. His jaw, caught in the midst of a yawn, hung open in astonishment.

"Are you the jailer?" Morrow asked.

The man closed his mouth and nodded.

"I have a prisoner. I want you to lock him up."

45

"Sí, capitán. The keys." He vanished for a moment, returned with two great iron keys on an enormous ring, and proceeded into the courtyard, where he turned to the Constabulary officers and the *pulaján* with a bewildered stare.

Morrow pointed at his prisoner and repeated, "I want you to lock him up."

The jailer was old and tremulous and anxious. "Sí, sí. Over here, over here." Making an effort at military bearing, he hurried to a grating in the opposite wall and put a key in the heavy lock. But he needed Ramos' help to get the grating open and then to get it locked again with the *pulaján* inside.

Still bemused, he watched them depart, only to come running after them when they were out on the street once more. "Capitán! Who will pay for his food?"

Morrow saw that this was a matter of great concern; perhaps, he thought, the old man is hungry himself. He asked, "Who pays for yours, amigo?"

The kind tone brought a frank reply. "Nobody, capitán. You understand, there is no money for the jail or for the police. I am the only police. You understand, I am no beggar. But I am given the crumbs left after the dinner of the presidente. It is enough for me. But for two, for the *prisionero* and me, it is not enough."

With the audience watching, Morrow put a ten-centavo piece in the old man's hand. "This will buy food for today. One day at a time, that is plenty to think of, *verdad, viejo?*"

"*Gracias, gracias.*" But after the thanks, instead of returning at once to his room in the *cárcel*, the jailer raised the coin for the crowd to see and repeated what Morrow had said. "One day at a time, that is enough to think of. *No es verdad?*" Then he laughed, saluted Morrow, and, swaggering in the spotlight of so much attention, walked back to the jail. To Morrow's surprise there was laughter in the crowd, too.

"That's done," he said to Lloyd. "I'll have to see the magistrate about our prisoner. But first I'll see the presidente to inform him officially that I'm here."

"His is the biggest house on the plaza, sir. I suppose informing him officially is all right, but don't expect anything of him. Zúñiga, old Don Florencio, that is, never did us any good, sir. He's as old as Methuselah and sick and probably loco, for all I know. You're wasting your time if—"

Morrow cut him off coldly. "That's enough, Lloyd. The place for remarks like that is not a public street."

"But I'm using English, sir!"

"You used a name and you used a loud, contemptuous voice and you used an insulting term that most of these people understand. And in any of those windows there might be someone who speaks English well enough to know every word you said. So watch your tongue."

Lloyd's head jerked as he swallowed. "Yes, sir." He added, "This is the house, sir."

It was the house from which the message had gone the afternoon before to bring Emerald Sands to get Lucy; it was the house facing the school building at which Lucy had knocked. In the bright morning she would have known that this was the house to go to for help; it was in the best repair, with the second story freshly painted, and with a new roof of galvanized iron, every corrugation of which reflected the sunlight so sharply that it hurt the eye.

"You'll remain downstairs," Morrow told Lloyd. "Or out here in the plaza if you wish. I can order you to watch what you say, but I can't control what you feel. Do you think they wouldn't sense your contempt? Relations are too delicate for me to risk taking you to my first interview with the mayor."

Lloyd muttered, "Maybe I'd better stay out here."

The door of the house swung open as Morrow approached. Ramos remained outside as if on guard, and the crowd scattered about the plaza waiting to see if anything else of interest might happen.

7

LUCY, waking that morning inside the white wall of the mosquito net, did not at first know where she was. Cocks crowing had often broken her sleep before, but the chorus of wild jungle fowl and of fighting cocks of Magtalisay, calling to the beginning day, was different from anything she had ever heard, shriller, sharper, fuller, somehow even more foreign than the dialect that was so strange.

She climbed over the Dutch wife that lay beside her in the bed, loosened the net, and set her feet on the cool bare floor. She felt extraordinarily rested and fresh. She crossed to the wide window, which opened one whole side of her room to the new morning.

Leaning out, she looked and listened, with eagerness that was almost anxiety. The cocks still crowed, but she ceased to hear them, or perhaps their chorus had become part of something greater. Her eyes and her ears were strangely keen, the two senses intermingling. She became aware, as she gazed, of straining to hear the sound of music that must surely be coming from some place beyond the clouds, that would reach her if she only listened closely enough. To this music the clouds were moving with majestic grandeur. Their glow altered from pink to salmon and from salmon to daffodil-yellow. Unbearably the yellow intensified, gained a metallic glitter, grew brighter and still brighter with a brassy brilliance like the clash of cymbals. For a protracted moment the whole universe waited in unendurable tension. And then the sun was up.

Lucy heard with relief the whisper of soft footsteps in her room and turned around to see the old muchacha placing a small tray on a table near the bed. "Buenos días," she murmured. Lucy nodded but could not answer; she could not even smile. She was trembling; she was frightened. What was wrong with her? Was she losing her mind? She had seen sunrises before; they had been a commonplace of her year of teaching a country school. She poured herself a cup of tea and drank it, and the trembling stopped. She told herself she had been cold; she had got out of bed too fast and had been giddy. That explained it. Or perhaps she was not yet over her seasickness.

She made herself be practical. Within an hour she had persuaded Emerald to accept her as a roomer and boarder and had arranged the terms. An hour later she had her trunk unpacked, and the old servant, whose name she learned was Engracia, had pressed a dress for her. Before another hour had passed, she was getting into the *calesa* with Emerald to call on the mayor and beg him to write to Manila, assuring them that she was badly needed in Magtalisay and would be safe.

She hardly recognized the plaza with the sun shining down on it and people standing under the trees. There seemed to be some excitement in the air, and she could feel that her arrival increased the earlier sensation.

"What's this all about?" Emerald said, and poked the *cochero*, ordering him to stop the carriage. With a wave of her hand, she summoned one of the bystanders to ask. "That new Constabulary officer," she translated briefly to Lucy. "He caught an outlaw last night, and now he's in talking to Don Florencio. Bragging, I suppose. Great man. New broom." She waved her hand in the other direction. "But you've got a reception committee of your own. News goes fast here, you know. Bamboo telegraph. Look at your school." She poked the *cochero* again. He cracked the whip, the pony galloped furiously over the cobblestones, and they pulled up in front of the door on which Lucy had vainly pounded for shelter the afternoon before.

A dozen small boys looked up at her. Unlike the other children in the plaza, whose garments, if they wore any at all, were ragged and scanty, these boys wore carefully mended pants and freshly laundered *camisas*. The sun was reflected from their neat, shining black hair.

Lucy, smiling, jumped to the ground and walked toward them. "Good morning, boys."

49

With serious faces concentrated in thought and effort, they answered her in a well-drilled chorus. "Good morning, Meestaire Hortone." Then they smiled.

Lucy caught her breath in the first poignant grief she had felt for Horton. He had been gone from Kansas for four years; her sorrow had been more a matter of the imagination than of the heart. But now she felt as well as saw that these were his pupils, his school, his unfinished work. For an instant he seemed to reach out to her across the impassable gulf, and she put out her own hands and took an uncertain step.

The pupils understood this as a gesture indicating that she was in a hurry to go inside the building, and two of them ran to open the door. Lucy entered and followed them up the stairs to the second floor. Here there was a wide, empty hall, where again the pupils opened a door. This was the schoolroom. It was dim and it held a damp, musty odor. At once a boy was at each window, sliding it open to the fresh and brilliant air.

Lucy saw near the door the small blackboard she had brought from the States, and there was a standard beside it with a shapeless mass at the top that she knew must be her map of the world after its hours in the rain the day before. Everything else, crude bookcases and benches, the teacher's desk with a pile of books on it and a stack of slates and even a sheet of paper with a pencil lying across it, all of this was thinly covered with dust and bound by cobwebs. Otherwise it looked, she realized, exactly the way it had when Tom Horton last walked out. Nothing had been touched, though the doors had been left unlocked.

She could have had no clearer proof of the truth of all Tom had written her about the respect for schoolteachers among this people. Even the outlaws, Emerald had told her, usually excluded teachers from their attacks. Horton's murder had shamed the people bitterly.

Again Lucy's eyes filled with tears. Holding her head high, she went over to the wall where some boards had been put up, as Tom had written her, and painted black. Her trembling fingers sought and found a piece of chalk. Winking back the tears, she stretched her arm up and

50

began to write as high as she could reach. Large A and small a, large B and small b, large C and small c, and on to the end of the English alphabet, each letter perfectly formed and smoothly written. The pupils gathered around her quietly and watched. When she had finished, her eyes were dry. And the school belonged to her.

8

WHEN the door of the presidente's house closed behind Morrow, it was hard for him to see anything at all at first, for the dim interior was doubly dark after the intense daylight. But he had already seen, while the door was open, the tile floor patterned in large squares of black and white, and the beginning of a flight of stairs. The servant who had closed the door appeared ahead of him now, a vague white figure in the darkness. "*Cuidao!*" the boy said, and Morrow thought it was good advice for the interview ahead. Take care!

At the top of two short flights of stairs they crossed a big sala, and entered a bedroom. In contrast to the sala, which was formal and empty of life, with chairs in stiff arrangement against the walls and a great expanse of dark polished floor, this bedroom had a crowded and lively air. There were three tall aparadores against the wall, with their doors slightly ajar and the contents ready to burst out; there were half a dozen floridly carved chairs and a broad table of red narra with a surface like glass; and beside the window there was a great bed with a high, handsomely carved headpiece about which hung a mosquito net. Morrow's eyes passed over these details to the old man who was the focus of the room. He lay in the bed, with his head and shoulders propped up on pillows. A man in middle life stood beside him.

Morrow addressed himself to the older man. "*Buenos días*, señor presidente. I have come to introduce myself and to tell you that your letter asking for reinforcement of the Constabulary here was very important and very influential. My name is Morrow, and I am at your service."

The man on the bed sighed in relief. "You speak my language, thanks to God. I can assure you that this is very pleasing to an old man who finds it difficult to learn new ways. And it is I who am at your service, señor capitán. As you were clever enough to see, I am the mayor of this poor town of Magtalisay, Florencio Zúñiga, and this is my son, Nicolás."

The son bowed, saying that he too was Morrow's servant.

"And may we inquire where you learned our language so well?" the elder Zúñiga asked.

"In Mexico, where I was born. And my mother, whom I never knew, was of a Spanish family from California. I have always felt that Spanish was as much my language as English."

He sat down beside the bed, while Nicolás kept his position at the head, as if on guard, and a circuitous and formal exchange of question and answer began. Leisurely and flowery, it delayed the real business of their meeting. But Morrow accepted it willingly. It was the custom. This morning it had a special value in giving them a chance to examine each other. Morrow never begrudged the time spent on these courtesies any more than he begrudged the time spent on oiling his gun.

There was a strong resemblance between the father and son, and in both the mixture of races was plain. Both had the broad forehead and the wide-set eyes of the Malay, and the full lips, but in both their Spanish blood had made the nose slightly aquiline. The father's skin was lighter in color than the son's, perhaps partly owing to age and illness, but largely, Morrow thought, to the fact that he had more Spanish blood; he was probably a true mestizo, half Spanish and half Filipino, and his wife, the mother of Nicolás, might have come from pure Filipino stock. The old man's face was patient and benign; the younger man's expression seemed, when Morrow could see it, similar.

Gradually and deviously they arrived at the subject of the outlaws and the Constabulary.

52

"*Pulajanes, ladrones, insurrectos,*" the old man said. "They are all of those. But I like best our Spanish word *guerrillas.* They fight the little war and they fight it everywhere, and often they win with very little trouble. For you see, if a snake attacks you, you kill it. But if a mosquito attacks you, you go behind your mosquito net. The mosquito and the guerrilla are alike. They annoy more than they hurt."

Morrow, using the same casual tone, picked up the analogy. "True. But sometimes the sting of the mosquito carries a deadly disease. And to come to practical matters, how many mosquitoes are there in Faustino's band?"

Don Florencio smiled. "Who knows? They do not stand still to be counted."

Morrow looked up at Nicolás. "How many do you think, señor?"

Nicolás' answer was not much more useful. "Any number between forty and two hundred."

"Who is this man Faustino? Where does he come from?"

"Such questions are very difficult," old Zúñiga said. "You ask things which are mysteries to us. We know nothing."

"Nothing at all?" Morrow looked from father to son. "Even very small bits of information might be of use. Is he a former soldier? An escaped criminal? Often to understand your enemy is to be halfway to victory."

"These are questions," Nicolás said, "for which we have no answers." He added, "He is considered very holy. No one ever speaks much of him. People are afraid, it may be."

Patiently Morrow tried from another angle. "Do you suspect part of his organization might be right here in Magtalisay?"

Who could say? Anything was possible. And so, too, they answered his other questions.

"If you hear more," Morrow said at last, "please let me know it, whatever it is. We are allies. I depend on you, and you depend on me. Together we can accomplish much."

"*Verdad!*" Don Florencio agreed warmly. "As our great leader Aguinaldo has told us, there has been enough of blood, enough of tears and desolation. That is why we do not want your Army. I am glad you have come."

Suavely Nicolás underlined this statement. "We would regret to see here, señor capitán, the reconcentration as in Albay, when the Army came in. Or the massacre at Balangiga. You know of that?"

Morrow nodded. He knew the story. The Filipinos had treacherously attacked the Americans and killed seventy or more, all but a handful of the men stationed at that place. They themselves had lost more than two hundred. And then the Army had been sent in, and had wiped out every male Filipino they could find over the age of ten. He said, "The time will come—and this is sure—the time will come when Americans and Filipinos, hearing of Balangiga, will refuse to believe it. Señores, you have now the future of your country in your hands. I wish to help all I can. If you will help me, my help to you will be greater."

Don Florencio reached for Morrow's hand. "We are going to be friends. I can feel that. No longer conqueror and conquered, but friends."

"Ojalá," Morrow said. "God grant it. For there's no other way."

"What will be your first move against the pulajanes?" Nicolás asked as his father sank back in the bed.

"My first move?" Morrow said. "I have already made it. A small one. It is part of my business here this morning. Who is the magistrate? I have just put a prisoner in the cárcel and I wish to swear out a complaint."

"A prisoner? A pulaján? I saw you from my bed, señor capitán, as you went toward the cárcel, and I wondered. What is the charge against him? You see, I am also the magistrate. Nicolás will put it on the record."

Morrow made his charge and told the story. "And now," he said, "I come to my last business for this morning. The Constabulary would like the use of the tower and the old cuartel on the cliff overlooking the bay. Who is the owner?"

"Who knows? It belonged to the Spaniards. Now I suppose it belongs to your government."

"Then I'll cable Manila about it, and we'll start repairs at once. Unless you know a better place for us?"

Nicolás answered, "The Escarpa would be good. But there is a story of the apparitions of Spanish soldados. Lights have been seen."

Morrow laughed. "Someone has been living in the tower, I think. If it is a ghost, he has no legal rights. And if it was the man we caught last night, he has no right there either."

"When do the new soldados arrive?" Don Florencio asked. "What island do they come from?"

Morrow concealed his satisfaction at the natural entrance of this topic into their conversation. He answered in apparent surprise, "But we will recruit them here. That's standard Constabulary practice."

"I hope it will not be too difficult."

"Do you know any reason why it should be?"

"Oh, no. No," the presidente said, and his son quickly echoed the reply.

"I thought, señores, that I'd find many brave men here."

"The men of Magtalisay are no cowards, señor capitán."

"Then perhaps you refer to the matter of the many who deserted, Don Florencio. Why did those men desert?"

The old man looked away. His face and his voice lost their warmth. "*Quién sabe?* Who knows?"

"The American lieutenants," Nicolás said, "must surely be able to tell you. If they cannot, who can?"

The atmosphere of the interview had changed. Better to end it for today, Morrow decided, end it on a still different note. He stood up. "Señores, I must go. There is only one more small request. I plan to enlist twenty men and train them before we accept more. Our full company will be forty." Knowing the value of confidence, he spoke with more than he felt. "I wish to have a parade and drill of those first twenty soldiers down there in the plaza three weeks from today. Or if that should be inconvenient for you, señor presidente, the day before or the day after. Will that be agreeable?"

The presidente smiled again. Yes, the parade would be very agreeable indeed. "You americanos! You move always at a run." He offered his hand. "Adiós, señor capitán."

As Morrow reached the landing on his way downstairs, a young Filipino with a patch over his eye ran up the lower flight and stopped him.

In a low voice, using English, the young man said, "You are Captain Morrow. I am Rufino Zúñiga, the grandson of the mayor of this so beautiful city." Morrow put out his hand, and the other made a violent gesture as if to strike it away. "No, I will not shake hands with you! But I wish to say to you welcome and to thank to you as I thank to every American for what they have so kindly gave to me." His fingers clawed at the patch and pulled it from his face, while he turned his head so that it caught a shaft of light reflected from the sala above. "See, Captain Morrow, see?" Morrow looked into scarred tissue and an empty socket. Before he could think of anything to say, the young man had run past him to the floor above.

Slowly, in deep thought, Morrow went on toward the door, reaching it as the servant threw it open for someone to enter.

Framed by the doorway, Lucy stepped over the high threshold. The sun shone through her hair and through the edges of her organdy dress, outlining her in brilliance that seemed to be her own. She passed so close that Morrow might have touched her, and he saw the youth, the almost childish freshness of her face, both in the flesh itself and in her expression. Coming into darkness from the blinding morning, she did not see him. With Emerald Sands following her, she crossed the tile floor to the stairs.

Morrow emerged into the sunlight with eyes narrowed against the glare. What a painting that girl would make! He had a sudden longing for brushes, oils, and canvas, a longing he had not felt in years. If a man could catch that radiance of youth . . . ! The emotion was sharp and deep, yet vague. He likened it to a sort of homesickness, something for which there was no room in his life, something to be conquered, buried, and forgotten.

9

IT was noon of that day before Lloyd saw Palmer. Palmer was sitting with his leg stretched out, as ordered, gloomily cleaning his revolver and his rifle. He said, "You might come in once in a while and let me know what's going on. If it was you instead of me alone all day, I wouldn't forget you."

Lloyd couldn't resist a chance to tease. "I was thinking of you, Harry," he said, tossing back the lock of soft hair that fell over his forehead. "I didn't forget you. I just never had a chance to come in. Trouble is, too much has been happening. I can't even start to tell you now."

"What was that shooting I just heard?"

"Well, that was sort of interesting. Though maybe not the most important thing that happened today."

"Are you going to tell me?"

"Sure, Harry. I want to tell you. But if I don't do it the right way, you won't believe me. Maybe I'd better let you find out for yourself. Seeing is believing, you know. And I don't really have time to sit down and talk. Now, I wouldn't complain about having to sit down all day like—"

Palmer picked up his crutch and hit Lloyd on the shin.

"All right, all right," Lloyd said, grimacing as he tried to make a joke of the pain. "You'll get the whole story. The shooting first. But you aren't going to like it. Morrow asked me, 'Are you a good shot?' I said 'Fair, captain, fair, sir.' I always say captain unless I say sir, and I always say sir—"

"Yes, you're a great handshaker, Jus. Get on with the shooting."

"I said, 'I'm not a sharpshooter, captain, but I can do a little better than hit the side of a barn, sir.' So he picked out a target and told me to hit it."

"With your Colt? You're better with a rifle."

"That's what I told him, and after I fired he said he hoped so. He said I'd better get some practice because we're going to teach every Constabulary soldado to be a sharpshooter."

"You can't teach a yuyu to shoot."

"That's just what I told him, Harry. So he called this Sergeant Ramos, and he said to me, 'Your initials are J. L., aren't they?' And then you heard the shooting."

"Why don't you tell it straight, Jus? Who did the shooting? Why?"

"Sounded like one gun, didn't it?"

"It was only one gun, damn it! I told you I heard it."

"You heard six shots, I suppose? There were twelve bullets fired, six by Morrow and six by Ramos. The captain took the J and the sergeant took the L, and they shot my initials in the post at the other corner of the house. But what makes me sore is that he didn't say, 'Here's one yuyu can shoot better than you can, Lloyd.' He just walked away."

"You're crazy, Lloyd."

"It's gospel truth. But what'll you say when I tell you there's a young, pretty American girl with curly hair right here in Magtalisay?"

"You're a bigger and better liar every day."

"Well, it's hard to believe. But I saw her myself. She's a schoolteacher. I'm going to ask if I can call, and then I'm going to drop in with that 'free' mandolin I picked up during the war, and we'll sit in the moonlight and sing. By the time you're well, it'll be too late for you. You'll never get her to look at you."

"I don't believe any of it."

"O.K. That won't change facts. And I'll get everything fixed just right for me. Maybe you can always get first choice with these cute little brown Filipinas, but this time I've got a head start. I'm way out in front.

"And there's still more news," he went on. "We're going to move. You and me and the safe and everything. Into that old barracks on top of the Escarpa. And no women are going to be allowed up there. I guess Morrow heard María and Encarnación when they were here last night;

58

Encarnación has that cute little giggle. He says we can find a house for them down here in the town, but the soldiers can't have women in the barracks and neither can the officers."

"What soldiers is he talking about, anyhow?"

"He says in two weeks there'll be twenty enlisted men."

"Twenty! Pearson never got more than twelve. So damn suspicious of Americans. Cowards, too. Where's he going to get them?"

"He didn't tell me that, Harry. But he did ask me if I knew any reason why men wouldn't enlist. He asked me if I knew why you hadn't been able to recruit any more men after the others deserted."

The two men looked at each other for a moment without friendliness, in a cold, appraising silence.

"Well, what did you tell him?" Palmer asked.

"Nothing. What did I have to tell?"

PART TWO

1

MORROW'S first prisoner escaped from the jail within twenty-four hours. The ancient *carcelero* was found tied hand and foot, lying in the courtyard and groaning horribly. Whether he suffered more from fright, from rough treatment, or from fear of the wrath of Captain Morrow, nobody could decide. His story was that a score of men had rushed the *cárcel*, beaten him into unconsciousness, and released the *pulaján*. Nobody had heard any noise, but the prisoner was certainly gone.

The escape did not surprise Morrow greatly, and his disappointment at being unable to question the stubborn prisoner again was balanced by an unexpected advantage. Now it would be possible for him to add to the barracks on the Escarpa a cell or two in which prisoners could be locked up securely, and the municipal authorities would have no excuse for being offended.

And the escape brought another benefit. All of Magtalisay was laughing over it. But they were not laughing at Morrow for trusting the *pulaján* to the old jailer. They were laughing over the ten-centavo piece that Morrow had paid for one day's food. From Morrow's point of view it had been simply a practical matter, for he knew that if he gave money for two days, it would all be spent improvidently at once. But the people regarded that small piece of money in a different light. Their interpretation reached

Ramos quickly, and he passed it on to Morrow. They were convinced, he said, that Morrow had put the fellow in jail with the deliberate intent of permitting his escape. So he left only ten centavos for food since he knew the man would escape that night. They believed that Morrow had, in effect, contemptuously tossed the man back to Faustino, saying, "Take him. He's worthless. I can't be bothered with him." It was such a good joke on the outlaws that people were forgetting to hide their laughter.

Morrow saw the first results of this stroke of luck at once. A few laborers had already been hired to begin the work of repairing the old barracks, but many more were needed. The wages and the daily hearty meal offered were an inducement, but this episode provided the additional appeal that was required, and men began appearing in sufficient numbers. Soon there were between ninety and a hundred names on the payroll, including the laborers and the men who supplied the building materials. Consequently the work went fast.

And this quick start was invaluable. Morrow knew the risk of an attack by Faustino was particularly grave at this time, with no enlisted men in the Constabulary and with their equipment stored in a vulnerable spot. Meanwhile he had to learn something of the terrain that was now under his protection. As soon as the work on the cuartel was well started, he put Ramos in charge and spent what time he could spare in mapping Magtalisay and its environs.

From the Escarpa he could see some of the country his patrols would have to cover, but it showed itself deceptively, hardly more to be trusted than a mirage. West, across the estuary and beyond the mud flats bared at low tide, were a number of salt beds, glistening yellowish-white inside their mud walls. But back of these lay the jungle, and the only way to learn any of the secrets of this part of the island was to go and find out.

It was the same in other directions. Magtalisay itself was plain enough and could have been roughly mapped from the top of the Escarpa steps. But everything else was buried, first under soft, thick foliage, then behind hills, and finally behind mountains. Even the coastline extending east and south around the bay held itself secret and remote, and by scanning this shore with binoculars, Morrow could discover little more than he could see with the naked eye.

Setting to work first on the nearest part of his territory, he paced the length and breadth of Magtalisay, from the plaza down into the fetid, evil-smelling sections and up into the pleasanter, higher ground. He mapped it with considerable accuracy but without too great detail, finishing the drawing during the long nights and tinting it delicately with the water colors he had brought for this purpose.

Next, he began a quick and superficial exploration of the water highways of his territory. He hired a banca with two men to paddle it, and took Corporal Fermín as interpreter. He had at first intended to take Lloyd to add another impressive uniform to his party, but decided against it. Until the matter of the desertions was better understood, he would have to be careful of what Palmer and Lloyd were given to do.

Taking a full day for the trip, he went first up the Sumpitan to Tuñgudnon, in the direction of Dos Picos, where Pearson had been killed.

Hardly large enough to be called a barrio, Tuñgudnon clung to a hill rising steeply from the water. The scattered huts were surrounded by irregular patches of partly cultivated ground on which grew camotes and sickly upland rice. On the opposite hill across the river were a few more patches under this crude cultivation, as well as some larger patches of coarse, light green cogon grass, the living death that steals the earth abused in this primitive culture.

Men had obviously lived in this place for many years, but on this day Tuñgudnon was empty. There was not a single human being anywhere to be seen. But there were warm cooking-pots. When he found those, Morrow knew that people had been warned of his approach; bamboo telegraph had sent them off into the jungle. He displayed himself casually, walking slowly about, or rather climbing, since there was no level ground. But no one showed his face.

They went back down the river to Canmanga, a settlement much larger than Tuñgudnon, built in a wide part
of the valley and surrounded by many hectares of rolling
country that offered the well-drained land best for Manila
hemp. This had once been a thriving barrio; there was
still about it an air of prosperity. But it was almost deserted. A handful of people—women, a few old men, a
half-dozen children, one of them with signs of leprosy—
crept out to stare at Morrow and reluctantly answered the
questions Fermín asked.

What they told amounted to less than could be seen
in what lay around them. Yes, they were almost the only
people left in Canmanga. Once it had been a big place
and they had lived in comfort, and they had had sons, but
everything had changed. Had Faustino's men stolen from
them? Oh, they had never heard of Faustino! Had Faustino's men killed their sons? No, they couldn't answer
that; they couldn't answer any more questions at all. Too
weak to be hostile, they were, Morrow decided, less afraid
of him than of the outlaws.

Again the banca rode smoothly and swiftly down the
brown stream between the green hills, and Morrow
checked the sketches and the estimate of distances he had
made on the slower trip up. It was surprising, he thought,
that there should be so much of the quality of silence in
the forested valley. He heard the paddles, and the men's
soft voices, and the murmur of the water, and even the
wind in the trees high up the valley wall; yet he had the
feeling that they were traveling in the midst of a great
stillness. It must come from the solitude; this valley was
completely empty of human life, except theirs, in this
small boat—

His thought was interrupted by the crack of a gun,
repeated by an echo. The boatmen shouted, and started
paddling faster. Morrow and Fermín, rifles ready, watched
for a sign of the life that threatened theirs, but they saw
nothing and they heard nothing; there was no movement
and there was no second shot. But instead of seeming
empty of human life, the valley now seemed full of it; a
hundred men, tens of hundreds, might be following them

unseen. They maintained their swifter speed; they kept their rifles ready.

Nothing more happened as the miles slipped by, and they came to their last stop at Sogod, near the union of the Sumpitan and the Negro. This barrio, a contrast in almost every way to the two already visited, was large, prosperous, and well populated with friendly people, who had already heard of the new Constabulary captain and were ready to show him around the village. Did Morrow want to see where the *pulajanes* had set fire to some houses in the last raid? Would he like to behold the very spot where a hero of Sogod—they pushed the hero forward— had fought one of the outlaws and almost killed him with his bolo? Over there was the hole in the ground where the robbers had dug up one man's hoard of money. Did Morrow think that meant a spy lived in Sogod, or could Faustino's eyes pierce the solid earth?

The whole barrio was a coconut grove. In every direction the eye was confused by the crowding host of slender boles; and the fronds, sixty to a hundred or so feet overhead, filled the air with a continuous sound like the crashing waves of a distant sea.

These palms were Sogod's life. As usual, they supplied food, oil for light, material for brooms and brushes and baskets and mats and clothing and other valuable objects, from building posts to toothpicks; but their greatest value in Sogod lay in still another product, called tuba. Morrow knew this as soon as he saw that the trees rarely carried their natural burden of coconuts. Most of them poured the juice of their flowering branches into bamboo vessels. This liquid, only moderately potable when fresh but greatly liked when fermented, explained Sogod's measure of prosperity even in these troubled times.

But to Fermín's direct questions about the outlaws, their answers were scanty. All they could tell about Faustino was that they had been robbed more than once. If they had more information, they were not yet ready to trust it with Morrow.

Still, it was here that he began his campaign for recruits by directing Fermín to announce that the time was coming soon when a man who wanted to fight the *pulajanes* might ask to join the Constabulary. He left it at that; merely an idea he hoped would have a quick growth.

Walking back from the landing place through Magtalisay, Morrow passed the school; and unexpectedly into his consciousness came the picture of the schoolteacher as he had had his single glimpse of her, entering Don Florencio's door in radiance. He stood still, feeling again the same nostalgia, aching and vague, unreasonable and unwelcome.

Why was he standing here? He had no time or wish for anything but work. He had maps to finish; he had to see what progress had been made on the barracks. He hurried away.

2

"THESE kids want to learn," Tom Horton's letters had said. "They can't learn fast enough to be satisfied. They want to learn everything at once. They hate to see the end of the day."

It was a late afternoon. Lucy walked between the benches, looking down at the heads of her pupils bent earnestly over their work. A child's soft and slender neck in this attitude of devoted concentration never failed to move her; she saw it as the most touching sight in the world. She loved children learning, children trying with all their might to do the tasks set for them, children feeding their hungry minds and training their unpracticed hands. And now, as usual, she supposed she would have to tell these children to stop and go home. It was four-thirty, and school was supposed to be over at four. But every child was still in the schoolroom. Emerald would soon be calling for her. It was certain these boys could never be punished by being made to stay after school; they liked nothing better.

But they were good. She could see already that they would need no punishment.

"Do you understand it, Teodoro?" she asked, looking over one boy's shoulder. She hadn't found their names easy, but she believed she was beginning to get them right. Teodoro was one of the easiest names. And the boy was one of her most advanced pupils, reading in a geography because he had finished all the readers.

"Yess, Meess Laisslee."

She still was not sure he understood. That was one of her few difficulties: they did not like to confess a failure to understand. And how could he understand that book? He was reading about wheat growing on the prairies. What could prairies mean to a boy who lived on a mountainous island, where, moreover, rice, not corn, was grown? She said, "Wheat is a grain. It is good to eat. Like rice. And the prairie," she pointed to the word and to a picture and then used gestures to illustrate her meaning, "is land as flat as water. You look and look and look, and everywhere, everywhere, north, south, east, west, you see no hill and no mountain."

She turned to a smaller boy who was writing laboriously on his slate. "C-a-t, c-a-t," she read. "That is very good, Paco." Putting her hand over his, she guided it in a smooth repetition. "And what is the word? Say it."

"Cat." The a was very broad, the t very sharp.

"That's right. Do you understand cat? I will make a picture on your slate." She made a crude sketch, a large circle topped with a smaller, ears, a tail, whiskers. "Now write cat again on your slate. Good!"

She moved on to the next. "Read it out loud, Felipe. Very slow, now. You like to go too fast."

"'Theess eess an apple tree. The boy will pick the apples. Who is the boy? The boy is John. John likes apples.'"

"Good, Felipe! Good! Now then, Eliseo. Let me see your slate. Good. Your numbers are right. And that is a pretty picture. What is it?" She repeated, pointing, "What is it?"

Eliseo, not finding the English word in his vocabulary

jumped up and ran to the window to touch the leaves of a plant.

"Of course," Lucy said. "It's a good picture and I should have known." She thought he might not understand all her words, but his smile showed he understood the tone of her voice. "I didn't know what a very pretty plant it is until I saw your drawing."

Looking down now into the plaza, she could see the calesa waiting for her. She hadn't noticed the clatter of the pony's feet or the scrape of the carriage wheels, and Emerald hadn't called, doubtless because the man standing there had come up to talk to her. She would have to go. She started to close the windows, and at once there were willing children all over the room, taking care of the small end-of-day tasks. She could see there was too much rivalry over this matter; the next day she must arrange for them to take turns.

She sighed a little, realizing that she was tired and hot, and probably dirty, too. The day had been long and she was learning at least as much as she was teaching. She knew by the ache between her shoulders and other small signs of weariness that though the hours had gone quickly, they had not drifted by unused. At this moment the gap between herself and her pupils, bridged so many times during the day, nevertheless seemed too wide for the next day's efforts. She had to remind herself that Tom Horton had done the most difficult work before she arrived. She brushed the chalk dust from her hands, patted a stray hair or two into her pompadour, and went out the door and down the stairs. Her pupils said good-bye and scattered across the plaza.

"So there you are," Emerald said. "I'd like to make you acquainted with each other. Señor Miguel Briones. Miss Lucy Leslie."

Lucy looked into the brown face, not old but with strong lines about the eyes and mouth, of a man about her own height. He bowed and said in very good English, "I am honored." His tone, she thought, was a little dry. Was he making fun of her?

"That's enough of that, Miguel," Emerald said. "Lucy

is working for your own people, wearing her pretty self out. And you are honored to meet her. Get in here, child, and sit down. You look made of eggshells."

Lucy stepped to the wheel, and Briones limped around from the other side of the carriage to help her up. When she was inside and had thanked him, he remained there, gazing up at her.

"Now what is it?" Emerald demanded promptly, not giving him a chance to speak. "You've changed, Miguel. You were a firebrand once, but now you're just a crab."

"I want to ask Miss Leslie a question."

Lucy said, "Why not? I'll answer anything I can."

"Why did you come to these islands?"

"But you must know. I came to teach the children to read and write and speak English."

"Who told you that is what the little brown brothers want?"

His tone brought color to Lucy's cheeks, though she had never heard of the resentment of some Filipinos against the teaching of English. But she answered simply. "They tell me every day in everything they do that they want to learn."

Emerald patted her arm. "That's a good answer, Lucy, and now he doesn't know what to say. You took the wind out of his sails. I told you, Miguel. You've been away too long. You don't know what's happening. Why didn't you come to see me as soon as you got to Magtalisay? You avoided me. And you've been listening to all sorts of nonsense. Kittens to make veal pie!"

Briones was still watching Lucy. "And how long do you think the children will be so anxious to learn English?"

This touched on something Lucy had been asking herself, and she answered Briones eagerly and warmly. "I wonder! The books we're using were written for American children. They're about apple trees and oak trees and snow and ice and skating and prairies. Well! You see? It's hard enough just to teach children to read and write, and I'm trying to teach them a new language besides. And then to have the books about things they've never heard of—

68

Now, you seem interested in the school, and you know all about these islands. I know the sort of stories that should be in the primers. If you and I could—" She stopped to look in surprise at Emerald, who was chuckling. "I didn't mean to say anything ridiculous."

"No, child, you didn't. I'm laughing at the expression on Miguel's face." To him she said, "Don't you doubt her. She means every word, or I'll eat my head. She doesn't know what you were trying to say to her. And now you listen to me. You're so bitter and so full of hate that you can't think straight any more. You've been believing a pack of lies. Why didn't you come right to me? All that nonsense about the Americans killing off your whole family! Your mother died a natural death, holding this hand of mine. I'm ashamed of you, Miguel, letting your politics control your head instead of the other way round."

She poked the cochero, who cracked his whip over the pony; and the calesa jolted and bumped out of the plaza.

"You talked to him like a Dutch uncle," Lucy said. "Who is he?"

"I watched him grow up. He learned his English from Arthur and me. Then he fought against Spain; that's what made him lame. And then he fought the Americans. He's a hero, I guess you'd call him, but I can still give him a talking to if I think he needs it."

"He didn't seem very friendly to me."

Emerald laughed again. "He'll know better next time. But he's a fine man, if he gets over his bitterness. You're tired?"

"A little."

"But not so much as yesterday, I think. I told you it was silly to wear yourself out dragging around three petticoats. One is plenty. And those stays! Take them off and throw them away. What does a girl like you need stays for? Your waist is small enough as the Lord made it. Women are fools. I'll say you have more sense than most, but you don't have enough."

Lucy stretched to loosen tired muscles. "Doesn't the air smell good up here? Aunt Em, I'm going to have a water-closet in that school. No. I'm going to have two.

One for the boys and one for the girls. Because I'm going to have girls, too. There's plenty of room. It's a shame not to have girls. They want to learn and they have a right to. This is the twentieth century."

"Were you listening to me? Did you hear what I said about your stays?"

"I'll admit you were right about the petticoats."

"I'm right about a lot of things."

"Now you're my Dutch uncle. Are you everybody's Dutch uncle, Uncle Em?" Glancing at Emerald, who was leaning against the side of the carriage, her eyes closed, she was afraid her joking had been misunderstood. Perhaps she was feeling faint again. Lucy had become increasingly alarmed over these spells, not knowing if they were symptoms of real illness or simply the effects that her inexplicable moods brought on. She noticed them even though Emerald tried to hide them from her. If Lucy spoke of it, Emerald would only say brusquely, "No, no. I feel perfectly all right."

"I'm sorry. You know I wouldn't hurt you."

"I know, I know. I'm not offended. Seeing Miguel made me think of old times. Tomorrow I'll go up to Punta Arenas and see about getting the next shipments ready. Oh, that place needs a man to take care of it! Sometimes it seems to me that the whole great teetotum, everything in the world, is running down since Arthur died. There's only one thing on earth worth having; I had it and I've lost it. You don't know, girl. You don't know." She rode the rest of the way in a silence Lucy did not try to interrupt.

3

TIME pressed on Morrow, as if Faustino were right behind him. But the outlaws had not been heard of. Perhaps it was true that they had crossed the island and were not at present in Morrow's territory. Still they were a constant threat. When no one knew where they were, they might be anywhere, even in the town of Magtalisay itself. Suspense was one of their weapons. They could never be forgotten.

Morrow spent a day on the Escarpa, where the building went well, and then decided on a quick trip up the east branch of the river, for it was important for him to see and to be seen in the river barrios. With Fermín again as interpreter, he set out in the same banca. The boatmen were better pleased than before, because the Negro was considered the safer branch, and one of them, Felizardo, who owned the boat, called one of the barrios they would visit his home.

The Negro meandered sluggishly through a wide, very fertile valley toward a series of peaks known as the Seven Sisters. But the rich land through which they traveled was sadly unproductive. The mud walls of the rice paddies were crumbling and the beds were filled with weeds. Near Tarnate, the first barrio, there were pitifully few people at work, only a handful of women planting the brilliant green seedlings in a flooded paddy, and a small group of taos laboring in another field. No more than two carabaos could be seen pulling plows through the brown mud. Tarnate itself was a neglected, hungry, sad, and frightened place.

"No tenemos ningunos carabaos." That was the chief complaint. "We have no carabaos. True; the pulajanes steal our rice. But if we had carabaos to plow the paddies, we could grow more."

"What's happened to your carabaos?" Morrow asked.

Some answered, "My carabao was sick. He died." They described the dreaded symptoms of rinderpest, from which all the islands had suffered. But more said, "My carabao was stolen."

"Who stole all the carabaos? Faustino? Where were they taken?"

Yes, Faustino was to blame. They could tell him that much. But that was all they knew. "And what can we do? When we could grow rice and sell it and get a little money, even then a carabao costs very dear, maybe as

71

much as twenty pesos. Now when we can raise no rice and have no money, a carabao costs one hundred and fifty pesos. We have hitched ourselves to the plow. But we can hardly grow enough to feed our families, to feed them a little, now and then."

"Whose carabaos are the two I saw in the paddies?" Morrow asked. "Can't you borrow them?"

The answers were vague, but it became clear that the animals couldn't be hired cheaply enough. Now other replies were evasive, too, and Morrow stopped his questioning and went about his task of sketching quickly the layout of Tarnate, directing Fermín meanwhile to drop hints, as in Sogod, concerning the opportunity to enlist soon in the Constabulary. They made, too, an announcement that if any of the uniforms and weapons taken by the deserters should be turned in, there would be a reward and no questions asked. A sign to this effect was posted in the small plaza of the barrio.

The inquisitive troop at Morrow's heels followed when he and Fermín returned to the banca, and it was there at last, in the mud of the river bank, that one of the men broke free of the silence that had gripped them all. He talked so fiercely and so fast that Morrow could not understand a word of his dialect.

He was a man smaller and darker than most of his companions, and, now that he was talking and gesticulating, composed of more passion than seemed contained in all the rest of them. He was, Fermín translated, Isidro Dapdap; he had been born in Tarnate and had never lived anywhere else; he belonged there; he never wanted to leave. But what was going to happen to him? Here was his story, and anyone would say it was true, for they all knew every word of it had happened.

It was a month now since the day, since the night, a dark night, after the moon had set. He had then a carabao he hid in a secret place and guarded every night. But someone had discovered the hiding place. And he himself had fallen asleep, because a man cannot stay awake forever, and he had started up at a noise and had discovered that his carabao was being taken away. He had run after it and someone had knocked him down, and he had been found there, looking like a dead man, the next morning.

But that wasn't all. Two weeks later he had gone to the neighboring island of Leyte where carabaos were for sale, hoping he could buy one, for he had saved a little money. And there were, it was true, carabaos selling for less than one hundred and fifty pesos. There were some for a hundred; they looked as if they might live another day or two, perhaps. And then there were the good ones. They cost too much. And among them, he knew it by a sort of roughness in its horn and by the slits he himself had cut in its ear, was his stolen beast. It knew him. When he shouted out the truth, they all laughed at him and threw him out of the place.

"Who was selling the carabao?"

Isidro didn't know his name, but he knew his face.

And then in increasing passion he went on to answer Morrow's earlier questions. Who were the owners of the carabaos now plowing in the paddies? The landlords who owned most of Tarnate. Where did they live? In Magtalisay in big houses. What were their names? Paterno, Zúñiga, Soriano, Villamor. Rich men. They owned Tarnate. Some of their carabaos had died, but only one or two had been stolen, and they had more than those Morrow had seen. They were used only on the land belonging to the landlords, and all the rice grown there by the tenants' labor would belong to the landlords, and the people were starving.

And he, Isidro Dapdap, wanted to enlist at once in the Constabulary and fight the *pulajanes*, though he had never before wanted to go away from Tarnate. He would go now with the Constabulary officers.

"Come to Magtalisay in two days," Morrow told him. "We can swear you in then."

Isidro waded out in the stream after them, clinging to the boat, but was persuaded at last to return to the land and wait until the time Morrow said. They did not know how long he remained standing where they had left him, but once, when a loop of the stream unexpectedly let them

73

look back across some empty rice paddies, he could still be seen, a solitary figure, looking after them. Morrow was tempted to return for him, but did not. He was a passionate man. Better to let him think it over.

The boatmen paddled on. It was noon and very hot. Gradually they drew nearer to the next barrio, marked by a grove of palms at the edge of the valley where the hills began to rise. "Punta Arenas," Felizardo said, pointing to it. "Before this time it was a barrio muy rico, but now the jungle is returning."

Leaving one man to take the banca around a loop in the river and meet them on the other side of the barrio, Morrow, Fermín, and Felizardo landed to walk through the streets. Quickly they had the usual procession, with Morrow taking notes and sketching, and a tail of villagers following.

In the center of Punta Arenas an avenue of royal palms stretched from the river to a house that, though built of woven bamboo and thatched with nipa, was still a large and pretentious dwelling. It belonged, said Felizardo, a self-appointed guide, to a señora who was the widow of an inglés; the inglés was buried under a stone they would presently see beside this avenue. As for the lady, they might see her too; he had just been told that she was at present in the barrio.

Morrow stopped at the monument; Arthur Sands, it said, 1825-1892. What sort of woman, he wondered, would live in an isolated and dangerous spot like this? Was she as remarkable as this man must have been? Someone like that could be very useful to the Constabulary. He went toward the house hopefully.

A muchacho, roused from his siesta, came yawning around from the back to say that the señora was in the bodega. He pointed to the road they were to take.

They went over a small hill, through a planting of young mangoes that were crowding each other badly, and finally down toward a loop of the river. There, on a bank high enough to eliminate danger from a flash flood, was the warehouse, a low, wide building with walls as well as roof of corrugated galvanized iron.

The doors were rolled open, letting in a square of light, but most of the barnlike interior was dim. Morrow could make out shelves and workbenches and various implements and machinery, but he could see no one. Yet he heard a woman's voice.

He was alone now. For some reason Fermín and Felizardo and the villagers had all dropped behind. He hesitated at the door, feeling like an intruder, wondering if he should knock or call out. Without a break the voice went on. It was really this that had made him pause, though he could not understand why the continuous flow of sound was so disturbing.

Presently he made out a figure at the rear of the building. "Señora," he said, and stepped inside, "may I introduce myself?" He started toward her. She kept on talking, though not to him, and now he could see that she was alone. And she was crying. The impulse to help sent him forward. "Señora, excuse me for intruding. Is there anything I can do for you?"

She was sitting on a box and had her arms on a workbench and her head on her arms. "Never again," she said. "Never, never, never again. I'll never see his like. Alone, alone." There was no expression in her voice, but the words, coming fast in an undertone, were more moving because of their very lifelessness. "Never again. Like the shadow over the sundial. Passing on. Merely a shadow and now gone." She repeated the last word over and over again. "Gone, gone, gone."

In pity Morrow turned away, but he could not leave. In pity, he turned back and touched her shoulder.

She sprang to her feet and whirled around, the box clattering as it fell. Though she was dressed in a man's trousers and shirt and they were much too large for her, the thin, elongated figure was unmistakable. She was the woman he had talked to on the pier that first day, getting hemp loaded on a casco, and he had seen her once more following the schoolteacher into the Zúñiga house. She stood straight and was fairly steady on her feet, but he realized now that she was very drunk. Her swollen, reddened eyes were fixed on him.

75

He repeated, "Is there anything I can do for you?"

"So it's you again, is it? Think you can bring back the dead? Go away."

Morrow nodded and turned around. At the moment there was nothing, probably, that anyone could do for her. He walked back to the door, noticing as he went much evidence to show that the man this woman mourned had dabbled in every possible native product for export. There was a huge coconut oil press on one side. There was a small distilling outfit from which, as Morrow passed, came a whiff of the perfume of the ilang-ilang. And there was more machinery and there were other sweet or aromatic fragrances in the jumble under the iron roof. Near the door was a drafting board with a paper pinned to it, and Morrow could not help hesitating to glance at it.

To his surprise, the woman was right behind him, and she said fiercely, "Those are *his* things. Nobody touches them." She seemed in good control of her feet, though her voice was thicker.

"I won't touch your husband's things, señora." Not knowing how else to end the uncomfortable interview, he saluted.

Either his reply or this gesture stirred her anger. "Stop laughing at me! Get out! Get out!" She searched with quick, darting glances and groping hands in the litter of the nearest workbench. "You'll be sorry, you'll be sorry—"

Morrow froze for an instant with the thought that she was going to throw something at him, that this was going to be a drunken brawl that would make a horrible and unforgettable scene for the Filipinos outside the bodega. Would it be worse to wait, or worse to overpower her at once? With a man, he would not have hesitated.

But her hands had come on something that diverted her attention, and she began again to cry and talk to herself. Morrow motioned to Fermín, and got out of sight as fast as he could. They hurried down to the river.

4

A DAY or two later, at the end of a hot and humid afternoon, Morrow met Lucy for the second time. He was returning through the poorest part of Magtalisay after inspecting some materials for the cuartel when he saw her leaning against a palm tree at the side of the street, her hands covering her face, her open parasol rolling in the mud at her feet. Several children stood about her, uneasy but silent.

His response to her distress concealed from him any other reaction he felt at seeing her again. He crossed the street, the children drew back, and he took her arm. "Miss Leslie, what's the trouble?" She shuddered and he felt her weight as she drooped toward him. "Are you hurt?"

She shook her head and whispered, "I'll be all right. In a minute."

"It's muddy all around here. I could carry you to a house—get a carriage—"

She shook her head again. "I have to go on. I'll be all right."

"Then let me take you where you're going. Can't you tell me what's wrong?"

She raised her head and looked at him. It was profoundly surprising for him to see her face so close. He had not known her eyes were gray. Even now, in her pallor, she had that radiance about her that had dazzled him before. A little color came back into her cheeks. She said, "You were on the *Esperanza*." Then she added hastily, "I'm all right. It was the awful smell. And a pig ran at me. A filthy pig."

Morrow knew how filthy pigs could be, since they were one of Magtalisay's substitutes, an ancient substitute, for a sewer. He said, "You'll remember that pork in this country is not fit to eat." She closed her eyes, turning white again, and he realized he could have said nothing worse. "Let's get to some better-smelling part of town. Don't you have a handkerchief in your bag?" He thought she nodded. "Then get it out and hold it to your nose and lean on me."

She murmured, "Bad manners to hold your nose."

"Isn't it time for bad manners? Let them see you do it and it will be worth a sanitation campaign."

She pulled out a handkerchief and the sentimental fragrance of violets made a brief conquest of the fetid air.

"Good," he said. "Now if you insist on going to the place you set out for, which direction—?"

"One of my pupils. I'm going to his house."

Morrow identified the boy by his expression of anxious responsibility, and said, "Sigue." At once the boy was off and they followed, with another child carrying the muddy parasol.

Lucy's arm was very soft in Morrow's grasp, and fragile-seeming, yet there was strength and resilience in her. Each step she took was firmer, and she began to hold herself straighter. As he guided her, Morrow watched her, wondering. She astonished him; but why? What was it that made her unique? Why did he feel that a dozen portraits might be painted of her and she would still elude the artist? Was that the reason he longed to try? What wouldn't he give for such a chance! The delicacy of her temple, the subtle line of her cheek—

Ahead of them a coconut dropped from a tree, and he felt her nervous start. He should talk to her, not walk along beside her like a bear, probably frightening her as much as the pig had done. But what should he talk about? He hadn't seen enough of his own people to know what he ought to say; he might as well be a Bontoc Igorot.

Frowning and looking down at the road, he began. "That was only a ripe coconut. The tropics are kind and drop food right in your lap. I suppose you've learned already to tell the coconut palm from the others? They're the most beautiful of all. The daughter of the ocean currents and the tradewinds. Coconuts won't grow in a greenhouse, you know. They won't stand around at weddings and funerals. They have to be where they can feel the wind. And yet sometimes the wind tears them to pieces."

Glancing anxiously at her, he saw she was looking at him. She had taken the handkerchief away from her nose and she was even smiling a little. "You're really very kind," she said. "And on the *Esperanza* I was afraid of you. I thought you'd warn the Bureau of Education and they'd make me go back to Manila. Even if I hadn't been seasick, I would have hidden from you."

"You were afraid of me? Well, you can see I'm harmless."

"Oh, I know more than that about you now." Her smile was brighter and even slightly mischievous. "The mayor wrote to Manila and told them that you would see that I was safe in Magtalisay." She added seriously, "Thank you for rescuing me today."

With relief, Morrow abandoned his lecture on the coconut palm. It had served its purpose. She was all right now. She commenced looking with lively and inquisitive interest at everything they passed, and she had a dozen questions for him to answer at once.

She made everything look new to him too. He forgot he had seen similar sights hundreds of times before: the woman weaving a hat, the girls at the windows combing each other's long black hair, the shriveled creature squatting in a doorway at the top of a ladder and chewing betel nut, her teeth black, her lips crimson, the ground below reddened where she spat. And all returned Lucy's interest with solemn curiosity. Two young women came from the river, each balancing a basketful of wet garments on her head, and they had to stand stock still in order to stare at the americana. "Look at her arms," Morrow heard one of them say. "She must be white all over!"

The boy reached the ladder of his home and his mother appeared in the doorway, with a look of apprehension at the schoolteacher.

Morrow asked, "Has the boy been making trouble?"

"None of them make trouble. He brought me a basket for the slate pencils, a lovely thing, and said his mother

79

made it. I want her to teach basket-making one day a week, and then maybe girls will come to school. You'll help me talk to her?"

Morrow said he would.

"I'm really very glad that pig tried to scare me to death," she said. "At exactly the right time." Her smile thanked him, as she intended, and charmed him more than she knew. She murmured, "Now I'm going to use all my Spanish at one blow," and looked up at the woman and said, "*Buenos días, Señora Flores.*"

Morrow followed her as she picked her way through mud, weeds, and dirt, and then climbed the bamboo ladder and entered the palm-leaf house.

Eliseo's mother was too nervous to talk until they began to examine her work, and then their praise made her shy. But she glowed under their interest, and displayed and named the materials she used, kawayang, buli, nito, salogo, malabago, junay. To Morrow's surprise her finished articles were of superior weave and design. He had expected a newcomer like Lucy to be impressed by the mediocre, but this work was among the best he had ever seen.

Watching the girl and translating for her, he was surprised again as, by her natural friendliness, she turned her errand into a warm success. His association in the islands with his own people, scanty as it had been, had too often shown him arrogance or its twin, condescension, building a wall between white and brown. Lucy had none of that. Her freshness and simplicity gave her a point of view that sophistication would have sneered at. But he could see she might accomplish wonders. By instinct she would go farther than anyone else could go by subtlety.

He felt that he was watching a dove with the wisdom of the serpent, and a young dove, at that. With the basket-weaving program arranged, they left the Flores house and walked together to the plaza, where she asked him to see her school and astonished him again with the simplicity and penetration of her understanding. On the blackboard was a chalk drawing of a nipa house. "Eliseo did that," she told Morrow. "He's an artist like his mother. And I've been thinking ever since we saw the house where

80

they live . . ." She paused, still working out her thought.

And he waited, idly correcting a line here and there in the drawing. What was she thinking, this girl with no more excuse for her sweetness than the wild rose needs? "Well?" he said at last. "What's the rest of it?"

She shook her head. "It's not ready yet. I must wait till the right time. I'll have to make it seem to come from the children and not from me. But if we had one drawing of a dirty house in a dirty yard, and another drawing of a clean house in a clean yard . . . Or if we should change the dirty yard and repair the house when the children tell how they've cleaned up their . . ."

A voice from below called, "Lucy!"

"That's Mrs. Sands. And I've kept you a terrible time!" With his help she closed the room for the night. "Come and meet her," she said, running down the stairs, "and we'll tell her how you saved me from a pig and a smell."

With her long face stiff, Emerald looked at him as he helped Lucy into the *calesa*. "I have met Captain Morrow before." She poked the *cochero* and he cracked his whip. Morrow had barely time to drop the muddy parasol on the floor of the carriage before the pony had gathered himself for a bound and was jerking the carriage away.

5

IN ten days the cuartel was ready for limited use, and the tower had been cleaned and prepared for Morrow. They moved the supplies and what furniture they had, and then they were established in their new headquarters. All this had been done with no interference from Faustino; it was almost as if he had cooperated. Since the attempt on Morrow's life on the day of his arrival, with the exception of that single shot when he was coming down the river from Canmanga, there had been no news from anywhere of the outlaws.

Morrow was grateful for the respite, though he wished he knew the motive behind it. Caution or strategy, fear or stupidity, even chance might have kept the *pulajanes* in the hills. Everyone had his own theory about it. Palmer told Lloyd that he was sure the Escarpa would prove more vulnerable than the heart of the town, and Faustino would show he was right and Morrow was a fool. Morrow himself thought Faustino might be waiting for men to enlist, when they would be given equipment worth stealing, uniforms and arms he might have been informed were yet to come from Manila, since the material on hand had been carefully disguised by the way it was packed. But Ramos said that Faustino and his men were plainly cowards, terrified of the señor capitán. If there should be an earthquake now, Ramos declared, everyone would know why. It would come because the *pulajanes* up there in the mountains were shaking with fear.

Like other sayings of Sergeant Ramos, this traveled around Magtalisay quickly, and its mild flavor held an intoxicating pleasure for people who found it a new and cheering experience to laugh at the outlaws. It was Ramos, too, who laboriously again and again pointed out how right it was for a man named Morrow to live in a Moro tower. Starved for humor and hope, the people took the pun to their hearts, and it comforted them.

Now more than half the time had elapsed that Morrow had allowed himself for enlisting the first new Constabulary soldiers, and almost half the time had gone before the day of the promised drill in the plaza. So far the enlistments totaled ten.

Though according to Ramos every man employed in the work on the barracks had inquired, more or less guardedly, sometimes for a "friend" or a "brother," about the possibilities of entering the Constabulary service, only eighteen had come to Morrow asking to enlist. These eighteen were carefully interviewed. Four were handicapped in sight or hearing, one was too old for active service, and three had six or more dependents each. Morrow kept their names and promised them work with the

Constabulary if anything suitable turned up. The other ten were sworn in.

In a private ledger for his own use, Morrow gave each of the ten recruits a page, where he wrote the important facts of each man's background. These were his first entries:

"Amadeo Sayos. 31. Married, one son, aged 2. Farm laborer. Moved from Tarnate to Magtalisay to live with relatives after *pulajanes* stole rice and burned house.

"Nicador Tiongco. 18. Chinese mestizo. Father's shop robbed by *pulajanes*.

"Emilio Pascual. 25. Will not say if married or unmarried. Farm worker and hemp-stripper. From Canmanga. Came to Magtalisay several months ago. Very bitter about *pulajanes* but will not say why. Possibly some friend or relative in Faustino's band.

"Gonzalo Alas. 19. From Sogod. Has been tuba collector, and has done numerous other small jobs. Says *pulajanes* have destroyed a man's chances to make a living in Sogod.

"Manuel Punsal. 25. Married. No fixed occupation. No fixed home. Father injured by *pulajanes*. Says he fought as *insurrecto* against Americans, but now wants to fight with Americans against Faustino. Understands guns. Good marksman.

"Juan Gaviano. 26. Farm laborer. Originally from Canmanga. House burned, father killed by *pulajanes*.

"José Lim. 20. Chinese mestizo. Father's shop robbed twice by *pulajanes*.

"Carlos Bautista. 26. Married, two children, 1 and 2. Carpenter. Former *insurrecto*. Good marksman. *Pulajanes* burned father's house in Tarnate, abducted his sister.

"Romualdo Mangubat. 19. Boatman, sometimes worked with fishermen, sometimes loading cascos. Had been part-owner of parao, which was stolen by *pulajanes*.

"Vicente Resurrección. 22. Married, three children, 1, 2, and 4. Fisherman. Part-owner with Mangubat of stolen parao."

The first ten. One thing they had in common appeared in the record: a reason for hating Pope Faustino and his outlaws. But also they were all men who seemed in fair health, with the possibility of improving to perfect fitness, and they were all men who had impressed Morrow as being courageous.

When there were still ten more men to be recruited and only two days to do it in, Morrow began to accuse himself of idle and harmful boasting. He needn't have set a limit of two weeks when fifteen days or even sixteen might see him with the full number and without a broken promise to live down. Broken promises are not forgotten. It was remarkable that ten men were moving into the cuartel, that ten men were having their uniforms fitted by old Lim, young José Lim's father, the shopkeeper-tailor. Ten men, when for two months not a man had been willing to enlist. But ten men were not twenty. Why had he set an exact number and an exact time?

Then the next day two more volunteers came in. Felizardo, the boatman, came to the tower to say that he had decided he wanted to fight at Morrow's side. He offered not only himself, but also his banca and his cousin, another quick-moving, eager young man from San José. The two were accepted and the banca was hired. The boat had been nameless but was now dignified by being called *El Buen Exito*, or The Happy Outcome. After those letters had been painted on the bow, Felizardo wanted to add an American flag on each side, and was dissuaded only when he understood that to have muddy water washing over the flag might look disrespectful.

That made twelve men, and Morrow thought they would shape up well. The only disquieting thing about them was their persistent questioning of Ramos, who reported it to Morrow, concerning who was going to drill them and lead them. Was it surely going to be Morrow himself? While leaving their reasons obscure, they made it clear to Ramos and he made it clear to Morrow that they wanted him, and not Palmer or Lloyd. It was Morrow who was their captain, wasn't it? Morrow, and only Morrow? They wanted to be very certain of that.

On what Morrow, angrily satirical with himself, called his last day of grace, two paraos sailed in from the south, skimming across the bay with top-heavy sails balanced by men standing on the outriggers. The crews, grim and intent, asked to be taken to the White Moro.

They told Morrow their story with passion and hope. Only two nights before, the *pulajanes* had attacked their village, Lopo-lopo, on the coast south of Magtalisay, coming like the typhoon, unseen until the work of destruction began, heartless, pitiless. Faustino's men were ladrones and murderers, and worse. Once long ago they had promised some wonderful and miraculous cure for all diseases, a remedy they called Independencia, but all they ever brought was death. This time five Lopo-lopo men had been killed and two wounded. A little girl of four had been beheaded by a bolo because a *pulaján* had stumbled over her in the uncertain light cast by her burning home. A girl of sixteen had been abducted. And all their hemp had been stolen. This was not so evil as the murders, but it would mean months of deprivation, for there had been many bales ready for shipment and everyone had suffered loss. So they had come for help.

It was the first time that Morrow had heard himself called the White Moro, El Moro Blanco, or realized that stories about him were spreading through his territory. There was a touching mixture of faith and fantasy in what these men expected him to do. They said they knew where Faustino's men had gone: they had flown at incredible speed to the top of a neighboring mountain. And there, they seemed to think, Morrow could follow them and exterminate them merely by his appearance.

When Morrow told them he could do nothing single-handed and couldn't act until his soldados knew how to hold a gun, they were reluctant to believe him. But they were convinced at last. And they confessed, too, when Morrow questioned them, that no one had seen the pulajanes actually going along the trail to the mountain. They agreed, finally, that Morrow might be right when he said the pulajanes would hardly carry stolen hemp up into the hills but had probably transported it by boat to a convenient market. Perhaps to Tacloban, which was nearest, but possibly much farther. The Constabulary in those places would be warned by cable, and something might be recovered.

Then Morrow explained to them the purpose of the Constabulary and the need for trained men—who would still be only a few against many outlaws—to clear the islands of Faustino's band. The interview ended with seven more recruits, all young and fiercely ready to fight the pulajanes. They included a pair of twins, Benito and Benigno Pulay, whose sister was the abducted girl, and the father of the murdered child, a man named Juan Reyes. The other four were the owners of one of the paraos, and this sailing vessel, the Obediente, was enlisted in the Constabulary service at the same time.

Late that night as Morrow lay on the palm-leaf mat spread over packing cases that made his bed in his solitary tower, he heard men's voices rising in interrogation outside. In a moment he was walking across the Escarpa. The moon, a few days before the full, hung close in the western sky, and the whole surface of the promontory and everything upon it, the cuartel, the cannon, the tower, the wall, the bushes and weeds at the edge of the cliff, the men, all were lighted with the clarity of day. Only the sun's yellow heat was lacking, and colors had taken on a new and unnatural beauty.

At the top of the steps the two sentries on duty, one of the new men and Corporal Saavedra, were arguing with a stranger. When they saw Morrow the argument ended. "This man," Saavedra said, saluting, "asks to see the capitán. We tell him the capitán is sleeping."

"I'm awake," Morrow said, "as you can see. And asleep or awake, I must always know if someone wants me. Who are you?" he asked the man. "What did you come for?"

Though he was a stranger, there was something familiar about him. It was quickly but painfully explained. "I am Pedro Dapdap, brother of Isidro, of Tarnate." Like Isidro, he was a passionate man, with emotions almost too strong for his voice. "My brother wished to join the Constabulary. I was there. I heard him tell you. I heard you refuse to bring him back with you to Magtalisay. If he had come, he would now be alive. They fell on him with their bolos.

86

they cut out his tongue, they killed him for speaking to you!"

"When did this happen, amigo? Who did it?"

Shrilly the man went on. "They were *pulajanes*, those who stole his carabao, some traitor in Tarnate. Some traitor in Tarnate who pretends to suffer like the rest of us fell on him yesterday and killed him with—"

"Quiet, amigo," Morrow warned. "We can talk as well by talking softly. Why didn't Isidro come here at the time I said? I told him to come in two days. That time is long past. I think he had changed his mind about joining the Constabulary."

"He did not change his mind. He wanted to fight the *pulajanes*, to kill them, to get back his carabao, to get the money they stole—"

"Quiet!" Morrow said again. "I think he changed his mind about joining us. I think he decided to act alone. Tell me? Is that right?"

"Perhaps. Yes. That is true."

"Then why have you come here? Did you come to give us the names of his murderers?"

"If I could name them, they would be already dead! I came—" His face, every change of its expression sharp in the moonlight, showed that a new idea had just come to him. Defiance and grief had brought him to say that Isidro's death was Morrow's responsibility, but that he himself was going to avenge it. Now he saw that Isidro's death was proof that one man was helpless against Faustino. "I have just made up my mind. I have come to enlist in the Constabulary in Isidro's place."

This offer, impulsive and passionate, was not quite welcome to Morrow, but it would be condemning the man to certain and immediate death to turn him back now. So Pedro Dapdap, fodder grass-cutter, no dependents, was the twentieth recruit.

"*Un verdadero milagro!*" Don Florencio said when he heard. "A genuine miracle. I am delighted. This is a true reason for joy." Others repeated his words. A genuine miracle, a joyful occasion. Morrow could not join them in delight. The price for these last enlistments had been high. Six butcheries in Lopo-lopo, one in Tarnate. Yet the butcheries showed the need, and without this sudden, terrible need to force them, the enlistments might have been too slow. Faustino was a tumor in the body of the people that could be cured only when it began to cure itself. Things were going, if not in the way Morrow would choose to have them go, then perhaps in the way they had to go.

6

WHEN told that Lloyd had asked to call, Emerald had approved. "And we can see what we think of him. I never paid attention to those young men when they came to live here. Why should I? But every Dora needs her David and every Caddy needs her young Mr. Turveydrop. Only you want someone proud and strong and handsome, like my Arthur." She had answered with a scornful sniff when Lucy protested that she was not looking for a husband. Now, while Lucy and Lloyd sat on the veranda and sang, she withdrew discreetly, returned to hover anxiously, and then withdrew again.

" 'Off agin, on agin, gone agin, Finnigan,' " Lloyd said. "What shall we sing next?"

"Do you know the Kansas song? 'Kansas sun, hot Kansas sun?' "

"Nope."

" 'Give me a home where the buffalo roam'?"

"Nope. How about *Nelly Gray*?" He played a few measures on his mandolin and then she joined in, their young voices thin and lonely. The sad melody did not seem alien to the island air. The moon, looking over the hill behind the house, lit up the palms and the roofs in the town below, made the Moro tower stand out very white on the Escarpa, and scattered brilliance over the black, unquiet water of the bay.

"What's that dot moving around down there?" Lucy asked as the song ended. "Can it be a man walking? Is it a sentry? I never saw such bright moonlight."

"It's probably Captain Morrow. I don't know when he sleeps. No matter when I'm supposed to be on duty at night, no matter when he's supposed to be on duty, he's always around. I guess he's crazy. No other way to explain him. You should see him and that Sergeant Ramos drilling the new yuyus—excuse me, I forgot you don't like that word—but anyhow they drill them until they're all ready to drop. They don't need drilling, you know. What if they can't form a straight line? Who cares? And then they make them take a gun apart and put it together again. And then target practice. It goes on forever. First one man for a while alone with Morrow or Ramos, and then another one. He hasn't issued guns yet; they just use two or three for all twenty men. Take turns. Drill with bamboo poles. And say, that band he's got! Have you heard them tooting and banging? Crazy! We don't need a band."

"What do you and Lieutenant Palmer do?"

"Oh, I keep the books. What books there are to keep. Palmer sits around with a sore on his leg."

"You mean he can't walk?"

"Sure. His leg's almost well. He thinks it's only an excuse so Morrow can keep him shut up. Harry has bad luck. Sometimes it seems a man gets all his chances taken away from him. Harry ought to be captain here. He could run this place and everything in it. But something always gets in his way. Harry's— How did I get started talking about Harry? Why don't I talk about myself?"

Emerald's voice startled them. "You seem to think a lot of your friend, young man."

"Yes, ma'am. There's nobody like Harry; that's right."

"Why does he stay in the Constabulary if it's not giving him a chance? Where's his get-up-and-get?"

"He says he'll stay long enough to bring in Faustino. He'll do it, too. Then he's going to have a big plantation. All coconuts. Maybe I'll have a plantation myself. It's like a dream. You get your land, plant your coconuts, and in

89

seven years they start bearing and you're rich. Did you know that?"

Emerald said, "I heard about coconuts before you were born."

"Is it true you get a nut a day from each tree? That's three hundred and sixty-five a year."

"Sometimes there's more."

"That's what Harry says. He says in ten years he'll be a millionaire. And if he can do it, why can't I? Maybe I'll plant gutta percha, too. Could be a big future in gutta percha. This soil is so rich if you plant a can of beans, it'll sprout right up. Maybe we'll both be billionaires. Harry's saving his money now, and I'm trying to save too. My luck'll change some day."

"Your friend Harry," Emerald said, "sounds like my Arthur. He always had big plans too. You bring Harry up here with you."

"Yes, ma'am," Lloyd said, somewhat disconsolately. "Harry's better than I am at a lot of things, and I might as well say so. I'm better with a baseball bat, though. If Morrow makes him play, he's not going to like it. Did you know we have two baseball teams? Don't ask me why. I thought we needed soldiers, but we're getting ball players. And what do you think! Captain Morrow strips to the waist to play, just like the Filipinos—you'd think the sun would kill him—and he wears a gold locket on a chain around his neck. Ever hear of a thing like that? Crazy. Oh, and I can sing better than Harry, too. He can't play a mandolin, either. He can't even play a mouth organ."

"Let's have something happy, shall we? Do you know this?" He plucked a gay tune from the strings of the mandolin and sang:

> "She was bread in old Kentucky,
> She was wine in New Orleans,
> She was beer out in Milwaukee,
> And in Boston she was beans."

7

FROM a few words here and a few there, spoken by the new soldados sometimes to Ramos and sometimes to himself, Morrow was gathering information about the *pulajanes*, and drawing a few conclusions, general but sound. Faustino, he learned, could strike in two places at once; Morrow knew then that Faustino's followers were numerous and that he had good deputy leaders. Faustino understood well the value of surprise. Faustino's attacks came sometimes from the mountains and sometimes from the sea; it was clear to Morrow therefore that Faustino's men must travel as easily over the bay as over the trails and rivers, and must surely have more than one well-established refuge. He heard also unending stories of cruelty, but they were an uninstructive monotony of horror.

The first specific, definite information that the Constabulary could go to work on came from Felizardo less than a week after he enlisted. He told Ramos first, and then went with Ramos to Morrow. He knew, he said, a secret place the *pulajanes* used.

"Where is it?"

Not far from San José. It could be reached easily by banca, and he, Felizardo, would be the señor capitán's guide.

"Is it a place where they live?"

No. It was a small place, a cave. Somewhere to meet, somewhere to leave stolen things after a raid.

"How many people know of it besides the *pulajanes*?"

He, Felizardo, alone, for as a boy he had found a secret entrance to this cave. Most people were afraid of the place. The last time he was there he saw signs of its use. If the señor capitán would go there, perhaps he would capture some of the outlaws, even Faustino himself. Who could tell?

Morrow questioned him in detail about the location of the cave, thanked him, and said he would consider going. He had, as a matter of fact, already decided that he must go. But why hadn't Felizardo told him sooner? Because his confidence was slow to grow? Or because a trap was being set? Against this suspicion of an ambush, Morrow could put only his faith in his own judgment of men, and Felizardo was one in whom his trust was strong. But he concluded that the wisest course would be to make an unexpected, secret departure.

So the new Constabulary company's first patrol began at night in a rain, when they would not need, for a while at least, to fear the moonlight. Felizardo and Ramos were in the party, with five others, the Pulay twins, Dapdap, Reyes, and Punsal. There were promising marksmen among them, but the important thing was that these five had the fiercest hatred of the outlaws. Morrow dared not overlook the possibility that one or more of the recruits had joined the Constabulary to acquire a gun and ammunition, and on this first trial of green men he was doubly careful.

In two bancas they went up the Rio Negro. A gusty wind flecked the water with whitecaps, and the boats were a double elongated blot across the irregular, flowing lines of the waves. The men had been warned not to speak, but they would, perhaps, have been silent anyhow. Morrow could feel their tension. They hoped, as he did, for a clash; they would welcome, as he would, the test of active danger.

Unseen, they passed the dark barrios of Tarnate and Punta Arenas and San José. By that time the rain had stopped, and when, at about five in the morning, an hour before dawn, they reached their first destination, the moon was shining. The river's course here was through a rocky, narrow valley. At Felizardo's direction they ran the bancas up on a stony beach and stepped out.

They were sheltered from the wind, though they could hear it rushing through the forests on the mountains about them. It was cold. In that heavy, wide-eyed silence that comes from watching through a night, they stretched cramped muscles and rubbed chilled fingers.

At Morrow's order, Felizardo repeated his description of the rest of the river. The cave, he told them, was not far now. Just above where they were standing, the Negro narrowed still more and the banks changed to limestone walls. Actually, then, the river ran right out of the mountain, for these walls rounded out and rose high above the water, and had in fact once had a ceiling of rock that had long since fallen in. In the wall of this former cavern, at the height of three houses above the river, was the mouth of the cave he thought the outlaws had been using. And at the back of the cavern, cascading from a cleft, the river flowed from the heart of the mountain.

How did one get into the cave? By climbing; it was easy enough if nobody stood on guard at the mouth to push an intruder back into the water. But the only way to enter the cave without warning was the way he had already told the señor capitán. You could not enter the cavern unseen; there was no chance of reconnoitering from that direction. Instead, you had to creep through the long tunnel he had discovered by chance; but why not go that way? He knew it well; he had explored it many times. He would lead them.

Morrow's plan was different. One banca with the Pulay twins and Reyes was to remain where it was. The other banca would take the rest of them upstream. He and Felizardo would enter the underground passage, and the banca would land on the opposite side of the river where there was another low bank. There Ramos, Dapdap, and Punsal would wait. Meanwhile, he and Felizardo would be approaching the cave.

The rest of the plan was twofold. If there were pulajanes in the cave, Morrow and Felizardo would frighten them into abandoning the place and escaping down the river. Then the two parties of Constabulary, who were placed so that they could fire at a boat on the river without shooting each other, were to capture them.

On the other hand, if the cave was empty, the capitán would signal to Ramos by floating down the current a piece of bamboo, which he would carry with him and mark by tying a handkerchief around it. Then the banca would come into the cavern. And they would all return to Magtalisay.

When the plan was understood, the single banca headed upstream again, Felizardo watching for his landmarks; a turn of the river, a rock, the shoulder of a hill, and then a mountain top with a projection like the snout of an iguana looking down at them.

The landmarks came into view. From the boat Felizardo climbed up the rock wall, carrying an unlighted lantern and holding to the pudlos vines that covered the limestone. Part way to the top he pulled the vines aside and vanished. Morrow followed, and the two began to crawl on hands and knees into the side of the mountain. After a turn or two they lighted the lantern and went on more easily, rising when they could from all fours and moving at a crouch over the rough, wet rock.

Morrow had his share of the common human fear of being buried alive, and he had no liking for being underground. It was difficult for him not to think how easily the slightest earthquake, in this land of frequent quakes could close them in. Felizardo, however, showed no sign of this feeling, though more than once they had to stop to clear away stones that he said had fallen since the last time he was there. He showed Morrow where he had marked the passage, on first exploring it, with a ball of hemp cord to guide him back, and although his marks were almost impossible for Morrow to see, Felizardo moved confidently ahead, never hesitating for more than a moment when there was a choice of direction to be made.

The small and twisting channel led generally upward. Morrow could not guess how many yards they traveled; he only knew it could not be as far as it seemed, because it seemed like miles. The chill had a peculiar power of penetration; though the air was not close and its freshness was proved by the steady flame in the lantern, it was hard to believe that it came from the outside world and had ever been warmed by the sun. A nightmarish fancy surprised and possessed Morrow, rivaling his awareness of the heavy rocks above: it was the childish idea that he had been swallowed by some prehistoric monster and was crawling up its icy gullet hoping to escape. The cave ahead, no matter what it held, became a goal as dear as it was distant.

In some places the passage was so constricted that Morrow had to remove his revolver and ammunition belt and pull them through behind him, and there was never room to stand upright. Then quite suddenly, coming out of a low arch, he sensed a change. The sound of running water, which had been only a whisper, increased to a noisy chuckle. The roof rose higher, the rock underfoot slanted down. From the recesses ahead came a foul odor to contaminate the dank air. But before Morrow had a chance to look about, Felizardo stopped short and the light went out.

Doubts of Felizardo pounded with Morrow's heartbeats. Was this a cul de sac filled with old bones? Was this to be the end of him, trapped in a black labyrinth? Was Felizardo still with him, or had he already turned back to find his way safely out into the day?

Morrow struck a match, and its flare was reflected close to him in Felizardo's large and startled eyes. "No light," the Filipino murmured. "We are here."

Already Morrow had blown out the match, hoping that his fear had not been seen. Felizardo's next words told him it had not. "The capitán will lead. Now I follow. But wait. In a minute our eyes will see. Then you will know how to go. *Cuidao, señor capitán!*" Having reached what he considered the point of real danger, Felizardo was resigning his forward position.

Very gradually the pitch blackness thinned, and a vague outline of rocky wall appeared on each side. Morrow began to move, testing each step before he trusted the footing. The floor narrowed and slanted to the slippery bed of a rivulet that washed over his ankles. The strong and repellent odor grew more powerful. Unexpectedly he found a grayish blur in the darkness ahead, indicating an opening that was the source of what light they had. At the same time he became aware of some movement besides their own. He stood still, straining eyes and ears.

There was a soft but swelling sound like water or wind, with an added shrillness that he could not at first understand. And then it came to him. He started to move again. Bats. Bats, after their nocturnal search for food, flying into the cave at dawn. And the odor was bat guano. It was hardly likely that the outlaws spent much time in such surroundings; it was almost certain they could use such a cave only for an emergency shelter. The passage turned, diminished to an opening that was little more than a crevice through which Morrow could hardly squeeze, and ended in the great vault of the cave itself.

It was high and long, with two arches through which the new day could be seen. The lower opening looked out on greenery, and the higher one was bright with the early morning sky. Except for Morrow and Felizardo, there appeared to be no human being anywhere about.

They made a search, and when it ended knew they were alone save for the bats, hanging from cracks and corners in the rock and covering ceiling and walls with gray, living drapery. Now and then during the search one of the creatures would be disturbed and would fly squeaking to a higher point and again suspend itself from a claw, furry wings folded about it like a shroud clutched and held close by skeletal fingers.

There was no other man, but there were traces of men. There was a small basket of empty cartridges, collected for refilling and further use, and now thick with guano. There were a couple of rusty bolos and some mildewed clothing, perhaps part of the loot from a raid. There were a dozen sacks of rice, doubtless stolen too, which had been left here to sprout and mold, a bitter waste. Faustino's men must have been here. But long ago. Morrow tossed the marked bamboo into the circular pool below.

In a short time he and Felizardo, both of them wet, filthy, and exhausted, were sitting in the banca. "Nada," Morrow told the other men. "No pulajanes." Seeing the men's glances turn from him to Felizardo and back again, he knew that he must not let this anticlimax be blamed on the young Filipino. He qualified his abrupt statement with detail and praise.

It was almost as cold in the open air as it had been underground, and everyone felt the cold more with the drop

96

from excitement. Each man hunched over in his damp clothes as if to conserve the faint center of heat within him. Even the men with the paddles had not yet warmed themselves with exercise. Morrow said, "We'll go back to San José and cook our food. The sun will soon be hot enough to dry us out. We'll soon wish we could be cold again." There were nods of agreement and a muttered, "Sí, señor capitán," but faces remained heavy and dull. It was time, Morrow decided, for one of the sergeant's stories. "Ramos," he began, "do you remember—"

He was stopped by the sound of a rifle shot from downstream, and a second, and a third. And a fourth, or was it an echo? At once, with Morrow's command hardly spoken, the paddles went deeper into the water. Now every eye was bright, every back was straight, every weapon ready. Ahead of them a curve in the river shut off their view, and, that curve rounded, another cut their vision short still more maddeningly, as shouting carried to them, and another louder, nearer shot. But at last, with the river, they swept around the final barrier—a rocky point, a mud bar, a clump of bamboo—and there was the whole scene before them.

The other banca had been pulled high on shore, an old habit in a land of sudden floods. Behind it, flat on the ground, with their rifles balanced over the edge of the boat, lay Reyes and the Pulay twins. Downstream from them another banca had been beached, and near it were three men protected from Reyes' and the Pulays' line of fire by a great boulder. A fourth man lay near the water's edge, and a movement in the bushes some distance beyond the boulder indicated that one or more others, perhaps well armed, were attempting to get behind the three Constabulary soldiers. At least one of the three men behind the rock was armed with a rifle. Outside the field of vision of the Pulay twins and Reyes, another banca carrying seven more men was heading toward shore.

The attention of the men in this boat was all concentrated on the landing they were about to make. Close as Morrow's banca was, they failed to see it as it glided around the curve. They were pointing and shouting, making it plain that once ashore they would finish off this encounter with little time and effort. One man rose to his feet, balancing himself lithely, and in a boasting shout offered himself as a target. When a shot fired by Reyes missed him, a shrill chorus of jeers rang out, and another man stood up, pounding his chest and daring the Constabulario to kill *him*.

Morrow whispered his orders quickly in Spanish and Ramos translated tersely.

What happened next took only seconds, but the feeling that time was suspended made each action long and slow. The paddles plunged deep, the paddlers' shoulder muscles swelled, the paddles lifted and came down again. The banca was around the curve and moving straight. The men braced themselves. Again the paddles dipped, and again, and again; and the banca, riding down the current that the other boat was crossing, leaped through the water for the side of the other vessel. The Pulays saw, and did not fire at the challenger. The outlaws on shore screamed a warning. And too late, much too late and very sluggishly, it seemed to Morrow, the *pulajanes* on the river turned their heads and looked upstream. Their faces, their cries, their gesticulations, changed, and froze.

When the sound of the collision came, it was dull, a disappointment; and the outlaws' dugout, guarded by the outrigger that balanced it on the far side, did not capsize. But the shock was great. Five of the enemy went overboard. As the two boats swung parallel, the remaining two men rose with their bolos high. Morrow's revolver sounded twice. The two men, moving like trained dancers, simultaneously stared at identical wounds in their right arms, dropped their bolos, and reached with their left hands to touch, incredulously, the blood that brightened their skin.

In another moment both boats had been grounded, somewhat downstream. Morrow ordered Felizardo to guard the two wounded men, and then, with Ramos, Dapdap, and Punsal, ran up the stony beach. He shouted a repetition of earlier orders: "We want prisoners, not dead men."

As the uninjured *pulajanes* outnumbered them, this was a bold command. It raised the confidence of the soldados, bridging those moments before the action started again when doubts of the outcome might have weakened them. It told them they were not caught in a trap; they were themselves the hunters and trappers. It gave them Morrow's assurance of victory.

For a little time Morrow could see the whole picture of this encounter. The *pulajanes* behind the rock were gathering themselves, waiting for the right instant to rush on Reyes and the Pulay twins. The violently agitated bushes revealed where an unknown number of outlaws circled to attack the same *soldados* from the rear. The outlaws who had come ashore after the collision, one of them a man of extraordinarily wide shoulders, waited at the water's edge.

With a sweeping gesture, Morrow sent Dapdap and Punsal into the underbrush, to go to the aid of the men crouching behind their banca. He and Ramos, moving more slowly, kept to the beach. Now the seconds dragged. The outlaws facing him began warily to advance. Then there was a sudden shout; the bushes erupted men; the outlaws dashed from behind the rock; and Morrow lost his picture of the whole and saw only the *pulajanes* running toward him. The big man wielded an enormous bolo, and two of the other three had revolvers.

Morrow fired, hit a man in the leg, and the man dropped, sending a wild shot into the air. Ramos fired twice, and a second man fell. Now in this part of the fight the odds had suddenly changed; there were two *pulajanes* armed only with bolos against Morrow and Ramos. Motioning to Ramos that the big man was his, Morrow fired. The bullet had no effect. Morrow aimed the next time with conscious care, but again there was no result. The man kept on coming, so close now that Morrow sent the last bullet in his revolver into the great chest. The man staggered. And Ramos shot and stopped his man. But the big man kept on coming.

Morrow drew his second revolver and fired and hit, yet incredibly the man remained on his feet. His mouth open, his eyes glaring, his wounds bleeding, he faltered and slowed but did not stop. His bolo, still lifted high, remained as deadly as the horns of a wild buffalo in his dying charge.

In amazement and consternation Morrow slipped his gun into its holster and prepared to fight with his hands, half hoping the man might yet drop, half fearing that no human power could ever stop him. And then Ramos with a leap was between them, his own bolo raised, and the man was down at last, dead before he touched the ground.

They looked toward Reyes and the Pulay twins. Reyes leaned over an outlaw who lay on the stones, and the twins were binding a prisoner's hands behind him. Punsal fought another, bolo to bolo, disarming him in that very moment. And little Dapdap, covered with blood, was triumphantly dragging a body toward his captain.

It was over. There were seven dead *pulajanes*, and six prisoners. One of the seven, the first boaster, had apparently been shot accidentally by one of his friends when the boats collided. They found him in the shallow water. Morrow's assailant had five bullets in him. And of the soldados, only Dapdap was wounded. Here were details for an epic tale to carry back to Magtalisay. As if, however, the truth were not enough, Ramos was already inventing decorations and amplifications. Morrow heard the story beginning to grow.

Towing the dead in one banca, with a covering of branches as protection against the sun, they started downstream, the captives distributed carefully and watched by proud and suspicious eyes. They were scarcely under way when they came on a bamboo raft tied to a tree near the shore, where it had been left by the outlaws when they discovered the Constabulary soldiers. It was loaded with miscellaneous loot, and it also carried two frightened young Filipinas. Felizardo knew the girls; they were from San José. And so was the loot. There had been a raid just before daylight. The *pulajanes* must have been hiding somewhere near San José when Morrow and his party slipped past silently on their way up the dark river. They must almost have met, almost have collided, earlier in the day.

Landing at San José, the victorious Constabulary turned

100

a morning of grief and helpless anger into a day of celebration.

They did not stay long to enjoy this glory. Morrow arranged for the burial of the dead outlaws and then delayed for one further purpose. From the neck of each body and each prisoner, he had taken the anting-anting. He displayed these publicly, showing their contents, which were very similar, three small bones in each, and a paper with meaningless scribbling mixed with an occasional Latin word and signed with Faustino's name. These papers and bones he tossed into a fire. Then he put the containers, which were of various materials, including a small bottle and an old cartridge case, on a row of stones at the edge of the river. With a shot for each, he blasted them into the water.

8

BY nightfall, after the return of the Constabulary from their first patrol, the sensation of their achievements had spread through Magtalisay and had quieted down. Weariness quickly overtook the heroes of the day, no longer sustained by excitement, and they unrolled their mats early, lay down, and fell asleep. Only Ramos kept himself awake, listened for a time to the talk of the others in the cuartel who had not been fortunate enough to take part in the great victory, and then went to the tower to see Morrow.

Few flying insects reached the Escarpa, but this night a large moth had flown out of the darkness to dash itself against the solitary lamp in the Moro tower. When Ramos reached the open door and stopped just out of the rain that had been falling through the past hour, he saw Morrow working at a picture of this moth as intently as he was usually working on his maps. He had to speak more than once before Morrow heard him and told him to come inside.

"What is it, Ramos? Do you want to go on another *patrulla* tonight? Haven't you had enough for one day?"

Ramos saluted. "Señor capitán, I am ready to go at any moment."

"Good. But that isn't what you came to say. What is it?"

"Something very important. Something the captain will not like to hear. Something the captain perhaps will not believe."

"Is this one of your stories?"

"No. I think this is the truth."

"All right. Let's have it."

"I have learned why those other men deserted."

"Yes, Ramos. That's important. You don't need to stand."

Ramos squatted on his heels near the wall. He looked up at Morrow and then away. "You will not like this."

"So you said before. But if it's the truth, I want to know it. Whether I like it or not. So tell me what you came to tell. Stop wandering around in the branches."

"I learned this today, not before, and I believe it is the truth." His glance showed Morrow waiting, and he sighed. Then he raised his head and began to talk freely. "I heard the first when the captain and Felizardo were in the cave. Faustino's men perhaps had been there once, but if then the cave was empty, the captain might say we had made the long trip for nothing. Naturally we did not know then that the *pulajanes* would be so obliging as to offer themselves to us for capture. So when the bamboo signal came floating down the current, and we knew no outlaws had been found in the cave, someone asked what Felizardo's punishment would be. Then all were very silent, and I could see that more had been said than it was desired I should hear. For still I am a stranger. They trust me, but not enough. And so with the señor capitán, also. They trust, but not enough."

"I know, Ramos. Go on."

"So we went to the cavern and then many things happened, and that moment was forgotten until tonight. But among those who did not go with us the same question

102

was asked. Was there no punishment for Felizardo? Would Felizardo have been punished if we had met no pulajanes? Much talk, señor capitán, much talk when I was not close. So I thought: Ramos it is time to learn more. And I made a plan." His eyes met Morrow's. "But perhaps I will not tell my plan and all the way it was carried out?"

"Save that part for some long cold night in the mountains, Ramos. What did you learn?"

"That part can be told in a few words, señor capitán. The reason for the desertion was la cura del agua."

"The water cure! Ramos, that is too few words. Tell me the rest. Were they afraid I'd give Felizardo the water cure?"

"Señor capitán, they trust you very much or they would not have enlisted. They hoped Felizardo would not suffer for leading you to an empty cave. But he had more daring than most of them. They would not have been so bold, they say."

"I want the whole story, sargento, all you have."

"Here is what I heard. And I believe it. There was a man who came from Tarnate and told the teniente Palmer he knew where the pulajanes were hiding. This was, you understand, soon after the deaths on Dos Picos. This man said he would guide the Constabulary officers and soldiers to the hiding place. And so he did. He took them to the hut of a montesino in the mountains north of the Rio Negro. When they arrived it was empty. All were gone, montesino and pulajanes. Now, that was not the fault of the guide. Perhaps it was the fault of no one that the Constabulary was too late. You will understand that, señor capitán."

"Yes. And I heard some of this from the tenientes. Do the men say there were signs the pulajanes had been there?"

"There were plenty of signs. The soldados could see them, but the americanos could not. Perhaps the tenientes say to you now that the guide and the soldados lied?"

"That's what they told me."

"Now comes the part they will never tell you, and you will not like to believe. Teniente Palmer gave the guide the water cure. He took him to a stream, and with a big bamboo and the other teniente to help, he poured the water in him. So in the next night, the soldados deserted, all together at one time. They said that this would make everybody hate the Constabulary, that Faustino's men did no worse, and they would not stay to be traitors to their own people."

"Ramos, who saw this happen?"

Ramos looked straight into Morrow's eyes. "Nobody, señor capitán."

Morrow nodded. He had expected that answer. Whether the story was true or false, nobody would admit he had seen it happen. They would have good reasons, from their point of view, for silence. They would not want to confess, in the first place, that they had deserted from the Constabulary. And the Spaniards had taught them not to bear witness against a white man.

Morrow asked, "What about the man that got the cure? Would he make a complaint before a judge? Or would he make the complaint to me? Why should I believe this story if he won't say it's true?"

"He cannot make a complaint. He died two days later."

Morrow turned away and put his head in his hands. True or false, the story sickened him. And he thought it might be true. If the soldiers had attacked their officers for any reason, they might have invented such a tale as their excuse. But that silent disappearance in the night, as if they were sickened, too, that helpless, dumb protest gave the whole thing the feeling of truth. And there was the distrust of the new soldiers for Palmer and Lloyd. On the other hand, evil stories had been invented before this as weapons against an American officer in the Constabulary. He must not let Palmer's surliness prejudice him. He had to be fair.

"Ramos, "he said, "there's no proof, but you say you believe. Why?"

"Cap, I had to come and shake your hand."

Morrow, startled, turned toward the open door. Phil Johnstone was standing there, closing an umbrella.

"I got your message and I sent that cable, cap, that you

104

had prisoners to go to Catbalogan and wanted to send 'em fast as you could, and then I got to thinking. Hardly more than two weeks ago that you got here, and you're rounding up these damn ladrones as easy as falling off a log. It's sure a big surprise."

Morrow had to take the offered hand, though he had never wanted congratulations less. "I don't deserve any credit. My men do."

"Well, if you look at things the way I do," Johnstone said, "nobody deserves credit for nothing nor blame for nothing when you come right down to it. It's fate. That's what I always say. Kismet. If a thing's planned, that's the way it turns out. Not planned by us, you understand. Planned Up There somewheres." In spite of the umbrella, the rain had soaked him. He looked like a wet terrier, apologetic, curious, too anxious to make friends to give himself a good shake. "Cap, you wouldn't have time for a little game of chess, would you?" Like a sleight-of-hand artist, he had a small case out of his pocket and was opening it.

"I'm sorry. No, I wouldn't. But we'll have a game sometime. I haven't forgotten you want to play, sergeant."

Looking into Morrow's face, marked by strong shadows in the light from the unshaded lamp, Johnstone saw the hollows under the eyes, the deep lines from corner of nostril to corner of mouth, the stubble of beard. Recognizing weariness and something more, he put the chess set back in his pocket. "I shouldn't've asked, cap. I moved out of turn. Another night, that'll suit me fine. I'll look forward to it."

"So will I, sergeant." Again they shook hands, and Johnstone plunged with his umbrella into the darkness.

Ramos had disappeared.

Morrow stood for a while looking out through the doorway, where he could see nothing but the drops of rain slanting through the feeble light reaching from the lamp on his rough table. Kismet, fate, whatever it was called, had to take the blame for a great deal. He wouldn't give it any additional burden; he'd carry this one himself. He was responsible. And he was afraid he was the wrong man for

105

this place. Capturing those outlaws had been an accident; they had dropped into the hands of the Constabulary as the durian falls from the tree when it reaches the point of perfect readiness. There was nothing in that simple victory to weigh against the inadequacy he was revealing at this moment. Here was a problem he couldn't handle. He didn't even know how to begin.

He glanced toward the paint brush he had put down, but then, putting aside his longing and ending his indecision, he stepped out into the wet night.

The rain died down as he reached the door of the cuartel and his voice as he spoke to the man on guard was loud in the sudden quiet. It floated in through the open window upstairs where Palmer and Lloyd were sitting. "The Little Admiral," Palmer said. "After his great naval victory."

Lloyd gestured to him for silence. "He'll hear what you say, Harry!"

"What the hell do I care?" Palmer demanded. But after that he said nothing more, and when Morrow arrived at the door he still said nothing.

It was Lloyd who jumped up and invited Morrow to come in and make himself at home. "I'd like to say again, sir, that the prisoners are a nice sight where they are now. Have some square-face, sir?" He pushed the black bottle of gin across the table toward an empty chair. "Sit down and I'll call the muchacho to bring another glass."

"Never mind," Morrow said. "I'm not going to sit down and I don't want a drink." He had almost said, I don't want to drink with you. Condemning them unheard, without waiting to listen to anything. He had to remember there was certainly a chance that the story was false. "I have something to say, something hard, and I'll say it quick. I've been told that the reason your men deserted you out there in the mountains north of Tarnate was because you gave your guide the water cure."

"It's a goddam lie!" Palmer was on his feet, banging on the table and shouting. "Who says so? I'll choke it down his throat!"

"Choke it down his throat with water? That's what they're afraid of. No. You won't find an accuser."

106

"I told you it was a lie."

"The story is that the man died. What do you say, Lloyd? I'm told you helped with the torture. Is that a lie?"

Lloyd's tongue sought to moisten his dry lips. "Of course. Of course it's a lie . . . sir."

"Then tell me what did happen. Why did the men desert?"

"They deserted because they were traitors," Palmer said violently. "Filthy black traitors! Nothing but damn googoos you can't trust anyhow! They didn't tell us why they deserted. They just got out and left us there, lost in the mountains. Deserters don't tell you anything."

"It's our word against theirs, sir," Lloyd said. He stood straighter, throwing his shoulders back, and looked straight into Morrow's eyes. "You have to take your choice. We can't prove that didn't happen. But they haven't any proof either."

"Their story fits," Morrow said. "It fits what happened and what I've seen and what I see now. You both look guilty."

Lloyd cried, "I thought white men stood together."

"White men do," Palmer said. "But when you say that you have to say what you mean by white."

"Shut up, Harry," said Lloyd. "That sort of talk won't help." Turning to Morrow he asked, "How can a man look innocent or guilty, sir? I'd say I probably look crazy with surprise."

Morrow stood regarding them in silence, thinking. Whether he believed them or not, whether the story was truth or lie, it made a problem that had to be faced. He said at last, "I put it to you. Your usefulness as officers in Magtalisay is very small. The men will not serve under you. Look at it fair. I suggest that you leave. I suggest that it's the only honorable thing men in your position can do."

Palmer said one word only. "No!"

"What do you mean, sir?" Lloyd asked. "Transfer to another district?"

That was the idea that had been vaguely in Morrow's mind, but when he faced it definitely, he saw that it would not do. How could he send them to another district? If they were guilty, they might repeat the offense, the crime, there. If they were innocent—and who could prove anything else?—then it would be wrong to send them away. He said, "You must see that would be impossible. I can only say what I said before. You're not much use as officers here. I suggest you leave. You're both young. You have plenty of time to begin something new. Something you'd be better suited for. It should be plain to you that such a story hurts the Constabulary, whatever lies behind it."

Lloyd's glance went back and forth between Morrow and Palmer. He had no answer ready.

Palmer had. "I'll be damned if I get out of the service! I'll be damned if I get out of Magtalisay! Just because you suggest it! Why don't you break us? Why don't you get us thrown out? If that's what ought to happen. Because you know you can't do it. That's why. I'm on my feet again. And I tell you I'm going to get Faustino! We'll see if my usefulness as an officer is over."

Morrow listened until Palmer was through speaking, and then waited a moment longer for anything more either he or Lloyd might say. "You damage the service by staying," he said at last. "Whether you want to see that or not, it's a fact. I could get you transferred or I could break you; I want to be sure you understand that too. But either might be unfair, to the new district or to you. So if you choose to stay, you stay. For the present. But listen to this, Palmer; I want you to hear every word. The men believe this story. It's true, to them. I don't dare use you as an officer. I can't risk what I've begun here, here where you had a chance and failed. No, don't interrupt me. Unfortunately your leg is about all right again. It's no excuse any longer for keeping you off duty. But you'll have to continue without duties if you choose to remain. You may not like the position, but you'll have to accept it. You, Lloyd, will resume your duties as supply officer. Neither one of you will have men under your command." He turned and walked out.

Palmer shouted after him, "I choose to remain! I'll get that devil Faustino! I'll get him single-handed!"

108

Morrow walked steadily away and the words faded behind him.

He did not return to the tower at once but remained on the Escarpa, walking back and forth looking over the bay. It was no settlement he had reached, since it really settled nothing. What should he have done? Perhaps he should offer his own resignation; he had not handled this matter well. But suppose he resigned; would they decide up in Manila that, with the new recruits, Palmer and Lloyd could handle the situation? Yes. That was what would happen. Unless he charged the two tenientes with torture and perhaps murder, they'd be given the command. And how could he make the charge with no proof?

And they might be innocent. He had to be fair. A man was innocent until proved guilty. The trouble was that he was almost convinced of their guilt. They had made none of the answers he'd expect innocent men to make.

He didn't want to resign; he wanted to stay. He had only begun. He wanted to see the new soldiers grow strong and skillful and confident. He wanted to see Magtalisay change into a good place to live. He wanted to see the people of the barrios free of fear. He wanted to feel that he had done something worth doing in the world.

He wanted to stay, and he would stay. Right man or wrong man, he had made his decision in Manila, and he would stay now to whatever end there was.

His mind did not turn to Lucy Leslie; she seemed to have been in it all the time. He wondered how she would look in this moonlight. It would suit her; it would bring out new effects in the modeling of her face and in her coloring. He would like to study her so. She would have a luminous quality, part real and part unreal, part her own and part the moon's gift. It was strange the way he kept trying to picture her face. Perhaps it was because he was a painter. He had thought that painter was dead, but he was coming to life again, remembering a girl he had spoken to on the *Esperanza*, had glimpsed in a doorway, had really seen and talked to only once. It was a strange thing.

9

DELAYED slightly by a heavy thunderstorm, the parade in the plaza took place in the late afternoon on the date set. Instead of twenty recruits, however, there were only nineteen. Gonzalo Alas had been called home to Sogod by his mother's sudden death, and he himself had been taken unexpectedly sick, and had died the next day.

Nevertheless, the parade was a success. There had never been anything like it before. The plaza had been cleared of weeds, and the fountain, though unrepaired, had at least been made to display a mild jet of water, and even the puddles left by the rain and reflecting the deep blue of the sky in dozens of scattered, irregular patches, seemed like a special decoration arranged for the occasion. And all of Magtalisay and much of Sogod must have been emptied of people to send such a crowd to stand before the houses and the church and under the trees, waiting for the Constabulario to appear.

The soldados formed in double file at the foot of the Escarpa, with the six-man band leading, and marched from there with the drum alone playing for them. As the band felt completely comfortable in only three tunes, they saved those until their actual arrival before an audience. Then the music blared forth, and the drill was performed, and the people listened and watched entranced. There was a Sousa march, and then *Old Black Joe* in a brisk and bright tempo, and, brightly also, a melancholy Spanish-Philippine song of a girl begging her soldier-lover not to go to Zamboanga, where he would be killed by the Moros. Each tune had to be played over several times, but that only made it better. It was all deeply enjoyed by everyone; and if the drill was as repetitious as the music, it was well done, and if the American shoes pinched and rubbed, they made a splendid effect. Uniforms were neat, backs were straight, heads were erect, and on this day every man carried a real gun and wore a heavy ammunition belt.

Morrow watched his men with pride, and he watched the crowd with anxiety. The afternoon was complicated by the matter of the guns and ammunition, and by his wish to have every man take part in the parade, and by the fact that Mayor Zúñiga was giving a reception afterward. It seemed to Morrow that the temptations for the *pulajanes* must be irresistible.

However, there was no suspicious movement in the crowd in the plaza, and he saw the Constabulary soldiers start on their march in glory back to the Escarpa, where they could remove their shoes and sit in ease talking over their triumphant performance. Through the dispersing crowd, which fell back to let him pass, he walked slowly to the Zúñiga house, entered and went up the stairs, and was taken at once to Don Florencio's side. Fortunately this placed him at the window, and he stayed there, uncomfortable through congratulations and introductions, until he saw the approach of Palmer and Lloyd, who had been temporarily useful as cuartel guards while the recruits were parading. That meant the soldados were back on the Escarpa, with Ramos in charge. Then, though still under some tension, Morrow turned his fuller interest to the people in the large sala.

The presidente was still propped up in the bed from which he had watched the drill. It was plain that he was tired, but it was also plain that he was not going to be persuaded away to rest. "Señor capitán," he said to Morrow, "our faith in you was great even before this magnificent demonstration that you have arranged for us this afternoon. The demonstration of a few days ago, too. Very startling! But less startling to us than to others, for we expected miracles. Here is one of the others, my friend Señor Villamor." He nodded toward the man sitting at his right, a thick-set Filipino in late middle age with a sad, square, heavy, pockmarked face. "When he heard that thirteen *pulajanes* had been killed or captured, he returned from Catbalogan. And my friend Señor Paterno"—his nod this time was toward the man beside Villamor, a younger man,

111

thin, rather nervous, who swung back and forth a pince-nez on a black ribbon—"has ventured to come back from Cebu. These are two of our important citizens. You will soon know them better." In his excitement and his wish to be complimentary to all, he was a little confusing, but his enthusiasm pleased Morrow. "And I must tell you that I myself sent for my daughter-in-law and my beloved grand-daughter. That proves my trust in you. They have been away a very long time. When Nicolás comes over here, he will take you to meet them."

Morrow could feel Villamor and Paterno measuring him, estimating his probable fortunes in the fight against the *pulajanes*, each man with his own private hopes that were beyond Morrow's divination. He remembered that in Tarnate the big landowners had been named. Villamor, Paterno, Zúñiga, and a fourth. What was it? Soriano. He would listen for that name, too. These were the *ilustrados* of the town, the people who would possess a mixture of the qualities, with a local flavor and in a relative degree, of any upper class anywhere in the world. They would have the "best" blood, and the most wealth, power, education; and consequently their greed or generosity, their arrogance or pride, their simplicity or love of display, and all their other virtues and failings would be more important to him than those of most of the other individuals in Magtalisay.

He knew there was not one of the *ilustrados* uninterested in the results of his pursuit of Pope Faustino. What he did not yet know was where and how their influence would be felt, which ones would help and which ones might already be hindering, and which ones, whatever their sympathies, would merely wait, like most of the frightened *taos* in their barrios, to see which side was going to come out ahead.

Nicolás accompanied him across the room. "You have met my son Rufino," Nicolás said. "There he is now, talking with the American *tenientes*, and with his amigo Luís Soriano, that *lechugino*, that sprout of lettuce, with the large diamond ring." He gestured disdainfully toward the group of four young men. "You will meet Luís later. After you meet another, an older friend. But first, *naturalmente*, the ladies. They are but few. The Villamor and the Paterno families have not returned."

The ladies were seated in chairs arranged in a stiff row against the wall, four Filipinas in the full-sleeved transparent *camisas* of the native dress, and Emerald Sands and Lucy. As Morrow and Nicolás came near, Emerald got up and walked away.

Beginning with the oldest, Zúñiga conducted Morrow down the row. "My mother-in-law, Señora Santiago." Morrow bowed to a plump, dignified mestiza in black, who was fanning herself, rather futilely, with a black lace fan.

"Señora Soriano, the mother of my son's friend Luís." Señora Soriano, also in black, smiled up at Morrow. By her coloring, the slant of her eyes, and the contour of her face, Morrow judged her to be half Chinese. On her fingers several diamond rings sparkled, and her dress glittered with beads.

"And my wife." Señora Zúñiga resembled her mother in feature, but was friendlier. She welcomed Morrow warmly, with praise for the performance of his men.

"And Señorita Leslie."

Lucy held out her hand. "Captain Morrow, I never saw a parade I liked better."

"You saw it, then?" he asked, a stupid question since he had looked for her and had seen her as soon as he entered the plaza.

"I wouldn't have missed it for anything."

"And my daughter Elena." Nicolás drew Morrow along. His suave voice was even softer than usual in paternal pride. And he had reason for pride, Morrow saw, turning from the Americana to the Filipina. Elena had a lovely face and appealing eyes. She smiled and murmured a few words that were too shy for Morrow to hear.

"And now my old friend." They left the women again to their sidewise conversation behind their waving fans, and joined two men at the window some distance from Don Florencio's bed. "My two old friends. Padre Gil and Señor Briones."

Morrow stepped directly to the window, where he could hear any sound that might mean the attack he still feared,

113

and where, with his back to the fading light, he could see most clearly the faces of the two men he had just met. They also were men who might be very important to him, whose influence could be strong either for him or against him. Padre Gil was the priest. In Briones he recognized El Cojo, the lame one, the exile who had returned on the *Esperanza*.

He said, "I am very glad to meet Padre Gil and Señor Briones, and I regret not meeting both sooner. Señor Briones and I arrived on the same small steamship; we should have met then. And since Padre Gil and I hadn't met before, I wished especially to meet him two days ago. One of our prisoners, I regret to say, died of his wounds, and I asked him if he desired to see a padre. But he refused."

"I am not surprised. I could have told you that he would not want to have me come." Padre Gil nodded as he spoke, nodded a number of times. He was an old man, short and wispy and wrinkled, with a whispering voice. "He would want his false pope or no one. I know this, though there have not, señor capitán, been many of them who have been captured, and I do not think the question of sending for me for one of them has come up before. But I know they have this new religion. I can understand; it is part of their hatred for the Spanish friars. Many people feel that. But I am a Filipino. They should come to me. So though I understand, I am very unhappy about them."

"Nobody is happy about them," Morrow said. "I don't suppose they're happy about themselves. The life they lead is a hard one. Men like a settled home, a family, and peace."

Briones said, "But they breathe the air of freedom." Quietly spoken, it was still a challenge. Though no one of the four men moved, they seemed to face each other in a new, more watchful way.

Morrow answered in a casual voice, "Yes, they have great freedom." The others relaxed, but their eyes were fixed on him. "They have freedom," he went on, "to rob and kill. But what about the freedom of the people who are robbed and killed? Is it right for one man to have freedom at so high a cost?"

"That is a curious question," Briones said bitterly, "for an American to put to a conquered Filipino."

Padre Gil watched them apprehensively. Nicolás Zúñiga's expression was unreadable.

"I know," Morrow said. "There is the difficulty. You see us as conquerors, and we want, some of us want, to have you see us as friends. I can understand your feeling."

"Can you understand this? I despise myself for having taken the oath of allegiance! I am a man of honor; I have given my word; my hands are now tied. I cannot fight against you. But I despise myself."

"Yes, I can understand. Though I regret the way you feel. I know something of your record. I know the admiration that is felt for El Cojo. I regret very much that you do not consider me a friend."

"I will quote your own Jefferson. 'Rebellion to tyrants is obedience to God!' But it is very reckless to talk this way to an officer in the Army."

"Not the Army," Morrow corrected him. "The Constabulary. Made up chiefly of your own people. And you should remember that under the American Constitution, which protects you as well as me, you have the right to free speech. But, Señor Briones, who is the tyrant? Am I the tyrant? Or the government that sent me here? I say the tyrant is this Pope Faustino. I wish you would ask the people of San José to tell you who is the tyrant. And do you know that two of these men of Faustino's are breathing the air of freedom in another sense? They have been identified as criminals escaped from Albay province to live by plundering the people of Samar."

"The principle remains the same."

"Señor, I put it to you. I saw you land here three weeks ago. I recognized you. But I have sent no message to Manila saying that you are here. I intend to send none. And I have been asked for no information about you, yet it is my impression that Magtalisay has been your home before and if that is so, the government must know it and must know you might return here. But they are not watching

115

you. You are free. Here is a question to answer. Answer it to yourselves, you, Señor Briones, and you, Padre Gil, and you, Señor Zúñiga. If the Spaniards had still been here, Señor Briones, if they had offered you an amnesty, would you have accepted? Would you have come back? Would you have trusted their promise?"

A servant coming in with lamps passed close to them. Their faces looked darker and more difficult to read.

But Padre Gil spoke. "El Cojo's return is proof enough that he knows he can trust the American promise. We have seen bloody proof of the Spaniards' faithlessness."

They drew a little apart, turning away and looking toward the archway into another room, where muchachos were moving around a table, carrying plates and trays of food. The room was now full of people, but none came near the four at the window.

Morrow wondered if he had been unwise to press his point at this time. Out of the corner of his eyes he saw Palmer talking to Lucy, and his wondering became certainty. He had been wrong; he saw the weakness of his position. How could he claim that Americans were not tyrants, that they intended nothing but friendship, when an American standing in the same room had done what Palmer was accused of?

If, of course, the story was true. Could he take the Zúñiga invitation to Palmer and Lloyd as evidence that the whole thing was a lie? Or was it evidence of submission to tyranny? He had no doubt that every Filipino in the room knew the story, and some must know with certainty whether the story was true or false. In this, as in other matters, they were waiting, and watching.

He made one further attempt to show to Briones that their interests need not run in different directions. "I think, señor, that your idea of freedom is not far from mine." El Cojo looked at him with cold, unyielding eyes, and Morrow shrugged. "Well, if sometime you should like to discuss it with me, you will find me always at your service."

Zúñiga said, "I think now we are wanted at the table to take some refreshment."

Smiling, concealing her secret anxieties, Señora Zúñiga saw that her guests were served. Would there be enough of everything? There were such scarcities these days! But there seemed to be plenty of the rice and chicken, and it was seasoned well with peppers and garlic, and the other dishes pleased the eye and the tongue, at least, though they were not so generous as she wished. She must remember to compliment her mother-in-law, who wouldn't appear in the sala at these entertainments, but was certainly invaluable in the kitchen. The cook always stirred himself for her. The preserved guayabano was very nice, and the roasted langca seeds, and the mampón boiled with sugar and sour tuba. Thanks to God for the little hanipa bananas! They were so good, and so filling, and there were always a lot of them.

But chiefly her anxieties concerned her daughter. Elena was a good girl, always easier to understand than her son Rufino—poor Rufino, with only one eye! She would like to keep Elena from harm, but things were changing so much that she was afraid she would be helpless. This americana who was teaching in the school was so different from anything she had ever seen before that she did not know what to think of her. But it was clear that Elena admired her. What would that mean? Would Elena want to try to be like the americana? The thought was frightening.

And those two young americanos! If Elena were only safely married! She was looking now at the one with the light hair falling over his forehead. She had been looking at him before. Señora Zúñiga had heard of the queridas whom the two tenientes were keeping, and she knew, as did all of Magtalisay except perhaps the other Americans, that both the girls were pregnant. And she had heard that sometimes an American did not see the difference between a muchacha who could be taken for the asking and maybe a present to the father, and a señorita like her daughter who was given away only in church.

The two lieutenants, plates in hand, were standing near her now, looking toward Elena. She wished she knew what they were saying, but she did not understand a word of English.

117

Lloyd and Palmer were talking, not of Elena, but of Lucy. "Wouldn't you say she's about the prettiest girl you ever saw?" Lloyd asked.

"I've seen prettier."

"Then you've been too lucky."

"I could stand on the street in Chicago and in ten minutes there'd be ten prettier girls go by."

"There aren't ten prettier girls in all Chicago. And anyhow, who cares about Chicago? We're here. That's the point, Harry. We're here and so's she."

10

EMERALD stepped down from the carriage and went into the softly lighted sala, where she dropped into one of the peacock chairs. "They tire me, Lucy, all the people at these parties. They tire me. I'm getting old and I'm all alone."

Lucy recognized one of Emerald's moods when she talked too much, her voice going on and on till tears and exhaustion came, and then a sudden decision to go to Punta Arenas followed. Lucy sat down beside her. "You're not alone. I'm here too, aren't I?"

"You are, you are!" Emerald cried, confused and ashamed. "And pretty as a picture. And everything you did and said today down at the Zúñigas' was exactly proper, with your mouth as small and nice as if you'd spent your whole life saying papa, potatoes, poultry, prunes, and prisms. You know I hadn't forgotten you, Lucy. There's one way of being alone, and that's when you look around and don't see anybody at all. Maybe it makes you feel lonesome and maybe it doesn't, depending on the other way of being alone. It's the other way of being alone I mean, when you can look around and see people close to you, even someone sweet like you, and still feel lonesome."

118

She paused, breathless, one hand at her throat, the other raised to keep Lucy silent.

"I met Arthur in a mining camp," she went on in a moment. "Ever hear of Gregory Gulch? That was the place. Arthur was an Englishman. He was a prospector, and my father was a prospector on week days and a preacher on Sundays. I looked the way I do now, except I was young. The tallest, lankiest girl west of the Mississippi. I could've enlisted in the Foot Guards and no questions asked. But Arthur was the tallest man I ever saw that wasn't a freak. We belonged together. That was in 1862. Never a cross word from him for the thirty years until he died. I wasn't lonesome then.

"I wasn't lonesome then," she repeated, her cheeks flushed and her eyes restless. "Sometimes on that station in the bush after we went to Australia I'd look around and wonder. Because I was so happy. There I was living in the back of beyond. Nothing to look at but gum trees. Unless it was a mob of kangaroo—and you call them a mob even if there's only two or three. But I knew Arthur was coming home to me. That was what mattered. Now he's not coming home.

"He used to say if I died he'd take to drink. Drink was a terrible thing to him. He wouldn't take even a nobbler of gin." She ended on a shrill note, and Lucy reached for her hand.

"Arthur would've liked you, Lucy," she said more calmly. "You're like the daughter we never had. I'm always thinking about you. Now, what's-his-name that comes to see you with his mandolin—"

"Justin Lloyd."

"That's it. Do you like him?"

"I like him."

"For a friend, or for a sweetheart?"

"For a friend. You know I don't want a sweetheart."

"Every girl wants a sweetheart. You can't bamboozle me. I am not a child in arms."

"I had a sweetheart and I lost him. I don't want another. Is that so different from you?"

119

"Don't make me angry, Lucy. It's as different as day from night. I was Arthur's wife. You hadn't seen your Tom Horton for four years." Her eye was caught by a movement on the other side of the room, and she sprang up. "Tigre!"

The cat saw her coming, and dropped from the top of a cage to the floor. In two bounds, then, he was out of reach.

Emerald clicked her tongue at the frightened occupant of the cage. "Poor thing, poor thing. I'll take care of you. Did you see that, Lucy? Tigre is half monkey. Almost a cousin to this poor creature that's part monkey and part bat. As soon as she's well, I'll set her free aga—" She broke off with a cry as the cat jumped to her shoulder and once more pawed at the cage.

Lucy pulled the cat away and pretended to cuff its ears. She was grateful for the diversion.

But she was grateful too soon. When Emerald had moved the cage to a safer spot, she returned to what she had been talking of. "That poor wild creature trusts me, Lucy, and you can trust me too. Every girl wants a sweetheart. You do, if you know it or if you don't. Now, if you'd admit you wanted a sweetheart, would this Justin Lloyd be the one?"

Lucy said, "I don't want any."

"And do you think I don't know what that means? It means you're looking around. I was looking around this afternoon, too. That other lieutenant, the one named Palmer, is handsomer than Lloyd. A girl should like that black curly hair and the bold look in his eyes. Lloyd is namby-pamby. But Palmer is different. He makes me think of Arthur."

Lucy had been holding the cat, stroking him. Now he turned suddenly and bit her, and she cried out and pushed him to the floor.

Emerald laughed. "You love that cat, Lucy, bad as he is. A girl likes something a little wild and bold. Do you think I don't know? Palmer has a wild, bold look about him. All Lloyd can do is play the mandolin. As for Captain Morrow, prying into things that are none of his business— Let him keep away from me, here or in Punta Arenas. But that dark young man, that handsome one— My Arthur was handsome. He was a bold man. There were days in his life, days before he left England, bold days he never told me about. But I could see them in his face. A woman likes that. Bold to all, but with softness for her. Oh, Arthur, Arthur!" Now it was time for the sudden tears.

Lucy went to her and touched her shoulder gently. "I'm sorry. I wish I could help."

But this time Emerald was not beginning to weep. Her flushed face was strange and her eyes looked through and beyond the girl. "Arthur, Arthur, Arthur . . ." It was long, anxious minutes before she recognized Lucy and let herself be taken to her room.

11

GLAD to be leaving the presidente's reception at last, Morrow lengthened and quickened his stride as his eyes became used to the night. He reflected that he might almost find his way back to the Escarpa by using his nose alone. One by one he passed these landmarks of scent. There was the ditch that served as a sewer and furnished the basic undertone to all the other odors; there was the *tienda*, which doubtless owed its smell to the articles it had for sale, though not one of them could be singled out as dominant; there was the *dama de noche* that grew near the corner where he turned, its sweet and powerful perfume briefly triumphing over the stench; there was the open road to the shore up which crept the salt and fishy odor of the estuary; there was a hint of the cloying fragrance of copra, stronger for some reason in a certain street; there was the green, moist, earthy pungency of the weedy shortcut he always took; and finally there would come the purer air, the increasingly fresh atmosphere that he would enter like a swimmer diving gratefully upward, when he commenced the climb to the barracks and his tower.

He had reached the point where the breeze came across the river's mud flats and over the fishermen's boats and nets, when he was stopped by Phil Johnstone.

"So the big celebration's all over, is it?" Johnstone asked. "Company all said they had a good time and went home, did they? I hope everybody used their party manners, and now they can put them away again."

"Where were you? I thought you must be down with malaria again."

"We wasn't invited. We don't belong to the Four Hundred of Magtalisay. Didn't you find that out yet? Nobody invites us to their parties."

"They know you stick too close to duty for anything like this. For me it was part of the parade. Otherwise I'd have been too busy myself."

"Well, I guess you're right," Johnstone said. He was for a moment somewhat cheered. Then he remembered the larger half of his grievance. "But Gracie's been crying her eyes out. She wouldn't even go to the parade because she couldn't go to the party after. I finally had to get out of the house."

"Why not come up now to the Escarpa?" Morrow asked. "This might be the time to have that game of chess at last. No use worrying about things like receptions. They don't really count."

"To a lady like Gracie they count. You'd know if you had a wife. It's about all that does count. No, I guess I better not go with you. Gracie might think I forgot about her. I better go back. Good night, cap. I know it wasn't your fault." He disappeared in the darkness.

Morrow went on faster than before, and quickly reached the last of the houses, where only open space dominated by the great mango tree lay between him and the Escarpa. He had seen no night so black that this tree and its shadow were not blacker, but tonight it was different. Its enormous globular silhouette was brilliant with the flash-

122

ng lights of a thousand fireflies. He stood still in astonishment and admiration before he circled it, avoiding as usual walking beneath its branches that had once dropped *pulaján* on him. He moved slowly, amazed as if he had never before seen this fairy transformation, and when he reached the steps up the rocky Escarpa wall, he turned to look again.

A hand slipped into his. Instantly his hand tightened and, guided not by sight but by a feeling of the presence near him, his other hand reached for and found the unseen person and held a shoulder in its hard grip. At the same time that the belated conviction reached him that this was a woman, there was a whisper, "Oh, you're hurting me!" A soft warm body sank on his breast, and a new scent, some cheap cologne, assailed his nostrils.

He asked sharply, relaxing his hold, "Who are you?"

"Don't you know? Can't you guess?" It was Gracie Johnstone's voice. She took advantage of his loosened grasp, not to step away but to come closer. "Guess! Come on. Guess! Who am I? It's a game."

He took a step backward to escape her and was brought up by solid rock, while she, following, stumbled and then rested still more heavily against him. He felt angry, embarrassed, and, above all, suffocated by plump femininity and perfume. Pulling her hands out of their firm clasp round his neck, he pushed her away and held her at arm's length. "I'm Morrow, not your husband. I just spoke to him. You'll find him at home now, Mrs. Johnstone, wondering what's happened to you."

She laughed. "You're not such a fool, are you? As to think I really made a mistake? I knew who you were. I was waiting for you." A little more loudly she said, "You hurt my wrists. Let go, please." As soon as Morrow had freed her hands, they reached for him again. "I knew who you were. I'm so lonesome. Aren't you lonesome too?"

Morrow's exasperation hardened his voice. "I am not lonely, Mrs. Johnstone. Now, are you afraid to go home by yourself, or shall I send a couple of my men with you?"

"What's your first name?" She leaned toward him with all her weight pressing against his hand as he tried to hold

123

her away. "I know you're lonesome. I know you don'
like these Filipinas like Harry and Jus are sleeping with
A little bird tells me things like that. But when I firs
saw you, I knew—oh, I knew I could love you! I—"

Morrow saw that he had to choose between freein
himself by force or calling for help. It was a humiliatin
choice, but he selected what seemed the wiser of the tw
and shouted to the sentry, ordering him to bring a lanter
down the steps. "Now," he said to Gracie, "the sentry i
going to take you home. Follow my advice and don't com
out alone again at night."

As the light began to bob down the cliff toward them
he heard Johnstone's voice. "Gracie! Gracie!"

He answered. "Here she is, Johnstone. Looking for you
I was going to send a soldado with her to be sure she go
back safely." Gracie, reluctantly, drew away from hir
"She ought not to be out like this."

Johnstone's white shirt appeared dimly. "Well, whe
she found you, cap, she was in good hands. Good nigh
to you again. Come along, Gracie. We don't need th
lantern now, cap. I can see all right."

Morrow climbed the steps slowly. Who would hav
believed that a colony of six Americans, a mere handfu
could give him so many worries? The answer was that h
himself would have believed it. What to another ma
might be an annoyance, to him was a trouble. He wa
ready to face Faustino, but he had not been ready to fac
Gracie. He had known he would have to deal with doub
ing, temporizing, perhaps hostile *ilustrados*, but he ha
not been prepared for dealing with the problem of Palme
and Lloyd.

And then there was Lucy. For a second he had though
that Gracie was Lucy. No; for less than a second, and
was not a thought but a desire. His response to the sof
ness of the woman's shoulder had been instantaneous an
strong. It angered him and disgusted him almost at onc
as soon as he knew who Gracie was; and he was still ang
and disgusted.

But he had not been surprised, he thought, enterin
his tower and striking a match. He drew out from und

124

some other papers a pencil sketch on which he had been working. Or, he told himself, on which he had been idling. Lucy's forehead and eyes were there; no more. Well, he could no longer deceive himself into thinking his interest was solely that of a painter. He had known the truth when he saw her in the window over the plaza, watching for the parade. His eyes had found her as if she were the only person there, and weakness had attacked his knees as if he were a boy in love for the first time.

The sketch was bad, abominable, grotesque, a caricature. He ripped it up and set fire to the pieces.

PART THREE

1

THE glory of that parade, marking the success of Morrow's first weeks in Magtalisay, had to last a long time. Working on his second monthly report, he reflected that it would have been better to start with a failure than to come to it after such a famous beginning. This report contained nothing but an account of bold raids by the *pulajanes* and futile though difficult, often heroic, pursuit by his Constabulary company. "Aside from destroying one outlaw stronghold, we have made but a single step forward," he wrote. "We have learned the identity of another *puláján* leader. A strong man, a man greatly feared. Perhaps as important as Faustino himself. And we learned of him from Miguel Briones, a man better known to you as El Cojo, one of the people's heroes of the revolution. Briones' offer of friendship is the best news I have to write."

It was a very warm night, and the lamp on his rough table seemed as hot as a stove. Though he was stripped to the waist, he felt weighed down and smothered by the heavy air. He put down his pen and stepped outside the door of his tower.

That visit of Briones, he recalled, had been a piece of unexpected good fortune, something he had not dared to hope for. Briones had limped inside the tower. Gravely and in silence he had accepted the box offered him as a

126

chair, accepted likewise the cigar, which he had lighted promptly. Seated opposite Morrow, with an expression withdrawn and perplexed, he must have waited ten slow minutes before he spoke of anything but the weather. Then, after a pause, he said, "Señor capitán, I should not interrupt your work."

Morrow gestured that his work could wait. "I remember telling you I'd be at your service. I meant it."

Again there was a pause, and Morrow made no effort to hurry his visitor into speech. Briones at last went on, "I must tell you first that I am glad you speak Spanish well. It is easier to talk to you." Here he paused once more, but this time to smile at his own words. "But as you see, even in Spanish it does not seem easy for me. You understand?"

"Partly. I'll understand more when I know what you're going to tell me."

This time they smiled together, and Briones leaned forward and his words came fast. "I will say it as it comes; that is best, without picking my way too carefully. The difficulty is that we have been enemies. Do not remind me that you and I have never been personal enemies, nor fired at each other in the line of battle. That is a subtlety we need not regard. The truth is that you have been on one side and I have been on the other. Enemies. Therefore it is not simple for me to give you information, for I feel that I am being a traitor. But I do confess that I have a wish to trust your word when you say you are here to help my country. I have a wish to believe that perhaps your interests and mine are the same.

"And yet I ask myself, is it only that I am tired of fighting? You see, I tell you the truth just as it bursts from my heart. Oh, I have argued with myself! I suspect myself. I suspect everyone, but myself most of all. I am a man in torment. Sometimes I think that whatever I do it is the wrong thing. So here I am, talking to you, and wondering if this time I do right or wrong.

"You must be thinking, señor capitán, that this is spoken as a little child might say it. But I am learning a difficult fact, and when we learn such things we are like little children again. I have learned all that I could learn of these raids by the *pulajanes*. I am beginning to see that what you said is the truth. They are fighting their own people. So I have come to you. But still . . ." Once more he paused.

After a moment Morrow said, "Señor Briones, I'll be as frank as you've been yourself. I want your friendship. But I don't want it until you're sure you're ready to give it. You see, I want it for a long time. If you've changed your mind about what you came to say, I'll wait."

"No. I must tell you. Here it is: On my return to this island, these *pulajanes* wanted me to join them. They sent one of their leaders to see me, and he talked of freedom and independence and foreign tyranny; they are strong words that mean much to me. I told him I had sworn an oath to the new government. Yet I tell you I was tempted! But now I know better what sort of man this leader is, and I am glad I was true to my oath. I have come to tell you this. And I will tell you also what sort of man this leader is. One must know one's enemies, *verdad?*"

Morrow had agreed, expecting a description at last of Faustino. "What is he like, this so-called pope?"

"Faustino? That I cannot say with certainty, for him I have never seen. I am told he is very frail, in poor health. That is why they came to me; because I am fortunate to have the respect of the people. Somehow he has that too, you understand. No, it was another leader who came, their strong man, strong in every way but in his heart and soul. A big man, señor capitán, with a big, square face across which a scar runs from the left eye down the left cheek to his mouth. A man of power and craftiness and hatred and greed. I know that now. His name is not spoken often; he lets them talk of Faustino. But he is your greatest enemy. Ola, he calls himself. Ola."

And for the first time Briones, departing then, had offered his hand to Morrow in friendship.

So much of good had happened, Morrow assured himself, looking through the darkness toward the glow that came from his tower and turning back to the night. So much of good. And then there was Lucy; it was good to

128

think of her, too, if he kept his thoughts careful and temperate. In spite of patrols and raids, he had seen her twice during the month. She had come up on the Escarpa to talk to him that first time, late in the afternoon. She had been wearing a pale blue dress and balancing the handle of a Chinese parasol on her shoulder, so that the deep blue circle framed her head but did not protect it and the declining sun shone full on her. He must have seemed to her as blinded as he felt, for she had said, "Don't you remember me, Captain Morrow? You don't see your friends often enough." And then she had said, "I need advice, and there's no one else I trust."

They had strolled together toward one of the old cannon, and she had said, "You're sure you don't mind having me come to you?"

"Mind?" He smiled at the absurdity. "I'll mind only if your difficulty is too big for me. Then you might never come to me again."

"It won't be too big for you. It may sound too silly to you. But I'm sure it's important. It's about Elena Zúñiga. You know her family and you must know what she's like."

He had watched her closely as she spoke, comparing lips and eyes with those he had put on paper from his memory of her face, seeing how he had failed, trying to store in his mind and heart the fluid, sparkling expressions. He listened, too, but heard as much as the words the simplicity and sweetness that lay behind them.

"Her mother doesn't like to have Elena help me," she was saying, "and she sends an old lady in a black dress to sit in the schoolroom while Elena's teaching and to walk back and forth across the plaza with her. Just the same, Elena feels terribly independent." She smiled. "Anyone would think she was as far away from home and as independent as I am. More independent. I'm sure she'd never ask anyone for advice."

Morrow knew so little of Lucy that this mild self-ridicule had astonished him. In fact, he asked himself then, what did he know of her? Almost nothing. And he wanted to know everything. The sweetness and simplicity were there, but they were not unspiced, and that was essential,

129

too. She was so young that no one could know her; she did not know herself yet. She was so young, and it was so brave of her to have come alone so many thousands of miles . . . He had forced himself to follow her words.

"So I wonder what I should do. Should I arrange to have her meet Jus Lloyd, and let them get to know each other? Should I pretend I haven't ever noticed that she seems interested in him?"

Morrow had confessed bewilderment. "I don't think I understand what you're asking me."

"Haven't I made it clear? Perhaps I'm ashamed to. It sounds so calculating. And unladylike. But I can say it very plain. Shall I encourage a—a romance between Elena and Jus Lloyd? She keeps asking questions about him, and . . . Oh, it's hard to put in words. But if I encourage anything, I'm sure her mother will take her out of the school and I'll lose a good teacher. Do you think this is silly? I'm glad you don't laugh at me."

Morrow would have liked at least to smile at her divided loyalty, her devotion to her school and her wish to help a friend. But he kept his face straight. It was not a silly matter. It was perhaps more serious than she realized. But he could not be sure how deep this girl looked into things; she had surprised him before. He had weighed his answer carefully.

"It's a big problem, and an old one," he had told her. "You want to do what's right for Elena. That makes it seem a smaller problem and a new one. But you can find your answer by looking at it from the larger point of view. Marriage between people of different races can be happy. But there are many things that can make them the most miserable marriages in the world. Now, who can say what's right for Elena? Can you? Can I? Can her mother? Even Elena herself doesn't know. But she ought to live her own mistakes and not yours, or mine, or her parents'. So my advice is, let it alone."

He had not been proud of his answer, which rolled out neatly as a product of long observation, but seemed as cold and detached as her problem had been warm and human. He felt cowardly, too, because he had not said boldly that Lloyd was not good enough for Elena. But how could he say that? He would have to go on to the rest of it: Lloyd and Palmer were not good enough for Lucy, either. But would he believe any man good enough for Lucy? Might he be merely envious of the gay young evenings the two tenientes and their mandolin spent with Lucy? If he could only settle that question about them and the water-cure story! He could be wrong in thinking them guilty. And as for their brown queridas— No, he could say nothing more.

But his answer had seemed to satisfy her, though she too thought it lacked courage. "I'll do nothing, then. But standing and watching doesn't look very brave."

"That's true. But did anyone ever prove that cowards are fools? They're often wise."

"I suppose they don't rush in where angels fear to tread. Perhaps I like to rush in too often, and interfere with people. . . . I think about you. Aren't you sometimes lonely?"

So she thought of him? He had been astounded. "Lonely? I don't know. I hadn't thought."

"I don't believe you ever take time to think of yourself. And I've taken too much of your time today." She turned toward the steps, and he walked beside her. "Elena tells me about you. Oh, there are stories! When a man stands before you, he wants you to see the best in him, and he fears you'll see the worst. Bolos or bullets cannot touch you."

"What nonsense! I'm an ordinary man."

"Then you must sometimes be lonely."

"Do you know what loneliness is?"

"You think I don't?" she had asked. "I do. I miss my brother. I'm so far from home I haven't yet had an answer to my first letter. Oh, I know what it's like to be lonely. If you have an evening to spare, spend it with us."

"Mrs. Sands has made it plain that I wouldn't be—"

There had been impatience for Emerald and warmth for Morrow in Lucy's quick reply. "She doesn't know you. And I'll tell you the truth, because it's so much easier to say what you think, isn't it, instead of hunting around for words to hide what's in your mind? I'll admit one reason I want you to come is so that she can see what you're really like. I'll confess that brought me here today, too."

She doesn't know you. Those four small words and the tone in which they were spoken had seemed to Morrow to linger in the air.

Strangely, he had gone to the Sands house that very night, but under circumstances no one could have foreseen. Lucy had sent a frightened *muchacho* for him between three and four in the morning, and he had thought at first that it was another raid by the *pulajanes*. It had seemed a relief to learn that the reason was Emerald's illness. Taking what few medical supplies he had, thinking that perhaps Emerald was only drunk, he had hurried through the silent town and up the hill.

Lucy, carrying a candle, met him at the door. Her hair hung in two braids over her shoulders, and her eyes were wide and dark; she looked like a child startled from childish dreams. "She's better now," Lucy said. "But I was afraid. So I turned to you. Again."

"Tell me about it. What seems to be wrong?"

"She's here in the sala. You can see her." She led him inside and to a couch, where Emerald lay, watched over by Engracia. "It's strange. She seems to be sleeping now. She looks all right."

Morrow counted the woman's pulse and found it exceedingly rapid, and then he reached for the candle and examined the quiet face. He no longer thought she might have been drinking, and he did not think she looked all right. There was a slackness at one corner of her mouth that he thought was new and that he feared might indicate paralysis. But he was no doctor. Returning with Lucy to the veranda, he reminded her of that. "I might be some use in a cholera epidemic, and I can set an ordinary broken bone and take care of an ordinary wound, but I don't know anything about this. It may be very serious. It may not. What happened?"

There was not much to tell. Lucy had been wakened by hearing something fall, and she had found Emerald unconscious on the sala floor. Once on the couch, Emerald had opened her eyes and she had talked, but Lucy had not understood a word and Emerald had not seemed to know where she was. And then, just before Morrow arrived, she had fallen asleep. "So I shouldn't have bothered you, Captain Morrow. And I'll let you go now."

"You're not afraid any more?"

"Yes. I'm a little afraid. But that's something different. It's . . ." She hesitated.

He waited for her murmuring voice to go on, straining his eyes to look at her and wishing he might see her more clearly, angry at the shadows and yet grateful for the way they enclosed her with him in a small world of their own. He felt he could have this sense of intimacy only as an illusion, and for the moment the counterfeit was almost good enough.

"I wonder," she began again at last, "if I can explain so you'll know what I mean. This has nothing to do now with her. I'm a little afraid all the time, and I like it. The island itself frightens me. The trees. The ground. The rain. That strange bird that cries in the night. And look now, out there. It's so different from the way it is in the day, so mysterious and so watchful. It frightens me, but I like it. It's as though everything were waiting for something to happen, and I'm waiting too, for something wonderful or terrible, I don't know which, but . . . I'm sure this doesn't make sense at all."

"It makes sense," Morrow said. He heard in her words a mixture of child and woman; he felt her youth and life and her readiness for love. "In a strange country the strangest thing is yourself, because you begin to look at yourself for the first time."

"Is that true? Is that why I'm frightened? Does it frighten everyone?"

"They don't always know they're frightened."

"I like knowing it. It's exciting. I never felt so alive before." She kept her voice low, but innocent ardor colored her tone. "Sometimes I wake up in the night trembling and run to the window and look out."

"What do you expect to see?"

"I don't know. And of course there's nothing, but I'm never disappointed. The air feels so soft and the night smells so sweet. And yet I am disappointed, too. But I don't know why."

There was a sound from Emerald, and Lucy ran back to her side. But she still slept, and Morrow, counting her pulse again, found the rate nearer to normal. "Better," he whispered to Lucy.

In the candlelight she was looking at him closely. "You're tired, and I've kept you here with my nonsense!"

"Not nonsense. More sense than most people talk. And I'm not tired."

"They say you never sleep. Are you made of iron?"

"No. Not of iron."

"They say, too, that you're never afraid. How silly I was to talk to you about how I'm frightened by nothing! They say you don't know what fear is."

"Then they've lied to you." He might have said, I'm afraid now, afraid because my hands want to reach out for you, my arms long to hold you. He saw nothing child-like about her then. But he was afraid that by a touch he might destroy this moment with her. For would she have so much confidence in him if she thought of him as a man? She trusted him as she would trust her brother. Couldn't he see that in her eyes? And what was she seeing in his? He hurried to put talk between them. "All men are afraid of something. The bravest man I ever knew would run from a kitten."

"What would frighten you? Why don't you tell me? Don't you ever talk about yourself?" Her eyes searched his face more directly than before; warmly, he thought, even tenderly.

But it was the night, he told himself, or the alarm she had had, or his own imagination. The moment had passed he had let it pass. Thinking of it now, on this other night that was so different, so oppressive, he was dully angry with himself.

But what was the use of regretting a lost opportunity especially one that had probably never existed? He had

134

better things to do with his time. He returned to his desk and the report.

He read over his paragraph about Briones, and then picked up the pen. "But we need," he wrote, "more information than this. I would like to offer bigger rewards, twenty-five pesos for each rifle surrendered, a hundred or more on the head of each outlaw. Even a thousand on Faustino's or Ola's head. It would save money in the long run."

That concluded everything he had to report on Constabulary affairs, but he had more to say about the town of Magtalisay and he was going to say it. Sooner or later his words would reach the right man. "I would like to suggest," he continued, "that the provincial health board consider the matter of the cemetery here, which is in noisome condition. It is badly overcrowded, graves are shallow, and the stench is bad from the pit where bones are thrown to make room too soon for new burials in the crypts. I mentioned this to the local health officer, who says nothing can be done without orders from above.

"That is almost always the attitude. Nothing can be done, they say. Well, the Constabulary can fight the outlaws and is going to fight the outlaws and beat them, but that alone won't make Magtalisay a paradise. More food must be grown and trade must come to life again, and then there will be taxes paid and there can be some civic improvements. But trade can't revive until the docks are rebuilt. So where do we start? The town needs help right now. I'd like to know where to write about this matter. The Engineering Department? Also there's the old tenant farmer problem. Until the poor aren't so poor and the rich aren't so rich and powerful, there's going to be trouble. Some of the poor taos can hardly be blamed for turning outlaw."

Having started, he could not seem to stop; it was as if he could only forget his own desires by counting over the desperate needs of Magtalisay. "These people need education, too; a school for more than the children. And they need doctors. There isn't a doctor within reach. I wouldn't want to think what an epidemic could do.

135

Disease should be hunted down the way the outlaws are hunted down. The people have to all join in. The women will make good nurses—when they're trained. There are young men who want to be doctors. They have to be trained, too. Magtalisay is living in the Middle Ages.

"I've heard our own people say that there's so much to be done for the Filipinos that nobody knows where to start. They say we've got to give them a good government, teach them to govern themselves. They say we've got to give them good schools. Encourage their commerce, give them modern transportation. Help them stand on their own feet. Help them recover from the heavy, grasping hand of Spain. They say we have the great, God-given opportunity to start these people on the road to being the leaders of the Orient, the most prosperous, progressive country in the Far East. A sort of Utopia.

"And all of this is true. Except that I know where to start. We have got to keep the people alive first of all or there is no use doing anything else. When they have doctors and nurses and hospitals, when they learn as much as the western world knows about preventing or taking care of smallpox and cholera and yaws and leprosy and malaria and dysentery and tuberculosis, and maybe even beriberi and pellagra can be cured too or prevented, well, then these people will have the chance they deserve. And if we can give it to them, is there anything that a nation could be prouder of doing? Well, sir, I—"

A scraping of shoes at the open door broke into the silence, and Morrow looked up to see Phil Johnstone standing there. "How about another game of chess, cap?" Even in the poor light his discolored teeth spoiled his smile, but he filled it full of pleading eagerness. "Tonight all right?"

"This report is about done, sergeant. Come in. Pull up that crate and sit down."

Johnstone was almost as quick as the words, and his pocket chessboard appeared on the table as if by magic. "Do you good to stop work for a while, cap." His fingers busily separated the black pieces from the white.

136

"You're probably right. I just have to copy this, anyhow. That can wait."

"I ever tell you I play chess with myself? I got a book. A book of gambits and a book of how to finish, too. Sure, I remember I told you last time how I play against myself. And never win. Neither of me ever wins, because we both always know what the other's going to do. But playing with you is something else again."

Morrow laughed. "You can always beat me."

"Now, I wouldn't say nothing like that." His tone was a trifle patronizing. "You really had me worried once or twice. The trouble with you is you don't think far enough ahead. You got to think what you'll do, then what I'll do when you do it, and then what you'll do after whatever I can, and then what I think maybe you want to do, and so what I do next after that. That's how I play, only sometimes there's two, three things we can each do, and you got to think of all of those. Your turn with the white, cap. Or look. Shall I set up an ending? That makes it easy. You can learn a lot that way."

"All right," Morrow said. "But I don't think you can teach a man what isn't born in him. I wouldn't be surprised if you were born with this chess set in your hand."

"I bought it in San Francisco, five, six years ago." His fingers moved rapidly, selecting certain pieces and placing their pegs in the holes provided. "Funny thing, but I never played till I got this. But when I was a kid, I seen two men playing once. I seen them through a window. I was a country boy, see, and I'd went with my old man to the mill town. So there was these two men, sitting over the board, and I watched and watched and they never said nothing and they never moved nothing for a long time. And then one of them picked up a piece and moved it, and the other man just shook his head. And I thought, there's a game I'd like to play. It would be a good game for winter on the farm.

"And then right after that I ran away from the farm, and now look at me, playing chess here. No winter at all. Fate, that's what I always say. Fate." He studied the board and made the final move. "Checkmate. What next, cap? A regular game? I'll show you a new gambit. I wish more than anything I could see that other board again, with the game set up on it just like it was when I looked at it through the window. I'd like to know which piece was moved while I was rubbering there."

As he talked, they arranged their men in new battle lines. "It's sort of as if there was some way to tell my fortune from it. Maybe it was a knight, galloping around the way I been galloping around the world. Maybe a queen that might've told me I was going to marry a lady like Gracie. Maybe a bishop, but I never had no use for ministers."

"There's Pope Faustino," Morrow said. "He has a lot of influence around here on everybody, including you. I should think you'd get news of him sometimes from that assistant of yours."

"Nope. I don't hear nothing and I don't want to hear nothing. I mind my own business. Just like when you asked if I ever heard about Palmer and Lloyd giving some Filipino the water cure. That's Constabulary business. I keep out. I do everything like I play chess. I look way ahead at all the moves."

"Faustino is everybody's business."

"Suppose you had a wife. I got to think of Gracie. I don't want nothing to happen to her."

"If you worry about living here, why don't you ask to be transferred to Cebu or Manila?"

"That's what I mean by looking at all the moves. I want to go back to the farm. That was a good life and I didn't know it. I like cows. And calves. I'm sick of mangoes, and I'd like some apples and peaches and strawberries and raspberries. What's prettier than a row of corn shocks when the summer's over? But Gracie don't like a farm. Now if she gets a taste of Cebu or Manila, I'll never get her home, but I figure she'll get so sick of Magtalisay that the time'll come when she'll want to get to the farm as much as me. Well, let's play." He settled in silence to the game.

He won again. "Checkmate, cap. But you made this

138

one harder. What do you think about the farm? Think I'll get there?"

"If you're doing it like that chess game, you will. Have a cigar?"

"Thanks, cap." He lit the cigar and moved the crate on which he sat so that he could lean against the wall. "I'd like to see wheat growing, and oats, and rye."

"But you can't get out of the Army any time you please, sergeant. What's your gambit there?"

"The malaria, cap. I got every move figured. The malaria'll get me out when I'm ready. Think I'll win?"

"I think you'll probably go back to that town and play chess with those men you saw. And beat them both."

"I'd like to play with them, all right. Folks are friendly, there. Not like this Mrs. Sands that's never spoke a word to Gracie, and it's the best part of a year since we come."

"Women have their own ways, Johnstone."

"You can figure 'em if you try. Like now, it's plain enough old lady Sands is after Palmer for that school-teacher. Gracie says the old lady's after Lloyd for herself, and her having a stroke, too, and dragging her foot when she walks. Gracie says—"

Morrow managed to stop him there. "Suppose we talk about your farm, sergeant, and then I'll get back to my report."

"No offense meant," Johnstone said anxiously. "It's the damn heat. I guess I better be on my way anyhow. Gracie gets lonesome. Can't blame her. This is one of the places God forgot. Game tomorrow night, cap?"

"Nobody knows what tomorrow will bring."

"No offense meant, cap. I forget you don't want talk like that."

"No offense taken," Morrow said. He might want to kick Johnstone, but he would never have the heart to do it. He watched the fellow walk out the door, and then he turned around to his desk.

Next month he'd have a better report to write. He was going to get to the bottom of that water-cure story, and then he could settle the Palmer and Lloyd question. That had to be done for Lucy's sake, and perhaps it had been good for him to hear Johnstone's gossip even though he despised it. The Constabulary would benefit, too, when that matter was taken care of. In effect, now he really had no junior officers. With Palmer and Lloyd reinstated or with new men in place of them, he could enlist more soldados, and then strike the *pulajanes* harder and faster. There'd be an end to the raids. And the Constabulary patrols would not come back to the Escarpa empty-handed.

2

AT the end of another month, however, an endless, frustrating, wearying month, Morrow's report was worse. Besides repeated small alarms, there had been two terrible raids, one in Magtalisay itself; and although in that one his soldados had captured half a dozen men and killed four more, the outlaws could afford the loss better than the Constabulary, which had lost two men.

It was another steaming night following a day of rain. Morrow had returned to the Escarpa late in the afternoon from a difficult and unsuccessful patrol in the mountains, and had found a note from Lucy asking him to come to see her when he could, telling him that Emerald had died suddenly and had been buried while he was away. His heart had gone out to her as he read the brief message, his only thought to go to her at once. As soon as he had got into a clean uniform, he had gone up the road, only to hear Palmer's voice before he was in sight of the house. He had turned around, gone back to the tower, written his report, and now he had picked up his paint brush.

There he sat, his tunic off, his hands sticky with sweat and unsteady with fatigue, working in a poor light that no painter he had ever heard of would have thought of using. But he was no painter, only a fool, trying to escape from his own thoughts, as if sketching Lucy's face were any escape. He threw his brush down in disgust, and gazed at the face on the paper. It would be lonely for her in that big house without the proud old woman whose sharp tongue she had never feared. He understood the sadness she must feel; he himself felt the touch of it. He saw Emerald's prejudice against him as part of the dissolution of her fierce and rare pioneer spirit; he held no resentment. Even to the end there had been something admirable about her. She deserved the tribute of grief. From him. From Lucy.

The stealthy sounds had been going on in the loft over his head for some time before he placed them. At first, when he began to notice them, he had not realized they were inside his tower; a wind blew in occasional weak gusts, and he blamed all unexplained noises on that. He was conscious of the origin only after he had felt, like a chill running along his backbone, that someone was behind him looking down on him. After a glance around to reassure himself, he wondered if the real reason for his disquiet could be overhead. Yet when he listened consciously, it was hard to pick out more than the night's customary sounds. Like an undertone, the waves washed in and out at the foot of the Escarpa. The sentry coughed. And then there was a new rustling, and he was sure.

It might be a rat, he thought; or perhaps an owl had entered through one of the slit windows near the top of the tower and now was trying to get out. But it might be a human being. He himself made, of course, a perfect target in the lamplight; it would be easy to shoot him. He blew out the light.

Yet he was not greatly alarmed; his next actions were no more than a sensible precaution. He walked noisily out of the tower, and returned very quietly. With a match in his left hand and his revolver in the right, he started up the ladder. When he stood on the fifth rung his head would be level with the loft floor and perhaps visible against the whitewashed wall; but when he was one rung higher, his arm would be free for easy action.

He reached the fifth rung and could see nothing but blackness, but now he heard more sounds, soft and unidentifiable. With another step he turned and balanced himself, released the hold of his left hand on the ladder, raised the gun to rest on the edge of the floor, and struck the match.

The flame was bright for less than a second, and then, not catching, was gone; but there had been enough illumination for him to see the intruder. It was Gracie Johnstone. She looked back at him with startled eyes, but before the match went out she had begun to smile.

His immediate reaction was no more than a tired relief because he had not had to shoot a man. "So it's you," he said. "Come down out of here."

But below again, relighting his lamp, he burned his hand on the chimney, and the pain increased his awakening anger. He made an effort to control it, for he was afraid it might cause him to say more than must be said to make her understand that her visit was unwanted and must never be repeated; and as he turned toward the ladder, he was sure that he was calmly ready.

The tower room was so small that almost as soon as he saw her she was at his side. With a little cry she threw herself forward to twine about him and hang heavily from his shoulders. She must have twisted a spray of dama de noche, the night-blooming jasmine, in her hair, because its scent, sickening when so close, assailed and stung Morrow's nostrils. She pressed her face, damp with the sultry heat, against his, whispering, "So lonesome! Love . . ."

He broke her hold and pushed her away. "Can't you see I don't want you here? You've got to go home."

She smiled coyly at him. "You know you don't mean that!" But he held her away, and her smile faded into bewilderment. Could he be refusing what she offered? "It's all right. Phil's dead drunk."

"Will you go by yourself, or do you want me to send a squad of soldiers with you? How would you like to have them march you through the street?"

She stopped pressing toward him. "What's the matter, anyhow? You don't have to scare me like that." With her eyes on his, she moved back a step. "And you don't have to look at me like that! As if I was dirt. Who do you think you are, anyhow?" Sullenly she went on,

142

"What do you think it's like to sit alone like I do all day? Nobody to come near me, nobody but Phil to talk to. That Mrs. Sands, alive one minute and dead the next. How do I know when it's going to be my turn? And that Leslie girl—now she's going to lord it over—"

Morrow interrupted her violently. "That's enough of that!" The harshness of his tone startled both of them, and she stared at him with her mouth a little open.

He was ashamed of what he did next; he could not understand how the impulse had taken possession of him. It was as though somewhere he must secretly have contained the bitterness he had hated in his father, the contemptuous raillery against life in general and women in particular that he had heard from his earliest years; it was as though his father took possession of him and spoke through him.

He said to Gracie, "How would you like to have me paint your portrait?"

Her expression remained smoldering and resentful. "Paint me?"

He had continued as his father might have continued, building up her eagerness. "There's a very beautiful and famous painting called 'Sacred and Profane Love.' I'd paint you as Love."

With a coquetry that he found utterly repellent she said, "I've heard about artists and models."

"And you've thought you'd like to be a model?"

"Well—of course sometimes models have to pose without their clothes on. I don't know." She was flattered but uneasy. "I don't know if I think it would be nice. Do you paint that kind of pictures?"

Perhaps nothing she might have said would have checked what he was about to say to her, but that question was the worst she could have put to him, recalling his father's jeers at his talents and ambitions. "You mean pictures of naked women to hang in saloons, Mrs. Johnstone? No, I don't. But I might have if I had tried. I might have made a fine career of saloon nudes, I suppose. It was often suggested to me."

143

"How could you paint me as love? How can you paint love? Holy love? What's that?"

"Sacred love. But you would be profane love. You know what the word profanity means? It's the use of God's name for the wrong purposes. There's profanity in love, too, Mrs. Johnstone. Do you understand that?"

"It's hard to understand, I guess." She began moving closer to him. "Why don't you call me Gracie?"

"Stay where you are!"

She stiffened and obeyed.

"If you don't stand still, Gracie, how can I see the picture you could make? It wouldn't be much like Titian's. But you're right. It would have to be in the nude. For the flesh tones I'd need gray and green, with a little yellow and purple. This lamplight is just right for the proper effect. Yes, you should be painted by lamplight. It shows best how your skin is beginning to sag, as if it was about to liquefy in decay, and rot and drip from your arms and your legs and your breasts. There must be green shadows around your eyes and at your temples, the green of corruption, and here and there some white where your grinning skull is starting to show through. But your lips would be red; you'd like that, wouldn't you? Your lips would be red, but they'd be drawn back from your teeth, and your hair would hang limp and damp with sweat, just as it is now. Where are you going, Gracie? You're not going home, are you? . . . I'd let you leave your shoes on. Your shoes are right, exactly right. That dirty yellow leather, and those high, run-over heels; and don't they have beaded toes, Gracie?"

She was white with fury. From all that he had said, she picked out his attention to her shoes; perhaps the rest she understood only in its contempt and not in its literal meaning. But the shoes were a concrete matter, and this criticism she felt she could answer, her uneven breathing making her words come jerkily. "Where do I get shoe-cleaner? Where do I get heels fixed? Where do I get new shoes in this terrible place? You tell me that, instead of insulting me because my shoes are old!"

But he had turned his back on her and was silent.

"Tell me that much, you painter, you captain, you black-hearted White Moro! You're a fine friend to Phil! If he knew what you said about me—!"

He didn't move until he heard her leave, when he dropped into his chair and put his face in his hands. He felt ashamed and guilty. He was sure that what he had done had been effective; he was sure that she wouldn't come back. But he thought he could not have felt worse if her intended temptation had been successful. However, before he spent any more time reproaching himself for brutality, he had something else to do; he had to make certain that this visit of hers started no gossip that might raise new difficulties for him in some unforeseen direction.

He went out to the sentry at the top of the steps and told him that Mrs. Johnstone was unwanted on the Escarpa and was never to be permitted to set foot there again. These were orders, and they were to be passed on to the rest of the men. He completed them by a description in the coarsest words of the dialect, telling why he was not interested in the woman, beginning with the fact that her husband was his friend, and ending with a characterization of her that made it clearer than any denial could ever do that he did not want her. He was glad Gracie did not hear this; a straight translation would have been easier for her to understand than what he had said to her.

The sentry's attitude proved to Morrow that he had done the right thing for his standing, if not for his conscience. The men would have forgiven their captain easily any casual moral looseness with women, white or brown; but at the same time there was no doubt that his continence raised his position and made him more of a creature apart. The sentry's response when Morrow said good night was very different from his greeting of a few moments before. It was again respectful.

Some of Gracie's jasmine must have been left in the tower but it was now only faintly sweet, irritating as a reminder rather than in its own right. Nevertheless he tried for a time to find the small green blossoms and get rid of them. He failed.

He leaned over the lamp to adjust the flame, and his "anting-anting" swung out, glistening in the yellow light. He had worn it so many years that he seldom noticed it, but now he had an impulse to look inside. He lifted the chain over his head and opened the locket.

And this was what was supposed to be the mysterious source of his strength! Two faces looked at him from the past, both smiling, hopeful, eager, vivid. On the left was his mother at the age of eighteen, a year before she died giving birth to him; opposite was his wife at the age of twenty, not long before she died giving birth to a stillborn son.

He thought of his father, who had seemed to come to life in him a few minutes earlier. His father had turned in anger and bitterness against the whole world. He thought of his father's women, good and bad, who had sometimes loved him but had always ended in the same humiliation, contemptuously discarded. Morrow himself had escaped early from that household, and he hoped he had escaped the bitterness. But he had abandoned his painting at his wife's death, beginning again only recently to use his brush. And, having already caused the death of mother and wife, he had kept away from women. Until now . . .

How young and trusting these two faces looked, how alive in the delicate coloring he had brushed in, how full of warmth and love! He gazed at them and tried to think of them, but Lucy's face came, clearer than ever before, between his eyes and the locket. He must send her a message that he would see her in the morning. He would see her and comfort her, if he could, and offer his help, if she needed help. And that was all.

As he wrote he could not help hoping that she might have sent for him simply because she knew the same longing that he felt himself.

3

WHY had she sent for Captain Morrow, Lucy asked herself, and what was she going to say when he came? How was she going to start? She ought to have the exact words ready, but it was not easy to plan. Whenever she tried to think, she ended in confusion.

And it was hardly surprising to be confused about this, for she seemed to be confused about a great many things. She had believed herself adjusted to this country, to the climate, to the people, to everything totally different from everything she had known before, and then at one blow she had lost her balance. Had she depended on Emerald so much more than she had realized? Had she never been the person she pictured when she thought of herself, that brave young woman of the new twentieth century, independent, standing on her own feet, facing the world unafraid, ready for any future, and sure she could make any future bright?

She wanted someone to guide her, but she was not sure she had a right to ask Captain Morrow for help, and she did not know how to proceed when he arrived. Should she tell him that Harry Palmer had asked her three times to marry him, and was going to keep on asking, though she had protested that she had not forgotten Tom Horton? How could she put into words her questions about Harry? They were simple enough. Perhaps that was the trouble: they were too bald. Did Harry really love her? Did he know about Emerald's will? Was Harry as wonderful as Emerald had said? Or could Emerald have been as wrong about Harry as she had been when she called Captain Morrow a snoop, a spy, an inhuman, heartless woman-hater?

No. She could ask outright none of these questions.

And she could hardly talk about Emerald's letter. Some sentences made her blush.

"I'm going to die, Lucy, but you're going to live. Live! Live and be happy forever! I want you to live in this house, when you and Harry are married, and I want you to sleep with him in the bed where I slept with Arthur ..."

She shrank from the thought, but wasn't that the way any nice girl felt? Tom had always been so far away, going off to war and then staying so long in the Philippines, that she had never had the same feeling of alarm.

"Harry is a real man, Lucy. Handsome and bold. I can see that you love him. I can read all the signs. And he loves you. You've forgotten your Tom Horton. That was a schoolgirl love, not a woman's love. A pale, silly love. You don't even remember what he looked like ..."

At least that part of the letter was right, Lucy thought. She had tried to imagine Tom beside her in the sala while she waited for Morrow to come, and all she could recall was the picture of him that stood on her table, perfectly flat, head and shoulders only, inside a frame. She would have to admit that Emerald knew what she was talking about there.

And now Morrow was at the door. His face was stern, almost hard, but it always changed when he smiled; and as soon as he could see her in the dim room, he would smile. She said, "Good morning," and there was the smile just as she had expected. As he came toward her she forgot for a moment that there were any tangled questions confusing her.

But it did not occur to her to say that seeing him was alone enough to ease all her difficulties; she was not aware of it consciously as a fact. She said, "I'm glad to see you. It's good of you to come." She added quickly, "I need more advice."

Morrow gave no sign that he had hoped for anything else from her. "I'll help if I can. Even if you hadn't asked me to come, I'd have been here as soon as I heard the news, to help in any way possible. I'm sorry I was away when it happened. Now, what about the advice? I'm not much good at it."

"You were right about Elena. You kept me from making a fool of myself. There was another man all the time. Señor Briones, I think, though she's still keeping it a secret. But this time . . ." She had reached the point where she had to make a beginning. He was watching her gravely. She looked all around the room, found nothing to help, and then asked, "You remember the night I called you, when Emerald had that first attack?" It was an unnecessary question, but it was a start.

He said, "Of course."

"Did you know she made her will after that, and wrote a long letter for me to read after her death?"

"I didn't know. But she was wise to understand the warning."

"Was she in her right mind?"

He thought that Emerald Sands had probably been as much in her right mind then as she had been for a long time. He asked, "Did she do something foolish in her will?"

"That's hard to answer. She left everything to me. I wish I knew what to do."

"If she left you her property, it's yours. You don't need my advice to tell you that."

"But there was a condition. Not in the will. In the letter. It isn't taking the property that bothers me so much. It hasn't been run right for years, and it's probably as much trouble as it's worth. It's the condition."

"If it's only in the letter, it isn't binding."

"But it's binding on the way I feel about it! That's why I wondered if she knew what she was doing. She knew she was going to die. It's a dying wish, a dying request."

Morrow said, "It's wrong for people to try to control others from beyond the grave." He added, "Usually wrong. You don't want to tell me what the condition is?"

Lucy evaded his question. "She isn't trying to control me," she said. "She's trying to tell me what she thinks is best." For some reason she dreaded explaining to him that Emerald's condition was that she should marry Harry Palmer. How could she say that she wasn't sure how she felt about Harry? That she wondered if Harry's interest in

149

her had been influenced by knowing she'd have the property, because he wanted to run a big plantation? She wished Morrow would say something more; if he would only talk to her, without asking questions of her and without waiting for her questions, he might almost by accident drop the words that would give her a hint, straighten out the tangle in her mind, help her see what she ought to do. He was very kind, but he was a thousand miles away.

Morrow felt her anxiety and disappointment; she had expected something from him that he had not been able to give. But how could he advise her on something she obviously considered too personal to discuss? He said, "Everyone has to decide, finally, what's best for himself, regardless of everyone else, living or dead. But why don't you wait before you make up your mind? Think it over a little longer. A sudden death is a shock. It takes a good while to get over it. Wait before you decide." Under the circumstances this seemed as sound as anything he might say. But it seemed also very cold, and he added, "I want to help you if I can. Isn't there anything else I can do?"

When he had gone, she knew she had been silly and foolish not to have told him all about the letter. Tears came too easily since Emerald's death. They began again to roll down her cheeks. She had never before in her life felt so wretched.

4

ON the steps to the Escarpa, Morrow met Johnstone coming down. "What is it, sergeant? A cable for me?"

"I just wanted to talk to you, cap." His words were slurred. "I get on Gracie's nerves, sitting around. I get on my own nerves." He swayed and Morrow steadied him. "Why don't you let me fall, cap? Maybe I need to bounce on my head."

Morrow could smell the whisky, but he suspected that

an attack of malaria was about to hit Johnstone, too. "You'd be better off in bed. Go home and—"

"And finish the bottle? I tried that yesterday. When I woke up, it was as bad as ever. Listen, cap. Gracie told me O.K., she's ready to go back to the States. So I start pulling all the strings, see? And then she tells me when I go she's going to stay right here. I don't know what to do. She's driving me crazy. How about a game of chess, cap? One little game?"

"You've got a fever, sergeant. Have you forgotten that your malaria is real? It's not just a way to get out of the tropics and out of the Army. You're imagining things. Need any quinine?"

"Only time Gracie told me to get out before, she was sweet on somebody. But who's she sweet on here? She don't have no use for Palmer or Lloyd, I know that. So who could it be?"

Morrow turned and guided Johnstone to the bottom of the steps. "Go home and go to bed."

"If she was sweet on anyone, it would be you. And I know it's not you. Think I never see those pictures you draw all the time? You've got a girl, cap. I'm not blind."

"Johnstone, I thought you made a practice of sticking to your own business. Better not forget it." He added more mildly as he started again up the steps, "Talking can get you into more trouble than talking can get you out of."

Johnstone turned, leaning against the rock wall, to stare up after him. He didn't want to go home. Gracie had told him, among other things, that she wished she never had to see his face again. He didn't want to go back to her right away. Either fever or alcohol alone might have sent him there anyhow, but the combination gave him a fuddled, restless energy that made him look for some alternative. For a few moments he debated the desirability of following Morrow to the top of the Escarpa.

Suddenly the thought struck him that it was true that Gracie was sweet on Morrow. He sat down on the bottom step to wrestle with the idea. Morrow? Yes, Morrow. But then it was all on Gracie's side. And Gracie was making a terrible mistake.

Slowly he put together a few simple thoughts about himself, Gracie, Morrow, Lucy Leslie, and Palmer, seeing them all like chessmen on a board, trying one arrangement and then another. He arrived at the conclusion that if Lucy's interest could be definitely turned against Palmer and toward Morrow, Gracie would give up her notions and be herself again. A little hard to please, maybe, but after all, she was a lady, wasn't she, so what else could he expect? With drunken resolution he knew what he had to do, and knew he had to do it then. He felt lightheaded when he got to his feet, but he started out through the town, crossed the plaza, and took the road up the hill.

By the time he reached the house, the fever had won out over the whisky; but to Lucy he seemed drunk. His flushed cheeks and glittering eyes, even his extreme politeness frightened her.

"Excuse me, Miss Leslie. I guess you don't know who I am. Our paths never crossed before."

"I know who you are, Sergeant Johnstone."

"Fine. Then we start off good. Is it all right if I have a chair?"

"Of course. Sit down." To her relief he sat near the door, across the sala from her.

"You must be wondering why I'm here."

She looked at him without answering, and waited.

"It's like this," Johnstone began, and came to a sudden stop. On his way he had planned what he wanted to say, but now the plan was gone.

The silence lasted so long that Lucy grew more afraid. She got up, trembling. "If you'll excuse me—"

"No! Wait! It's not your move. It's mine." And now he was sure of himself again. "It's like this, Miss Leslie. You're a queen, see? So nobody's going to let you be captured by a pawn. You're too good. A queen belongs to a king. A king can't get along so good without her. You ought to remember things like that. Or maybe you don't know a pawn when you see one. Or a king. He's a king, though. I'll say that for him."

"What are you talking about? Excuse me—I'm going to call—"

152

"It's about Palmer. Palmer's a pawn. Not worth nothing. Don't you understand? There's things you ought to know. Nobody'll tell you but me."

"I don't want to hear anything." She had begun to move cautiously to the door.

He got up and came unsteadily toward her. "But you have to listen to me, after I come all the way up here! Why, I know things about Palmer nobody thinks I know. Why don't Captain Morrow put him on active duty? For cruelty, that's why. He gave one of the Constabulary men the water cure. The cap can't prove it, but I know it's true. I know it! And what about that pretty little Filipina? Ever hear about her? Wait, why don't you? Let me tell you!"

He stared a long time at the doorway through which he had disappeared, but she did not come back, and at last he turned, crossed the sala and the veranda, stumbled dangerously down the steps, and started down the hill. "I put a bee in her bonnet," he said aloud to himself, but he was not sure. All he really knew was the buzzing in his own head as the fever mounted in his blood. By the time he reached home he looked so bad that Gracie helped him to bed without a word of complaint.

Lucy excused herself when Harry came that evening. She was not condemning him unheard after what Johnstone had said. She was simply too bewildered to talk to him, too exhausted by the day. She wanted to see Morrow again first. She'd beg him to come back; she'd send another note to him in the morning. She wasn't sure what she wanted to say to him, but in the morning she'd be able to think everything out.

153

PART FOUR

1

JOSÉ Felizardo was the sentry on duty that night. Placed by chance near the top of the steps when his mother climbed painfully to the Escarpa, he was the one who met her there and he was the first to hear her story. But he hardly knew her at first, she was so changed, and when he had heard the story, he could not believe it, though it left him incoherent with grief. It was Ramos who had to question the woman gently, translating so El Moro Blanco could understand.

Where had this happened?

In San José.

When did this happen?

Two nights before. A man dressed in Constabulary uniform had appeared in the barrio just at sunset, asking for old Felizardo, saying he was a friend of José, sent to collect information. Were there any guns in the barrio? If so, where were they kept? Where was the rice kept?

He didn't get much information. Old Felizardo had no gun, and if anybody else had, it was a secret from the rest of the village. As for the rice, if the Constabulary wanted information, why didn't they send José himself? José' father felt that his son had been slighted.

At other houses likewise there was little told the man in uniform, because there was little to tell. And then he disappeared. Nobody had felt alarmed.

Two hours later the attack commenced, and it was the worst San José had ever known, the worst they had ever heard of. Every house was ransacked, every scrap of food was taken, people were stripped of their clothing, no matter how poor and old it was. And there was not only the leader in Constabulary uniform, but there were two or three others in uniform also, though most looked like *pulajanes*. Finally, old Felizardo, very boldly, had denounced the leader and the others as *pulajanes* in disguise.

Then came the hardest part of the story for the woman to tell. Ramos gathered the faltering, broken words and sentences, and translated them into sentences broken by his own angry exclamations.

One of the men in uniform had been ordered to take off his tunic, and old Felizardo had been forced to put it on. From Felizardo's house, where it had proudly decorated a wall, they took an American flag. They tied it like a turban around old Felizardo's head. Then they tied him to a tree, poured kerosene on the flag and the uniform, and set fire to them.

"And this happened two days ago?" Morrow asked. "God knows where they've got to by this time. Ask her why it took her so long to get here."

"Señor capitán, she says that nobody wanted to bring her down the river. They told her it was no use coming to the Constabulary, when the Constabulary and the *pulajanes* were working together."

"And they couldn't see the truth? We've inspired a lot of faith!" Morrow said bitterly. "Well, we'll try to earn some. We'll start at once. Ramos, wake the men that are asleep, and I'll pick the patrol party. You'll go, and Felizardo, of course. And listen, José," he went on, when Ramos had started, "ask your mother if she can describe this *pulaján* leader."

The thought of revenge cut through the woman's grief, and she stood and faced Morrow while she spoke. The short, sharp syllables of dialect burst from her lips too fast for him to understand, but he could read her gestures. The man's height, the width of his shoulders, the way he carried his head, the way he stood, all these she showed. And

155

Begin at the beginning. Was there such a man? And a gun?"

"Yes, sir," Lloyd said quickly. "He brought in Captain Pearson's revolver. It disappeared when Captain Pearson was murdered on Dos Picos."

"Well?" Morrow asked. "Is that all? Did he tell you how he got it?"

"I questioned him," Palmer said. "He wouldn't say anything. I had to let him go."

Lloyd said eagerly, "He told us he found the gun. Near a river or something."

"Well?" Morrow said again. "Is that all? Did he collect the reward?"

"No, sir," Lloyd answered. "No, sir, he didn't take it. He went off without it. I tried to give it to him, but Harry—" He looked uneasily at Palmer.

"You keep out of this!" Palmer said.

"Then who's going to tell me what happened?" With each word, Morrow's voice lost a little more of the weakness and hoarseness of his illness. "Why didn't the man take the reward? Are you telling me he brought the gun in simply because he wanted to help us? That's a rather dangerous thing for him to do, if he's an ordinary tao or a montesino. Faustino's revenge can be terrible. Do you want me to think he wasn't interested in the money? Who was he? Where did he come from? Why did he come?"

"I told you he wouldn't answer any questions!"

"He doesn't seem to have been much different from you, Palmer. You aren't answering questions either. How do I get you to answer? Perhaps that's the question I should ask; perhaps that's the crucial question. Did you talk to him the way I'm talking to you now? Or do you have some other way that you can recommend of persuading a man to reply to you?"

"I tell you he wouldn't answer!"

"And you just talked to him like this, did you?"

"Of course I talked to him like this!"

"And that was all? Or do you have some other way of asking questions? A way you'd like to have me try on you?"

178

then with her fingers she showed his face. It was large, the chin was like this, and the forehead so. And the scar, twisting cheek and mouth, ran this way.

Morrow recognized the man beyond a doubt. It was Ola.

In less than an hour Morrow and Ramos, Felizardo, the Pulay twins, and six more men were on their way up the Rio Negro toward San José.

They found the people of that barrio convinced that the outlaws had not arrived or departed by boat but had used a trail leading toward the mountains known as the Seven Sisters. Certainly there were signs on this trail of recent use. "And it is an old *montesino* trail," José Felizardo told Morrow. "We in the village never use it. You will not find a guide for it, señor capitán, but I will hunt it out. I will follow it if I have to cross the whole island of Samar to where they say there is a great sea. I will overtake the murderer of my father if it takes the rest of my life!"

From the beginning Morrow found this trail curiously depressing. It seemed to run on forever through wet forest and over wet earth, with the giant trees moving endlessly past in silent, dull monotony. Yet it was not a monotonous expedition. They passed through leech country, in which every branch and twig bordering their path held its hungry annelid, ready to catch at mortal flesh and begin a feast of blood. Ramos invented a new character to accompany them, Uncle Dewlap, an immoral old man hunting for a virtuous woman through many surprising adventures. And Morrow suffered an attack of dengue fever that added variety to his days and nights with aching bones and evil dreams.

At noon on the third day they came unexpectedly into a cogonal large enough to give them a deep view down a long valley and past a dozen small mountains and foothills whose profiles showed one against another far into the distance. Except for themselves, there was nowhere a sign of human life. With their usual caution the men crossed this open space singly and bending over so that they were hidden in the tall grass, but Morrow, walking like an automaton, moved erect from the shelter on one side to the shelter on the other.

A response came almost at once. One of the Pulay twins held up his hand and hissed for silence, and all stood listening with startled eyes turned toward Morrow. There was a confusion in his head that dulled his hearing and he could not distinguish the sound they heard, but when it ended, they told him what it had been: the mountain telegraph, the irregularly spaced, dully booming notes of wood striking wood, of a club beating on one of the buttress roots of a great tree. They could not doubt that notice of Morrow's appearance in the cogonal was being sent ahead of them.

"That means we're on the right trail," Morrow said. A little of his apathy fell away. "Maybe they're getting ready to run." The thought set the soldados more keenly on the chase.

But Morrow's excitement soon died. The day seemed endless to him, and he grew clumsier than ever beside his men. His legs ached, pain shot through his knees, and his breathing was laborious. He seemed to have reached the limit of endurance and was about to order a stop for the night, when surprisingly ahead of them there was light between the trees. They hurried forward.

The forest ended, beginning again at about a hundred meters distance, not gradually but like a solid wall, the face of which, instead of showing the everlasting green of the jungle, was alive with white orchids as a cataract is alive with foam. The space between was a deep river bed, down the center of which flowed a stream. Where the path came to the brink of the drop stood a bamboo ladder, and across the stream another ladder reached up.

It was too inviting, especially after the warning that had been sent through the jungle. Was there quicksand below? Or an ambush on the other side of the river? Or did the real trail stay on this bank?

A search lasting into the twilight finally revealed a fork in the trail. They would follow it in the morning. But for the night, trying to equal Faustino in duplicity, Morrow took his men across the stream, and there they made their

157

camp. If any spy was watching them, he could carry back the story that they had used the ladders.

Before daybreak they were back on the first side of the river again, starting in a new direction, and by the middle of the morning they came in sight of a deep, tranquil valley along which were scattered some twenty brown-thatched huts.

At once the peace below changed to confusion. Men and women burst from the huts and ran back and forth, meeting one another, stopping, starting again, vanishing and reappearing, with all the inexplicable busyness of ants, while no sound they made reached the ears of the Constabulary men. It seemed that they themselves must somehow be responsible for this activity, but the forest around them remained silent and undisturbed, as if it held no hostility. It was strange, but now everything was strange that filtered in to Morrow through his illness, and he could find no energy to use in thinking. Lifting his hand, he set the soldados in motion once more.

The trail down was long and difficult, turning back on itself and winding through thicker and thicker jungle. What they reached finally was a squalid group of huts, stripped now of the beauty distance had given them, and empty.

"Let me go after the *pulajanes*," Ramos begged. "With half the soldados. I want to show these cheese-bugs how to fight."

Morrow refused permission. "You'd never catch up. They have at least an hour's start. You couldn't go fast. You'd have to watch for traps. No. We'll stay here. If we can't get our hands on them, at least we can destroy the cheese." He set the men to a systematic search of each shack, with instructions to set fire to it as soon as it was proved empty. They found kerosene to help, and in spite of recent rain proceeded to make the dwellings unfit for further use.

Leading the way down the valley, Morrow and Ramos came to a newer, sturdier hut standing apart from the rest, the only one they had seen that was closed, with door and window shutters fastened down, and the only one around which the ground was swept clean in a circle containing no banana trees, no shrubs, no weeds, and no litter. Near the ladder a woman sprang to her feet, screamed thinly, turned as if to run, and then sank down again.

They approached carefully, guns ready. But no shot, no sound, came from the house. Soon they could see that the woman squatted beside a man who seemed to lie motionless on the ground, but they still went forward slowly, watchfully, expecting at any moment to hear or see the first indication that this was an ambush.

At last they reached the man, and Ramos, while the woman whimpered, pulled him to a sitting position. He lolled, heavy and inert.

"Put him down," Morrow said, and knelt beside him, touching his skin, listening to his breathing, feeling for his pulse. "I don't see what's wrong, but I think he's dying. Better stand away." He spoke to the man. "Can you hear me? Are you hurt?" Bending over, listening, he noted the saliva that ran from the man's lips and the swollen tongue that pushed against his parted teeth. He asked the woman, "How long has he been sick?"

She whimpered again, her head lowered against her bent arm.

Morrow got to his feet. The woman looked little more than a child, and he spoke to her softly. "*Muchacha*, what has happened to him? If you don't tell us, we can't help. If you tell us, maybe we can. Stand up and tell us. Don't be afraid."

She turned her head and looked up. And she was transformed, fear vanishing, and wonder, surprise, joy, appearing. She cried out again, but this was a different sound, and it ended in words." Benito! Benigno!"

Then Morrow, dull with fever, realized she was looking beyond him, and he discovered that the Pulay twins had come up. This girl could be, must be, the sister they had lost. But there was no delight on their faces to answer her joy. They were frowning at her, standing in identical poses with identical expressions. It might have been comic, but instead it was almost frightening. Morrow understood. The brothers had thought of her as an unwilling victim of the

159

pulajanes. They had found her weeping over a dying out
law.

She read their condemnation, and with eyes suddenly a;
fiery as theirs, she began a passionate defense. Ramos in
terpreted for Morrow the rapid words. "She says this mar
is a good man. She says he saved her from Ola. Ola i;
wicked and has many women. She says this man is dying
and her brothers can go away and leave her and she wil
die too. Or if they wish they can kill her and she will be
glad. She is very excited."

"I can see that," Morrow said. "Ramos, stop her. Tel
her if there's anything we can do to save this man, we'l
do it, but it has to be done fast. Ask her if she knows what';
wrong with him."

Ramos caught her attention by leaning over the man or
the ground and speaking to him. At once she squatted
again, with a sad and anxious face.

Morrow repeated his questions.

Now she answered. "He showed me this. But I knov
this could not hurt him." The man's *camisa* was un
fastened, and she pulled it down to reveal his shoulder anc
to point out two tiny holes something over an inch apart
"I was not here. He takes care of the god, and I came to tel
him to carry the god away. And I find him like this. H
can talk only a little then. And now he cannot talk at all."

Looking at the marks on the man's skin, Morrow knew
it had been hopeless from the beginning. "You see what i
is," he said to Ramos. "And a huge one." To the girl he
said, "*Muchacha,* I am sorry, but there is nothing we car
do. He has been bitten by a cobra, and a bite in tha
spot—"

"No!" The girl refused to believe him. "Snakes do no
bite him. He knows how to make them tame. Or if the
bite, it does not poison him. He will not die for that."

Ramos told her, "He is already dead. Just now h
stopped breathing." Morrow saw it was true.

But the girl cried, "It is a lie! Oh, I will breathe for him!
She put her lips to the man's, and blew.

One of her brothers reached down to pull her away, bu
Morrow stopped him. "Leave her. Soon enough she"

160

know that Ramos is right. Wait. And then be good to her. She will need you." He added, "And we need what she can tell us. Bring her to me later."

He walked to the silent shuttered hut and climbed the ladder to the small veranda. The door, he discovered, was fastened on the outside. This knowledge he should have added to the other facts that were evident about this house. It was a better house than the others, and it was isolated; and the girl had spoken of a god; and her man had died of a snakebite. If Morrow had been well, he would have realized that caution might be necessary. But he was tired, feverish, and in pain. He was thinking only that this was another hut that had to be searched. With his pocket-knife he slashed the strands of bejuco that tied down the door, and he swung it on its hinges. His shadow then lay across a rectangle of light that cut through the darkness of the interior and fell on the bamboo floor. He stepped inside.

He knew instantly that the room was not empty. There was a dry rustling, and there was an odor, so faint that when he tried to identify it, he could no longer smell it, though the chill it had brought to his nerve ends remained. He said, "Don't move or I'll shoot." It was a purely reflex defense, for he could see nothing but shadows. The rustling continued.

Perhaps he already knew, except in his conscious mind, what it was that shared the room with him, for he was silent then and stood absolutely without motion, breathing no more than the man who lay on the ground outside. And into the rectangle of light on the floor moved a dark, sinuous form, and it was drawn erect in the light before him. The sun glistened on the shining brown body, on the orange throat, on the eyes level with his own, on the slightly enlarged hood of a king cobra.

Morrow's thoughts struggled sluggishly in the instant that he knew was all that was allowed him. If he moved for his revolver, the snake would strike before he could shoot. It would strike anyhow, and strike for his face. But if he could catch those fangs on his hand, or, better still, on his arm where the sleeve of his tunic might hold some of the venom—

161

He had his elbow half raised when the shot deafened him. The snake fell, knotting, coiling, writhing. Its tail lashed Morrow's legs like a whip, but its head was blown to bits. Morrow, turning, saw Ramos' face, grinning with satisfaction. "How did you know I needed you?"

"I hear the señor capitán speak in English. I think— No, I do not think. I jump and I fire."

The sound of his own words came back to Morrow. "Don't move or I'll shoot." Yes; he had spoken in English. He put his hand on Ramos' shoulder and gripped it hard. English, Spanish, or dialect, he could not find any words to serve him now. But Ramos' eyes were still watchful, and Morrow's senses were sharpened to the realization that there was no time then for gratitude. "Tell the soldados to open the window, and we'll see if this devil has a wife."

They found nothing else, however, in the single room of the house except a large green-glazed pottery jar, which stood opposite the door and was covered with a piece of richly embroidered Chinese silk. It was empty.

Morrow returned to one of the yet unburned shacks and gave Ramos orders for the rest of the day. He had taken, he felt, the last step he could drive himself to, and he spread his blanket and lay down on the floor. At intervals then he was aware that his orders were being carried out. The smell of burning reached him, and the sounds of destruction. Various reports were brought to him. As evening and fever closed in on him together, each piece of information came as if from another world in which he no longer had any existence. No guns had been found, he was told, but some ammunition had been left behind by the outlaws. The dead man had been buried. The cobra was more than three meters long. Ramos had the skin.

Sometime during the night, early or late Morrow never knew, the Pulays brought their sister to him. She was glad to leave the outlaws, they told him, now that her man was dead. And she would answer Morrow's questions.

He seemed to himself to be far away, talking to her across an immense distance in which his questions echoed and re-echoed and her answers were only a whisper. "How many people ran away?"

"Seven, no, nine, women and girls." She counted on her fingers. "Fifteen men. Children, two or three. I do not know. Maybe more."

"Was Ola one of the men?"

"Yes."

"Where were they going?"

"To a place where nobody can find them. A place I do not know."

"Was the snake the god?"

"No. The snake was a guardian of the god. My man was the guardian of the snake and the god. The god lives in the great jar."

"But the jar is empty."

"The god is there, though you cannot see him. I cannot see him, either. But I know he is there. I have heard him speak."

"Why did Ola run away? He is a coward."

"He is bad, señor capitán. But he is not a coward. But he learned that the White Moro was seen walking here alone. Then the White Moro was seen with soldiers, as if they had come up out of the ground. And then he crossed the river and followed the wrong trail, and yet very quickly reached this valley. All this was magic. Ola said he would always fight men and he would fight magic, too, when Faustino was safe. But Faustino was here, with us, and Ola said—"

Morrow raised himself on an elbow, his chest laboring, his head throbbing. "Faustino was here and—" He fell back, with the words loud in the hollow air. "Faustino was here, here!"

"Sí," the girl said softly. "El papa was here with the god."

"Muchacha, you believe Faustino is holy?"

"You know to look at him he is a holy man! And he talks to the god, and the god answers him. His anting-anting is very strong. And here is the proof: In each anting-anting of each man he puts the true bones of the small finger of his right hand, and that shows he is a great saint, for it is a miracle that for one finger only which has been cut off his hand there should always be bones for every anting-anting!"

The soldados left the valley early the next morning, carrying Morrow in a litter shaded by leaves and swung from poles. Following the trail by which the *pulajanes* had fled, they came rather quickly to a stream that led them to the bay. There they built rafts, and staying close to shore, they poled the rafts up the coast toward Magtalisay.

2

LUCY lay in a long chair on the veranda. The evening air was soft and warm; though a breeze blew, it was loving and delicate, only the gentlest whisper. She felt content with everything, the air, the earth, the sky, the sea, the trees, the flowers whose perfume she breathed, and even with herself. She was at peace mentally because she had postponed a decision about any problem, and especially about Harry Palmer, until Morrow should return from the Constabulary patrol beyond San José.

She dozed a little, dreamed, and woke, disturbed by some sound.

Harry Palmer stood at the foot of the steps, looking up to the veranda. He had been in her dream, so seeing him was natural; but the dream had been in Kansas, and where was she now? The moon had risen above the mountain behind the house, and it shone down full on his face, smoothing it and purifying it in its cold, deceptive light.

Unable to see her in the blackness under the wide eaves, he said, "Lucy? Lucy?"

"I'm here. I was dreaming about you. I dreamed you were coming." Her voice was low and drowsy, filled with unconscious seductiveness. "I'm here." She raised an arm to show where she was, and to him it looked like an invitation. He climbed the steps, passing from the moonlight

164

into the darkness, leaned over her, and lifted her into his arms.

So much of the strangeness of her dream remained, and so much of the feeling of being in harmony with the whole world, that for a moment or two she had no impulse to resist. He murmured, "Princess! Lucy, Lucy! Princess!" It was only when he turned her face with one hand and held it firm while he pressed his lips to hers in a long and fiercely possessive kiss that she began to struggle. "Pull away if you want," he said then. "But now I know you're going to belong to me."

"No! No! I'm not!"

He laughed. "Those no's don't count," He was still holding her by one arm, and he drew her closer again.

"Harry, don't! I told you to wait. I want to think. I need time."

"I'm helping you to think." He kissed her once more, a rougher and longer kiss, his arm so tight about her that she was powerless, and then he put her back in her chair. "If I hurt you then, next time you'll know enough not to fight me."

She shrank back, covering her face with trembling hands, though in the darkness he could not have seen the color that warmed her cheeks or the look in her eyes. He had hurt her; her jaw was sore where his fingers had held it and her lips were bruised. But she was not thinking of that, and she did not notice the little swagger with which he walked over to the railing. She was at the moment unable to notice anything outside herself or to think at all. She was frightened, frightened because she had hated his kiss and yet had liked it. She heard the scratch of a match, and covered her face more carefully as he lighted a *cigarillo*.

Then he said, "I've wanted to kiss you for a long time— I get what I want."

After a little he spoke again. "I like courage. There's nothing better than courage. I like a good fighter. But don't fight me, Lucy. That won't get you anywhere!"

Lucy's mind was working again, though not very much above the level of emotional reaction. Had he said these things, or anything like them, to the Filipina he had been

165

living with—if there was such a person? What about her? Did she exist? How were such stories tracked down?

But these were among the questions to be postponed for a while. Lucy tried to keep them shut away. And they rebelled. She could smell the tobacco smoke, and when she looked up again, taking her hands away from her eyes, she could see Harry's silhouette against the moonlit trees rising on the other side of the road. He was a handsome man, with a bold, clear profile. A bold man, as Emerald had said, bold and a little wild. She had not wondered until now just how much wildness or what kind of wildness Emerald had meant. What had Emerald known? But Emerald had wanted her to marry him.

She formed a question, apparently innocent but a little guileful, to bring her some sort of information about one of Johnstone's charges. "Are you in command now that Captain Morrow is away?"

With a violent swing, he threw the cigarillo into the road, but when he spoke his voice was more sullen than angry. "No. I ought to be, but I'm not. When you look at me, Lucy, you see an unlucky man."

"How do you explain it?"

"How can anyone explain luck?"

"I mean, how do you explain the fact that you ought to be in charge but you're not?"

"It's a long story, too long to tell now. You've heard a little of it, some from me and some from Lloyd. It's been one run of bad luck after another. And now Morrow's afraid to let me have my chance. He knows how I want to get that devil Faustino. And I could get him, too. That's the trouble. He knows I'd get him. I'd go out after him and I'd bring him back. What was left of him."

"Captain Morrow has gone after him now, hasn't he?"

"Sure. With more soldados than I ever had. But he'll come back without Faustino, just like the other times. Wait and see. I ought to be captain. And he knows it. So he'll never give me a chance."

"He doesn't seem like that sort of a man to me."

"What do you know about him? Remember, Mrs. Sands didn't like him either."

166

"But Harry, she just took a notion; she didn't know him at all."

"She was a smart old lady. My notion about Morrow gets stronger all the time; the better I know him, the less I like him."

"Harry, are you telling me all there is to tell about it?"

"About what? About the way Morrow treats me? How can I, and put it in language you want to hear? I can't tell it all and say it nice too. I've had bad luck ever since I came to the Philippines, getting cheated out of what I deserved. Until I met you. Now I'm going to have you, Lucy. When? It's got to be soon."

"No, no!" she cried in a sudden panic, afraid he would touch her again. "I haven't promised. I haven't promised anything." She wanted to run from him, and she got to her feet, but she was slow. He had her arm in his hard grip before she could move away. "Let go, Harry! Don't you care if you hurt me?"

"Take back what you just said."

His face was very near and she could see he was smiling. He enjoyed her panic. That fact made her angry, and she was angry, too, at this new sensation that pushed her from him and pulled her toward him at the same time. When she spoke again her voice was controlled and icy. "Go away and don't come back until I send for you. Go away at once, or I'll never send for you."

"What's the matter with you, anyhow?"

"Go away."

He jerked her closer to him, and peered down at her face. He must have been able to see enough to know she meant what she said, or perhaps he could feel it in the rigidity of her body. Abruptly he let her go, turned, and went down the steps to the road.

3

"YOU haven't said a decent word today, Harry," Lloyd told him. "How about a little sunshine inside, to make the home happier?" They were in the office in the cuartel the following noon, Lloyd at his desk, Palmer at the window, looking out at a snarling, gusty storm of wind and rain. "I'm serious about it. I'm going to marry Encarnación. I bet that kid she's going to have will be cute. And where'll I find a wife any crazier about me than she is? She'll run my coconut plantation. I've got it figured out how I can buy a piece of land—"

"Oh, shut up, Jus, for God's sake! Always talking about that plantation!"

"I'm only going ahead on my own, that's all. Our plans together fell through when you started thinking about Lucy Leslie. Have I complained? No. I think I've been very agreeable about it. But there's no getting along with you. You lord it over me one day, and the next day you're so sour—"

"You'd better keep your mouth shut."

"In my own office? You don't have to stay. You can walk out, the way you walk out on—"

"Hey, Jus," Palmer said, pointing out the window, "look at this. No, you're too late. They're inside now."

"Who?"

"The sentry and a wild man from the mountains. Maybe it's news of Morrow."

"Bad news, you hope."

"Shut up. They're here."

They were at the office door. The robust sentry in his grass raincoat and hat was like a small thatched house on two bare feet, and beside him the stranger looked forlorn and very wet. His ragged camisa and his short, frayed pants clung, transparent, to his thin brown body; his ribs, swell-

168

ing and contracting in his anxious breathing, could be plainly seen. His long and matted hair was glued to forehead and neck in black points from which water dripped. With his darting, timorous eyes, he was like a creature brought from the heart of the jungle.

The two tenientes understood only a few of the words that he dared to say in his low, fearful voice, as he kept patting the bundle he carried under his arm. But the word *dinero* was repeated several times. Money. He wanted money; that much was clear.

At last Palmer seized the bundle, put it on the table, and said, "We'll see what you have to sell." He unfastened the bit of knotted vine, unrolled with a jerk the covering of soft matting and then a second piece of matting, and gave a startled gasp as a revolver slid out on the board. "Jus!" he said harshly. "Jus! Look here!"

Lloyd was already staring at it. It was unlike the revolvers they carried, not only of a different caliber but of an entirely different style, with a highly decorated and beautiful handle. Palmer picked it up and balanced it on his hand. "No mistake about it, is there? No chance of a mistake with a gun like this? Well, Jus? You say it. Go on. You say it. Whose is it? It's rusty, but look—there's where he marked it, and there's the marks. Go on, Jus. Say whose gun it is. Or maybe," he turned and spoke savagely in broken Spanish to the Filipino, "you can tell us whose gun it is!"

"It's Captain Pearson's!" Lloyd's voice was an adolescent's squeak. "But it's no use asking this fellow anything about it, Harry. You can tell by looking at him he don't know whose it was. If he did, he wouldn't've come in with it. No use getting excited. I'll give him the reward for bringing in a gun and then he can go. It's ten pesos he's supposed to get, isn't it? Morrow never got permission to offer more. But ten's plenty."

"By God, he's not going to get the money and walk out just like that. Are you crazy? He can answer a few questions first!"

"Give them the reward, and no questions asked. That's

what we're supposed to do." He went to the safe and began turning the dial.

"It's no wonder they think we're all fools! They send in Pearson's own gun, and get a reward, no questions asked! Can't you hear them laughing at us? By God, I'm sick of being laughed at!"

"Give them the money, and no questions. That's Morrow's orders, and I'm going to stick to them."

"I've had too much of sticking to Morrow's orders! Think they don't know he's tied our hands? Think they don't know he's away now? Looking for them some place they left a month ago. They're laughing their damn heads off at all of us. Everybody's laughing at us. Calling us fools. Calling you and me cowards because we sit around the cuartel all day."

"Shut up, Harry. You make me forget the combination. Now I have to start all over again."

Palmer was silent for one brooding moment. Then his resentment burst out again. "I'm sick of sticking to Morrow's orders. Here this fellow is, he could take us straight to Faustino, so we give him ten pesos and turn him loose. They're making fools of us. Everybody laughs at us. Even Lucy. She asked me why I wasn't in command here."

Lloyd pulled out the cash box and opened it. "What about Lucy?"

"Mind your own damn business. But nobody has any use for a coward."

Lloyd began to count out the silver coins.

"Don't you see, Jus," Palmer began in a tone that was almost pleading, "this is my chance? Maybe the only one I'm going to get? You used to try to see what I meant. Can't you—"

"I'm obeying orders. That's all I'm interested in doing. Now let me count this." He set the coins on the table and swung the safe door shut. "There it is, amigo."

Hurriedly but carefully the man moved the coins into the center of a piece of matting. Then Palmer leaned forward suddenly, gave the matting a pull, and knocked over the neat stack. "Hold on. It's not that easy. Where did you get this gun? Dónde? Dónde? Answer me!"

The small brown man's eyes moved back and forth from the money to the face of the man towering over him.

"Leave him be, Harry!" Lloyd warned. "You've been ready to fly off the handle all morning. I tell you, you ought to know by looking at him that he don't know where it came from. Looks to me as if it was buried somewhere all this time. He just found it, that's all."

"And that's all from you, too. You said your piece. Keep out now while I handle the rest. I ought to be in command here while Morrow's away and for once I'm going to act like it." He returned to the Filipino. "*Dónde, you God damned yuyu! Dónde? Dónde?*"

Lloyd got between them and shoved the coins into a heap over which he began folding the wrapper. "You'd better get out of here, amigo. Pronto."

The man came closer, reaching out to help with the package, and Palmer caught his shoulder and flung him back. The money spun across the table and off, ringing and rolling over the floor.

"Let him go, Harry! Let him go, for God's sake!"

"Let him go, and laugh at us? Let him go, and tell his Pope Faustino what fools we are? I'm not afraid of Faustino and I'm not afraid of Morrow." He shook the man slowly back and forth as he spoke. "Look me in the eye if you can, you God damned yuyu! Tell me you didn't kill Pearson. Tell me you didn't rip open his belly. Ah, you're guilty as hell!"

"Harry, he couldn't kill a dog. He's scared to death right now. You can't get anything out of him."

"I don't need you to tell me what to do."

"Harry, stop. You've been working yourself up all morning. Stop now. Stop before it's too late."

"It's too late for Pearson. Ever think about that? Everything's too late for Pearson because of this filthy ape and all the rest of them. I'm not going to let him go until he tells me the truth about where he got this gun. And I'm not asking you to hang around. I don't need any sickly yellow cowards to help me do my duty. He got the gun somewhere, didn't he? Let him tell me where."

"I'll talk to him, Harry. Take your hands off, and I'll try

171

to get an answer. Or all right, don't take your hands off. But give me a chance." He changed to Spanish, addressing the shivering Filipino. "Don't be afraid. Tell just where you got this gun. Then you get the money. Just where. That's all."

The frightened eyes flashed wildly toward him. "I find it, señor. I find it. Near the river. Near a big rock."

"Harry, he just found it. He just picked it up. I tell you, nobody that had anything to do with Dos Picos would dare come here. So calm down and let him go. Let him pick up his—"

Palmer interrupted him. "So you want to believe that, do you! Well, you can get out. Send my muchacho. He's a good interpreter. Get out, I said." He took his hand from the man's shoulder and turned toward Lloyd. "Or shall I throw you out? I can do it with one hand, you know. Maybe it's about time I did."

"O.K., Harry. I'm going. But call your muchacho for yourself. I don't want to have any more to do with what's going on. And don't lay a hand on me. Sure, I know you can lick me, but it might not be so easy as you think. I don't like what you're going to do."

"What do you know about what I'm going to do?"

"I know you pretty well, Harry." He saw, behind Palmer, that the Filipino was sidling to the door, and he tried to hold Palmer's attention. "Come on, Harry, think it over. You've gone far enough. Think it over before it's too late to stop yourself."

Palmer had been watching him with a frozen stare. Now he answered in a voice carefully slowed and softened. "Are you trying to say that I'm not in perfect control of myself? You're a fool and a coward. You always were." Then in a roaring, angry shout he called for his servant, and, with a quick turn, caught the wretched Filipino just before he reached the door.

Lloyd went into his own room swiftly, but it was no escape. Through the flimsy partitions of woven bamboo he could still hear plainly what went on in the office, and could picture too clearly the cowering Filipino, the muchacho, growing steadily more frightened himself, and Palmer

172

the inquisitor. The same questions over and over again. Where did you get the gun? Where did you find it? Or did somebody give it to you? Where did he find it? What's his name? What's your name? Who sent you here? Where do you live? Where did you get the gun? Who did you kill for it? Where did you get it? The same questions, now soft, now loud, and the answers, never the same, incoherent, inconsistent, and terrified.

Lloyd knew how Palmer's face was changing, very gradually; he might as well have watched, he thought, as to see it this way in his mind. The flesh would seem to swell, making all his features heavier and coarser. The long lines from his nostrils, past his mouth, down the chin, would be deepening. And his shoulders would hunch and double their bulk. His hands would swing before him in slight but constant, impatient action.

That sudden rustling, that moan, meant that he had seized the miserable fellow and was shaking him. That thud meant that he had thrown him to the floor.

And then the questions again.

Lloyd couldn't stand it any longer. He went back to the office and looked in. "Harry, you'll never learn anything from him. If Faustino's men sent him, they picked him because he don't know where they are or probably even who they are. Harry, twice before I saw you begin like this and I know how it ended. Stop it before it's too late!"

Palmer had glanced at him, but did not answer. But the Filipino took advantage of this slight change in attention, or perhaps took courage from Lloyd's appearance. Moving warily back to the wall, he drew the bolo that hung at the back of the rope tying up his ragged trousers. He had either forgotten or had not dared to touch this weapon before. But he had no chance to raise it, no chance to make even a threatening gesture. Palmer was on him, a kick had flattened him on the floor, the knife was wrenched from his hand and thrown aside. But the loss of the bolo did not mean the loss of the man's suddenly discovered spirit. Like a wild animal he was up again, and he flung himself on Palmer and fought, like an animal, with tooth and nail.

He inflicted little damage and was quickly overcome.

173

Panting, head hanging, hair falling over eyes, hands held behind his back in a cruel grasp, he was beaten and helpless. Palmer said, "That was thanks to you, Lloyd. I told you to get out. Now I'll never get anywhere by asking questions." He spoke in an ordinary, conversational tone, but Lloyd, shivering, backed away and returned to his room. Behind him he heard Palmer say to his muchacho, "Get me a couple of cartridges out of that box. Raining harder again outside? Well, a little more water won't make much difference to us." Lloyd heard his feet tramp out of the office and down the stairs. He knew that the soundless bare feet of the two Filipinos accompanied him.

In the loneliness of his room, with the rush of the rain loud in his ears, Lloyd could still, he felt, hear and see what was happening below as clearly as if he had been down there. They would go out of the barracks and around to the back, where the bamboo pipeline brought water down from the mountain. Harry would tie the fellow's hands behind him, and throw him on the ground. Maybe Harry could make the muchacho hold the fellow's feet; maybe he'd have to find some other way to keep them quiet. Then he'd prop that miserable, terrified mouth open with the cartridges. And then he'd start pouring in water.

And Harry would ask softly, but in English, so the questions meant nothing, "Ready to talk? Got something to say? Ready to answer?" And he'd chant, the way he chanted before, that time near the end of the war, when they were alone with a couple of prisoners, and that time up in the hills when seeing this had made those other Constabulary soldados desert, " 'Damn, damn, damn the Filipino, Pockmarked, murdering ladrone, Underneath our starry flag, Civilize him with a Krag . . . ' "

Lloyd made himself go back to the office and was at his desk, writing, when Palmer came in again. Lloyd looked up but said nothing.

Palmer walked to the window and spoke with his back to the room. "That damn monkey of a muchacho got scared and wouldn't hold him down. I had to give up. I didn't get anything out of him. What's a man going to

174

do without cooperation? This was my chance. Maybe I'll never get another."

"Where is he?"

"Where's who?"

"You know who I mean. Where is he?"

"Out there on the ground."

"Dead?"

"God damn you! No!"

"Somebody ought to see that he gets away from here all right."

"He'll take care of that himself."

Better keep out of it, Lloyd warned himself; better not have anything to do with it. But after a moment he said, "His bolo's still here on the floor. And his money."

Palmer picked up the bolo and threw it out the window.

After another long moment, Lloyd got up from the table and picked up the money. He recounted the coins, wrapped them up, and then walked slowly out the door. Palmer, still at the window, with water dripping from his clothes into little pools on the floor, made no indication that he was aware of what Lloyd was doing.

The man was gone from behind the barracks. Returning to the front of the building, Lloyd looked for the bolo that Palmer had thrown down. That was gone, too. He crossed the rocky Escarpa, bending against the rain, to the sentry. "Where's that man that was here?"

"He is gone, señor teniente."

"Was he all right? Could he walk?"

"A friend came and helped him."

Lloyd showed the bundle he held. "I wanted to give him this reward," he said.

"Sí, señor teniente. But he has gone."

Glancing at the sentry's face, Lloyd for an instant caught his eye and was filled with a sickening sense of guilt. He said, "Tell him it's his, if he ever comes back. Tell him I'll take it to him. Tell him—" He broke off. Every word increased his shame. He turned back to the cuartel.

Palmer was still standing in the window. He gave no sign that he noticed Lloyd there below him.

4

IT was pneumonia following dengue fever that had sent Morrow home from the Seven Sisters Mountains on a litter. He realized that later, and at first blamed his illness for the fact that everything seemed strange in the world of health from which he was an exile. But though he progressed each day on his way back to normal, he found the strangeness was not disappearing. Palmer's single, brief, surly visit to the tower was not surprising, but Lloyd's embarrassed and oversolicitous attitude was. The soldados he talked to were uneasy about something. And Ramos, who was constantly in and out, supervising everything done for Morrow, was silent. Silence in Ramos was almost as startling as a shout from a dumb man.

When Morrow asked what was wrong and insisted on being told, Ramos was still so locked in taciturnity that he could give only a few words in reply. "Teniente Palmer. La cura del agua." His response to further questions was equally meager. But Morrow learned enough to sicken him.

He sent at once for Palmer and Lloyd. It was a spontaneous reaction, moved by the feeling that if a man is accused of a crime, he must be given a chance to defend himself. But as soon as Ramos had gone to call them, Morrow began to see the size of the danger, if the story was true. Everything he had done and everything he had said, everything he had promised and everything he wanted to do, might be turned to failure. And the truth of that earlier story of the water cure was involved, the story he had never been able to prove or disprove. Morrow had no time to plan what he was going to say to the two tenientes before he heard their voices as they came toward the tower.

It was very early morning. Intense sunlight streamed through the doorway, melting the coolness left by the night. Morrow watched this patch of radiance, waiting for shadows to darken it, and when they came, he pulled himself up from his straw mat, swinging his feet around so that he sat facing the door. The scarlet blanket in which he was rolled slipped down, revealing tanned and muscular shoulders, arms, and body, bare except for the locket, their healthy strength incongruous under his haggard face, which was marked with new and deeper lines and was dark with his unshaven beard. To the tenientes as they entered he said, "From the beginning. The water cure."

An answer was slow in coming, and Morrow could see their eyes, peering toward him while getting used to the dimmer light in the tower, but seeming to him to question, to be all of blind youth trying to see and to understand. He regretted his brusqueness. "Sit down, Lloyd, Palmer. Pull over those boxes. We'll talk about this."

But now their eyes were adjusted. Palmer stood straighter, and Lloyd's glance flicked anxiously, warily, back and forth. Palmer said, "I'd rather stand."

The illusion of their youthful innocence vanished from Morrow's mind. "All right. Stand. Now talk. Begin at the beginning."

"There's nothing to tell. Lloyd reported when you got back that nothing important happened here while you were gone." Palmer's tone was hard and contemptuous. "Nothing happened on your patrol, either. You didn't bring back Faustino, did you?"

"Have you anything to say, Lloyd?"

"Well, sir, I don't know what you want me to tell, sir."

"I thought I made that clear. The water cure. I have been told that a man came to the Escarpa to claim a reward for a gun. He was tortured. So I was told. I'm asking you, both of you, to tell me about it. I'm asking you before I talk to anyone else that was here while I was away. Is there any truth in the story? You didn't even report the return of a gun."

"Torture!" Palmer spat out the word. "You have to love the little brown brothers, you have to kiss them. Or it's torture!"

"I want to know about the man that brought the gun.

177

"For God's sake," Lloyd cried, "you don't mean you'd give Harry the water cure!"

"Are you suggesting that, Lieutenant Lloyd? Is it a good way to get an answer?"

"You don't—you can't—"

"Oh, shut up, Jus!" Palmer cried in angry disgust. "Don't you know what you told him? Don't you see what he got you to say? He wouldn't give me the water cure, even if he could. You don't give the water cure to a white man. Oh God, what's the use of this! Let's get out!"

"Don't leave this tower"—Morrow's voice was very cold and very clear—"until I dismiss you. I see your hand move. Don't draw your gun. Sick or well, I'm faster than you are. Sick or well, I think I could see that you got the water cure if I wanted to give it to you. Don't misunderstand me. It isn't that I wouldn't give it to a white man. I wouldn't give it to any man. But I say that if any man deserves it, it's a man like you, with the brutality to treat another human being in such a way. For I've got the truth now, haven't I? Are you going to deny it, either one of you?"

"I didn't help this last time," Lloyd's answer burst out. "I swear I tried to stop him. I was going to tell you, sir. I wanted you to know I didn't help him this time. I was waiting till you got well. Even that other time I got sick and went off and left him."

Palmer sneered, "Coward then, coward today. But I'm no coward, Morrow. That was Pearson's gun he brought. Pearson's! I saw Pearson dead. I cut him down. He was crucified. I swore revenge. And I'm not going to let them make a coward out of me like Lloyd, or a sucker, either. It was my chance to find out where he came from, to get Faustino. You thought you took all my chances away. You want all the medals yourself. But I'll get Faustino yet. I'll get him before you do."

"I see," Morrow said. "A coward like Lloyd, or a sucker like me. That's what you meant, though you didn't go quite so far as to say it. No, don't interrupt me, Palmer. I have something more to say. If we were looking for

179

revenge, that debt would have been paid long ago. How many men were killed on Dos Picos? Three. And how many outlaws have died, one way or another, through our Constabulary pursuit of them since? Ten, twelve, perhaps more. But at least three of theirs for each one of ours. How much vengeance do you want? Anyhow, our duty here is to give the people security, a chance to live again in peace, to grow their rice and eat it in safety.

"Well, I can see I might have left all that unsaid. But the rest of what I have to say will be plainer yet. This is the Philippine Constabulary. We belong to the people of the Philippines. We have no room for a man like you. You are no longer an officer." He called to Ramos to come inside the tower, and gave him, in rapid Spanish, instructions to get a penknife from the desk and stand with revolver ready. To Palmer he said, "Take the knife. Cut off your shoulder straps and the rest of the insignia."

Palmer stared at him with his lips parted and moving a little, as if trying to talk but unable to make a sound.

Morrow answered what might have been his words. "Oh, yes. I do have the power to do this. I was told before I left Manila that my decision in regard to you would be supported without question. In the Constabulary you are through. As for you, Lloyd, I'll think of asking them to give you another chance. Away from here. I'll think it over."

"But I don't want to leave Magtalisay, sir. That is, I was thinking of getting married—"

"I've given as much consideration as I can to personal matters. Too much. You can't stay with the Magtalisay Constabulary." Morrow turned his attention again to Palmer. "If you can't cut those off by yourself, I'll have Ramos do it."

Flushing suddenly, Palmer jerked at his tunic. Two buttons flew off, caught by the starch-stiffened button-holes, and one sleeve tore as he pulled. And then the jacket was in his hands, and he was ripping at the initials, P. C., and at the shoulder straps. Without speaking, the others watched him throw the threads and the bits of

·cloth on the floor and, finally, the knife. Then, turning to leave the tower, he stumbled against Lloyd, swung a fist at him, missed, and hit the wall. For an instant he stood absolutely still, and the others waited, motionless too and silent, as if frozen in spite of the growing heat. He drew a deep breath that they all could hear, and with his tunic hanging from his hand, he walked out, a dark figure, through the brilliant doorway.

"Captain Morrow," Lloyd began. "Captain—"

Morrow shook his head and gestured for him to leave. Then, pulling the blanket around his shoulders, he lay down again and closed his eyes.

5

THERE was an immediate change in the atmosphere on the Escarpa, with renewed confidence spreading among the men. Ramos reported to Morrow that Palmer had gone straight from the tower down the steps into the town, returning to the old Constabulary headquarters and having his belongings sent after him. At once, Ramos said, there wasn't a man who didn't look and act as if a threatening shadow had been removed. Morrow was certain he could tell the difference in the sound of the soldiers' marching feet when they drilled; and one soldado after another disturbed his quiet that evening by coming to the tower door to inquire about his health.

The next day the reaction in Magtalisay made itself apparent in a visit from Briones.

El Cojo limped in out of the rain, leaving his umbrella near the door to dry. He pulled a box close to where Morrow lay, sat down, drew out a cigar case, and offered Morrow a cigar. "Are you well enough to smoke, señor capitán? No? Then do you mind if I do? These are very good; I have them sent from Manila. Though even these are not the best I have smoked. Those best cigars—but there was only one of them." Smiling, he lost himself a moment in recollection. "May I tell you a story?"

"I'd be glad to hear it."

"I was young then. Sixteen. I saw myself as a fine *caballero*; I went to Manila; I was to enter the *colegio*; I was seeing the world for the first time after growing up in provincial, backward Magtalisay. You will know the way I felt, perhaps? Well, I visited a cigar factory owned by my uncle, and a beautiful girl rolled the tobacco into a cigar on her bare thigh. They say there is something about the touch of the skin—Well, it was the finest cigar I have ever smoked. Now I am only thirty-four, but I feel like an old man when I think of that time."

Morrow gave him an understanding look, and Briones smoked in silence for a little time. Then he said abruptly, "I shall never understand Americans. No Spaniard would live in a place like this tower. No Filipino who could afford a good house would live here. With boxes and crates for furniture. You could have a good house. You could command the best in Magtalisay."

"This suits me."

"No, I shall never understand you. When I heard that *teniente* Palmer was out of the Constabulary, I did not believe it. I said to myself that Captain Morrow, even Captain Morrow, could not do this to another *americano*, no matter what that other man has done. But I have learned it is true. True! You prove to me the principles of democracy. An American uses torture on a Filipino, and you do not say that the Filipino is an ignorant native, that his skin is brown, that he is nothing but a yuyu or a googoo, that he doesn't matter. You do not say that whatever the *americano* does is right because he has a white skin. No. You say, here are two human beings. If one abuses the other, he must be punished. Señor *capitán*, this is something I have never seen before. It is something I did not expect to see."

If Morrow had thought of a reply to make, he could not have made it. He lay without speaking; he could not even meet Briones' glance. To him this was not thanks, not an expression of trust, but an indictment of men of his own color; and he had no words for what he felt.

Then Briones began to talk again. "I did not think that I would ever come to regard an americano as a friend. My brother Ricardo was killed by americanos, and we are certain also that my brother Andrés died with him. My mother perished of grief for them both. That I must also blame on your people. Once I blamed them because I thought they had killed my sister too. But I know now that she is among the living dead, the lepers. And we have the Japanese to thank for leprosy— So I have believed that all countries and all peoples are enemies of one another. Until you do what you did yesterday.

"Now I wish to help you. I remember Aguinaldo's proclamation after he had been captured. He said, 'Enough of blood, enough of tears and desolation!' And he was right. I swear that I will do everything I can to help you capture this Pope Faustino, and Ola, and their outlaws. Outlaws—though many, perhaps, still think they fight for independence. It may be I will hear myself called a traitor."

"You'll hear them calling you a greater patriot than ever before."

"Ojalá! A man's life can take many strange turns." He shrugged and changed the subject. "I have heard of a jar that you brought back with you from some pulajanes' lair in the mountains. Is it here?"

Morrow sat up and turned to point. "It's right there with a blanket over it. Did you hear the story that a god lives in it? I'd like to have you look at it. It certainly looks empty to me."

"Do not think, amigo, that I shall see in it anything that you cannot see. This is it? Under here?" At Morrow's assent, he lifted the blanket and then the piece of embroidered silk beneath, and revealed the large green jar. "So this is it! And they said it held a god, you say? Did they tell you anything else?"

"You seem excited about it, Briones. I wish I knew more to tell. Faustino left it behind in his hurry to escape. As I understand it, nobody ever saw this god that lives

183

in the jar, but they've heard his voice. Faustino talks to him. Ventriloquism, I suppose. Know what I mean?"

"Ventriloquism? Sí, señor capitán. I know that word. But this is something different, I think. We shall try to learn. The air in this tower moves, no es verdad? Where does it enter now? Not by the door; I can see the rain blowing past the door."

Morrow pointed to a window halfway up to the left, beside the ladder. "There's usually a strong breeze up there."

"Good. I think I can get this up there. It would be a pity to drop it and destroy it; these old wine-jars are very rare. Especially this kind, if I'm right about it."

"It's old?"

"Sí. Several hundred years." Moving carefully, with the jar in one arm, he mounted the ladder and braced himself. "We shall soon know if I am right. There's a good wind coming through here. Plenty of rain, too, which we could do without. The window is narrow, but it will hold it, I think. It will be perfect. Ah!" He raised the jar and tilted it a little so he could set it on the edge of the sill. "Now listen." He gave it a push and straightened it.

At once above the sound of the rain a delicate and musical tone, not a sigh and not a voice but something like both, floated into the air of the tower, growing fainter and then stronger, and again dying away only to return in even greater volume and then fade to nothing.

"Muy rara, muy hermosa!" Briones said in awe. "I have never heard a finer one. I have only twice before heard even a poor one. Very rare! The wind blows over the lip, you understand?"

"I understand," Morrow told him. "I understand why they believe it holds a god, too, and I'll be surprised if they don't try very hard to get it back."

"Yes. They cannot be happy to think you have it. Shall I bring it down again?" He lifted it out of the window and carried it, in response to Morrow's gesture, to the matting-covered packing case beside the American. "It must be their most valued possession."

Morrow turned the jar around, tracing with his fingers

184

the raised decoration on the swelling sides. "What is this design, Briones? I haven't ever had a really good look at it. Do you mind lighting that candle?"

"It is a dragon," Briones said, as they examined it. "There is the head; and the body and the tail coil around this way. The scales are well done; there is nothing crude about this jar. A Chinese dragon, you understand, amigo; these jars were brought to the islands long ago by Chinese traders. Here's a claw. You can count the sharp talons. Four."

"Four? Do you know, that's a very curious thing. I wonder if it has anything to do with Faustino's *señal*. He often leaves a sort of trademark of a claw or hand with four fingers. Superstition's a funny thing. It has a sort of logic, if you want to figure it out. Like this dragon's four-toed foot. And the *pulajanes'* anting-antings that always contain three finger bones to work part of their magic. That's all tied together by an insane kind of reason to something I learned on this patrol. Faustino himself lacks the little finger of his right hand. Apparently that fact is a secret, and yet it's used as part of all the rest of this superstitious nonsense. What do you think of that?"

"Extraordinary, extraordinary!" Briones murmured, and then stood for a few moments in silence, in deep and remote thought, with his hand locked so tightly over the rim of the vessel that when Morrow tried to turn it for a better view of the dragon he could not move it, and Briones seemed unaware of the effort.

"Well," Morrow said presently, "I can see what this must mean to them. The center of Faustino's hold over them may be here. I suppose it's safe enough in the tower, covered up as I had it? As safe here as anywhere. Shall we put it back?"

"Yes, yes! Cover it over again." Briones moved the jar himself, replacing hurriedly the embroidered silk and the blanket. "I have heard, señor capitán, that you yourself wear an anting-anting."

So that's what was bothering him, Morrow thought. The superstition touches even him. And it has touched me, too. There's something about that jar, about the

185

voice it speaks with . . . In superstition Faustino had a powerful weapon. "An anting-anting?" he repeated. "You must have been told about this." He took off the locket and opened it. "My friend, you have given me a confidence. I will give you one. Perhaps I wear this for superstitious reasons. But it is a reminder of bad fortune, not a promise of good."

He waited until Briones had taken the pictures to the door for better light, and then continued, "The one who smiles was my mother. I never knew her. She died when I was born. The other, perhaps you have guessed, I was allowed to know and to love for a short time. She was my wife. She died when our child was born. The child died too."

Briones held the locket a little longer before he closed it and returned it. He said only, "They were very beautiful."

"Beautiful, and too young to die." Morrow slipped the chain back over his head. "You have been neglecting your cigar, amigo."

"I cannot stay longer," Briones said. "And we have already told much to each other, I think. Enough for this time. I am your friend. I will try to help bring peace." He hesitated, and then went on in a lower tone, as if talking more to himself than to Morrow, "I must try. It is my first duty. I can see now I should have helped long ago. There have been these attempts to persuade me to join Faustino. Perhaps somehow . . ." He picked up his umbrella. "Hasta luego, amigo. Together we can do much, I think."

Morrow walked unsteadily to the door, impatient with the way his illness confined him, and watched Briones limp across the Escarpa and disappear haltingly below the level of its rocky surface.

6

BY breaking Palmer, Morrow had raised Constabulary morale and, unexpectedly, won Briones' offer of active aid. Another consequence, but an expected one, came soon after Briones departed: a note from Lucy asking to see Morrow as soon as he was well enough.

He had foreseen this interview with her from the moment Palmer walked out of the tower, dragging his tunic. Fortunately, he had not thought earlier that she might be affected; his decision had not been influenced in the least degree by the thought that Palmer's disgrace might set her free of him or might, contrarily, bind her closer. But he had been wondering ever since what would happen when she learned the truth. Would she believe it? Was there, he wondered, a promise that bound her to Palmer? Would she be warned in time? Or would she resolve, without reason or foresight, that nothing should turn her against the man?

Anyhow, he had been bracing himself for her possible reproaches, or for her pleading to have Palmer reinstated. Although he had not yet walked farther than the doorway of the tower, he sent her word that he would meet her the next morning at her school. He would take no more time for convalescence, and spend no more time dreading this interview.

But as soon as he entered the plaza and saw her, a slender figure in a white dress, sitting in the balcony-like window alone, waiting for him, his reluctance to meet her vanished. What they were to talk about was no longer important. All that mattered was being near her.

His elation lasted almost until she met him at the top of the stairs, but by then it had left as suddenly as it had arrived. His haggard, tired face made her exclaim in self-reproach when she saw him; she thought, however, the walk from the Escarpa deserved all the blame.

Her words of regret for having made him come so far and her sympathy for his illness were sweet to him, but bitter too. He felt that they were more than he deserved, but nothing of what he wanted. He protested, "I'm well again. And nobody has been as good to me as you have. Soup, jelly, custard—something every day."

"Don't you know that in Kansas we'd lynch a neighbor who didn't do that? Come and sit down."

Their chairs faced each other across a small bamboo table, on which she leaned, watching him. Below in the plaza men and women passing through stared up at them. Sitting there with her was very pleasant, Morrow thought, and he wished he could prolong the minutes while they both waited for his breathing to steady after the climb up the stairs. But the subject he dreaded could not be postponed, and he himself began it. "You want to talk about Palmer."

"Yes." Her eyes met his with the grave and frank simplicity he loved. "I tried to talk to you about him once before, but it all went wrong. I couldn't say the things I wanted to say. I guess it would have been wrong to say them then. But now I have to. I must know all about him."

This was not the way Morrow had expected her to begin. His reply was awkward and blunt. "Isn't he the one to tell you about himself? I can't praise him to you, you know."

"Did I ask you to praise him?"

"I didn't mean that the way it sounded. But under the circumstances—"

She moved her hands in a shy, beseeching gesture. "Captain Morrow, we don't understand each other, but we must. We did once. I'm sure we can again. But I don't know just how to start. Did you think I was going to ask you to give Harry a second chance? I don't think he wants it. He says he's glad to be out. But anyhow, I wouldn't ask you that."

"He went to you, then."

"Yes, he came to me."

"He told you his story, and you think he's been badly treated."

"Did I say that? No. I trust you. I don't think you would be likely to treat anyone unfairly. Do you know all the facts?"

Was that the wall she'd hide behind? It could be the sort of wall to withstand every attack except that of Palmer himself, and Palmer might break it down too late to do her any good. Morrow said, "I knew enough facts for the action I took. What I did had to be done." He hoped his words showed none of the love or pain he felt, but only their own truth.

She said, "Maybe *I* don't know all the facts."

He was astounded. Wonderingly, he studied her face. Had he misread her completely? What did he really know of this girl he had fallen in love with? Very little; almost nothing. Almost nothing except that she was young, simple, and direct, and, because of those qualities, vulnerable. Did she realize that in effect she had told him that she trusted him more than she trusted Palmer? He echoed her. "Maybe you don't know all the facts?" He realized suddenly that he had let a few words of gossip, enlarged by his own fear, illness, even jealousy, perhaps, persuade him that Lucy might be deeply in love with Palmer. Now he understood that he might be wrong. It was like thinking it was night and then opening his eyes to discover the darkness had been of his own making.

Her eyes were open wide, and they met his unswervingly as if inviting him to look into them. "I've been trying to make it clear. I have to know all about him. I have to know the facts. It isn't easy to ask, but I have to."

"He must have told you—"

"Let's forget what he told me. Don't you see that I don't know whether I can believe him or not?"

"How important is this to you?"

The color deepened in her cheeks, but she did not look away. "You make me say it all, don't you? Emerald wanted me to marry him. She wanted him to run her plantation. Emerald told me I loved him; she said that she could see all the signs, that she knew, if I didn't. And he's been

189

asking me to marry him. But I told him to wait, and let me think—and then he came back again when this happened. Do you see? Oh, I haven't said it plain enough yet. I don't know if I love him. Sometimes I think maybe I do. Sometimes I think I don't. Now do you see?"

"Perhaps I see a little." He wanted to add, If you're not sure, it isn't love. But was that right? Would it be fair to say that? Would it be wise? He leaned back in his chair, gazing at the neatly woven bamboo in the top of the table. He could tell her what love was; there was nothing uncertain about what he felt. But her uncertainty, pathetic, charming, and frightening, was that of youth. What is love? He had a hundred answers to give her, but dared not offer one.

She broke the silence to say, "I have nobody but you to turn to." She put her hand on one of his, which were lying on the table. "It might take just a word to decide me, one way or the other. What did Harry do? I have to know the truth."

A word could turn her? Yes. That was the danger. What a child she was, to think a word could have any influence on love. But a word might turn her toward a step she would regret.

"Why is it so hard for you to answer me? It should be easier than what I've just had to tell you."

"Should it?" He could not resist taking her hand in both of his and holding it strongly and warmly clasped, but only for a moment. He released it then and began his reply, trying to be careful but still direct, as she had been herself. "You want to know whether you can believe his story. You want to hear from me the reason for what I did. Then are you going to decide between the two versions—if his story and mine are different? Or are you going to someone else?"

"I trust you."

Trust is a part of love, he thought. He said, "The charge against him is cruelty, torturing a man with the water cure."

She nodded but she was not satisfied. "He told me that was the charge. But—"

"And this confirms an earlier charge of the same thing that couldn't be proved. Did he tell you that?"

"No. But I'd heard. Sergeant Johnstone claims it was true."

"Johnstone?"

She nodded again, and shrugged quickly. "But who would take his word for anything? It's this last charge that really matters. Harry says it can't be proved. Is that so? Weren't there witnesses?"

"There were no eye-witnesses. The victim has disappeared. Palmer's muchacho ran away. Lloyd kept out of it. But there's no doubt of Palmer's guilt. Would you like to talk to Lloyd about it?"

"Oh, no! I couldn't! I'd be ashamed. I feel ashamed now." She shrank away, for the first time turning her eyes to avoid his. "And sick. When you said 'victim' . . ."

Morrow waited. He had had to tell her what she asked, and it was really no more, probably, than Palmer had already told, but for the first time she was seeing the ugly picture in her imagination. He could not guess at her next reaction, but he dared not feel hopeful about it. He watched her bent head, almost afraid to see her raise it. What would she ask next that he would wish he did not have to answer?

She looked up and said, "I feel sorry for Harry, too. Of course you can't give him another chance, but I think I ought to. I think Emerald would want me to. He says you're down on him; you won't see his side of it." She spoke slowly, giving Morrow a chance to comment after each statement; but he was silent. "I can't let him think that about me. Maybe another chance is all he needs, so that he'll know the world isn't all against him. Then we'll see; then I'll know what he is. Don't you think I should do that? I want to be fair."

Fairness! It was Morrow's own principle, but he did not welcome it now. He got up, habit helping him stand straight in spite of the giddy weakness he had not yet thrown off. "I can't advise you. I swear there was no prejudice behind the official action I took. None. I had

191

no choice then. But I can't judge now. Fairness to him? Mercy to him? What about you? What would be fair to you?" Her steady gaze held his through a long pause, and he discovered that he was trembling. "How can I tell you what to do?" To keep his voice from shaking, he hardened it until it sounded angry. "I love you. More—more—from the first—" He could find no other words. Her wide eyes were still on his; they seemed to tie him there. He made a prodigious effort and turned away, walked to the stairs and down them, out of the school building, and through the plaza.

What did he know about women? Everything he had said had been wrong, or he had said it in the wrong way. He was sure of that. He was surer when he learned the following day that Palmer had gone up the river to Punta Arenas to act as manager of the Sands plantation.

7

JOHNSTONE looked at Morrow with pleading eyes, like a dog that knows he deserves a whipping. "Sorry you been sick, cap. I should've got up to see you, but . . . I don't know. I didn't get here. I guess I thought you'd send for me this way as soon as you felt like seeing me."

Morrow was blunt. "You're ashamed of something, but that's not it. You gave yourself away, didn't you? No, don't say anything. I'm doing the talking. A long time ago I asked you for information about Palmer and that water-cure charge. You told me you knew nothing. But you told Miss Leslie—"

"I don't know what I said to her that day. I wasn't responsible. I was a sick man."

"You seem to have a good idea of what I'm talking about."

"No. I don't know a thing!"

"Johnstone, it's time to give me the truth. She wasn't

convinced that you knew anything about that affair. I think you do. I want—"

"I tell you I was out of my head with fever!"

"It's too bad you never talked to me when you were out of your head, if that's the only time you don't lie. Johnstone, we're not in the same service, but we work for the same government. It's our duty to see that Americans out here deserve respect, and get it. But getting it comes second. You failed."

"You ought not to be so hard on me, cap! I went to see her to help you. By telling her a few facts about Palmer."

"And if I'd had those facts when I asked for them, she would never have met him. Did you think of that? Well, it's too late, now, but I still want it. The truth, Johnstone. What do you know about that earlier affair? You weren't there, were you?"

Johnstone's answer was slow in coming; it was a struggle to bring out what had been so long concealed. "This boy," he said at last, "you know, my assistant. This boy I been training. His cousin was one of the deserters." He raised his eyes about as high as Morrow's chin, and then looked down again, but he stood a little straighter. "It was only his story, see?"

"But it was a way for me to get the whole story."

"It wasn't none of my business," Johnstone said in sullen defense. "I didn't want to make no trouble for nobody."

"Trouble?" There was exasperation mixed with Morrow's anger and disgust, but there was pity too. He tried to keep the pity out of his words and voice. "I don't suppose you'll ever understand how much trouble you've made. I hope you keep thinking about it. Johnstone, there's no room out here for people like you. You want to get away; perhaps you'll be glad to hear what I'm going to do. I'm going to your office and have that assistant of yours send a cable to Manila about you—"

Now the anxious eyes met Morrow's in fright. "But what if they give me a dishonorable discharge?" He added, "sir," and then went on, "Maybe they wouldn't pay our fare back home. And Gracie, she'd never forget it! Don't you remember the chess games we played, sir? I thought we was friends!"

"I thought we were friends, too," Morrow began, and then gave up. What was the use of reproach or condemnation? The same ignorance that guided Johnstone's acts put him out of reach of what Morrow might have said; it would have been as impossible to stir in him any deep regret as it was unthinkable to say that Gracie, too, was no credit to her country. "That's all past," Morrow said. "The cablegram has to go. I'm sorry. Really sorry."

He noticed that as they walked to Johnstone's house the man's spirits began to revive. The reason soon appeared. "You know what, cap?" Johnstone said. "I been thinking. I already asked to be relieved. Maybe this'll just hurry things along. Yes, maybe it'll work out that way. After all, like you said, you and I are in different services. It isn't like you was a captain in the Army. No use in worrying until I have to."

8

MORROW walked the Escarpa in the systematic exercise by which he was rebuilding his strength. He had always paced this rock; his feet knew it well; but his solitude here had changed. It was disturbed and enriched by the company of Lucy's image, by what he had said to her and what he wished he had said, by hopes, resolutions, doubt, self-reproach, and despair.

Trying to force his mind to other thoughts, he stopped and looked west over the estuary toward a part of his territory of which he knew very little. Action was what he needed. He would take a patrol there; at least an exploratory patrol. While he had been lying idle, this neglected rectangle of mountains between estuary, river, bay, and strait had begun to attract him with the mystery

194

and promise of a dark continent. He himself had sailed along the bay and into the strait, and he had brought back sketches of the mountainous profile rising above the coast. A patrol there. That must be made. As soon as he was strong enough to keep up with the men.

He was walking again, busy with this plan, when he saw Briones reach the top of the Escarpa. He had not seen Briones for several days, since their examination of the green jar, and he had been told that no one else had seen him about the town. He crossed the rock to meet him. "I hope you are well, amigo. I heard that you had been confined to your house."

Briones' answer was bitter. "I wish I had been! But no. I have been to confer with the outlaw leaders, hoping to bring peace. I did not succeed. In their minds was only the hope that I would join them; that was the only reason they wanted to see me. For my offer to be a go-between they had nothing but contempt."

Morrow came rapidly to a decision. "Señor Briones, I put it to you. You have said you and I are friends, and you have proved it. But forget the friendship. That is another matter. You are the friend first and always of your own people. Well, you have met the outlaws. You have talked perhaps with both Faustino and Ola. You have been, perhaps, inside their fortress. Pues, you have learned much that could help the Constabulary. If you can tell me all this, if you will—who knows? It could be your information that would cure this sore and make Magtalisay and its barrios healthy again. Now for the first time I am asking, begging for your assistance. Will you tell me what you have learned?"

Briones was not slow in answering. "You do not need to ask. I came to tell you everything I know. But I do not know much to tell. The truth is that I do not even know where I went."

"You can probably tell me more than you think."

"I do not know where I was, amigo. They took me at night, blindfolded. They kept me under guard. I am surprised to be back here alive. They must think there is

195

still hope I will join them. So I came to tell you all, but the all is nothing."

"If you were there, you must know something. More than you think. Suppose I ask you questions and you answer."

Briones nodded. "All right. I will answer what I can. Understand, amigo? What I am able to tell, I will tell. Only what I do not know, only what is concealed from me will be concealed from you. You trust me?"

"You needn't look at me so anxiously. I knew a long time ago that I could trust you. Now, here's the first question. We begin at the beginning. How did this message or these messages from Faustino reach you? Who brought them?"

"Now you will perceive what I mean when I say I know nothing. Ola visited me once, as I told you. Besides that I have had four messages. Each one was tied to a stone which was thrown in my window at night. I could never find who had thrown them."

"When did they come?"

"The first one came the day I arrived here. The day you and I arrived together, amigo."

"Then someone here in town, someone who lives here, must have written that first message. Do you have any suspicions that there is a connection between Faustino and the Zúñigas, or Paterno, or Villamor, or young Soriano?"

"I, too, think there is someone here in Magtalisay who is a friend of Faustino, someone who is powerful. Someone who must be one of those you name. But which is it? I cannot yet see."

Morrow made a gesture that brushed aside this part of the problem. "Then we'll talk about your visit. How was it arranged?"

"I was to signal them any time I was willing to meet Faustino. I put a small coconut-oil lamp at night in the window where the stones had passed. The second night a voice I did not know told me to go down to the end of a certain pier. A banca would be waiting. I was to step into the banca."

Morrow exclaimed with satisfaction, "There's something definite. You went by water. That's the first step."

"But does it tell you so much? It was almost certain I should have to go by water. Where can one go outside Magtalisay without going by water? For that is all I know. They blindfolded me. I saw nothing until they set me ashore, and there they had to unbind my eyes, because I had to climb a mountain trail. But that was not until we were away from the water and it was as dark as the inside of a wolf's mouth. I don't know where I was."

"Amigo, when you were in the banca, did you go up the river or across the bay?"

"But how can I tell? I could see nothing!"

"But you could hear. You could smell. You could feel the lift of the banca and how it rode on the water. Tell me, did you smell the salt of the bay?"

"I don't remember."

"Think about when you were coming back. Did you know when you were close to Magtalisay?"

Briones said in surprise, "But yes, amigo! I could smell the salt and fish of the estuary. You think, then, I had been on the river? But of course!"

"Now then, which branch? One runs fast and one runs slow. On the Sumpitan you can hear the rush and whirl of rapids here and there, but the Negro flows languidly."

Briones closed his eyes. "Wait. It is not easy to recall. I had many things to think of. But wait . . . Coming back, yes, coming down we came swiftly, and the men joked because they had only to guide the banca, for it moved with the current. But I cannot tell you how long it took us either way, for that I do not know. I left my watch here. For some reason, though I thought I might take a chance on trusting my life to the *pulajanes*, I did not want to trust my watch."

Morrow gave no indication that these answers were satisfying any theory. "And do you know if you went north or south away from the river when you landed? Were you in the forest? Could you see the stars? Or the moon? No, the moon would have set."

"We stopped soon and waited for dawn. The sun came

197

up on my left. I think it did, but how can I be sure? The trees were thick, and the path kept turning. We may have gone south and then north. Or east, or west. When we came out of the forest the sun was directly overhead, and I do not know where we were."

"Never mind that, then. Tell me what this outlaw's nest is like. How many houses, how many men? Did you recognize any of them? That sort of thing."

"It is a valley with a small stream. Ten houses or twenty, I cannot tell you. No less than the first, no more than the last. They told me they had a hundred men, but I saw nothing to make me think they had more than half that many. I talked with Ola. You know I knew him before."

"You didn't talk with Faustino?"

Briones answered slowly, "Yes. I talked with him also."

"And what do you think of him?" When Briones did not reply at once, Morrow added more questions. "Is he the man behind all this? Or is Ola more influential? What about the idea that Faustino is holy? Is he really missing a finger of his right hand?"

"Yes. The finger is gone. And that idea of holiness, it is easy to understand. In a sense he is behind it all. He holds it together. You would have to see him to know. But Ola is the fighter. In that way Ola is the leader. He is a very wicked man."

"And Faustino is not?"

"You would have to see him to understand." His eyes evaded Morrow's.

Morrow had the feeling that Briones himself had to some degree fallen under Faustino's spell. He dropped his direct questioning, and showed the Filipino his map of the region around Magtalisay. "Briones, the valley where you went must be somewhere on this map. Would you want to do any guessing?"

The two of them leaned over it together, and with his finger Briones traced the course of the Sumpitan. "Somewhere up this river, you think?"

"Or possibly up some branch of it of which we know nothing."

"Yes, there is that, too," Briones said, and sighed. "I wish I knew these mountains. It is my shame that I know the city of Manila better than my own province."

Morrow put his hand over the part of the map in which he was now most interested. "Amigo, under my palm is the spot where I think you were taken. You have said nothing to make me change my mind. Tell me, do you remember anything unusual or characteristic about the mountains surrounding that valley? Any landmarks?"

Briones reflected, and shook his head. "They were mountains, señor capitán, and to me a mountain is a mountain. Yet there was one, I believe, that was different. I saw it with the sunset behind it, and it was like a head with hair on it."

"Let me show you some of my sketches," Morrow said. He concealed his sudden hope and excitement, but he was almost certain that he had seen a peak that might be described in such a way, and his hands fumbled in haste as he shuffled the pile of drawings. At first he could not find the one he wanted. But the paper was there and he picked it out at last, and held it for Briones to see.

"I am sorry," Briones said. "But no. No, that is not it. That is not what I saw."

Morrow let the drawings fall to his desk. His hope had been strong, and his disappointment equaled it.

"I am sorry," Briones said again. "That trip of mine was for nothing. I want to help, but I am of no use."

Morrow tried to reassure him. "Don't think that, Briones. We can't afford to be discouraged. And what I can't learn one way, I'll have to learn another."

"Ojalá!"

Morrow echoed him. "Ojalá! God willing. And if you get any news, I hope you'll bring it to me."

They shook hands then and Briones left.

Late that evening a message from Morrow brought Briones back to the tower.

"Though I'd rather have you see this by daylight," Morrow said, "I didn't want to wait till tomorrow. It's near enough finished, and maybe these lamps are good enough to give you a fair view. Now then, have you ever seen this before?" He set up on a box against the wall a large watercolor landscape, and waited for Briones' reaction.

"Have I ever seen this before?" the Filipino repeated "I cannot tell. The light is bad. It shines back at me. But anyhow, why should I know this picture when you have just painted it?"

Morrow changed the angle at which the painting stood "Now look again."

"Good. I can see it muy bien." His tone sharpened with excitement. "Amigo, you painted this yourself? Then you have been there! You yourself have been there!" He pointed, and his finger shook. "That mountain! You must explain. When have you seen this? I am confused. But that is the mountain I saw with the sunset behind it."

"It's not hard to explain," Morrow told him. "I haven't been there. Yet. But you described a mountain that wa like a head with hair on it. Well, from the parao I had seen a peak that might resemble that very thing, and showed you my sketch. But it is difficult to imagine scene reversed like that, shown from the other side, with out its natural colors. So I did the imagining. I painted the other side of what I had seen, as if I were in tha valley, and I put the sunset behind it. And do you recognize it?"

"You have painted very true. I can see that the detail of the valley are a little different. It is wider, I think Señor capitán, you are a great painter. This is a work o genius. It is more than that. It is magic. Do you know that Faustino is convinced that you are a magician, and that bullets and bolos turn aside when they come nea you? Well, I think he must be right."

"Magicians know some tricks, and this is a trick. Bu that's all the magic I have."

"So now you will find this valley? Of course. Well perhaps that is the way it must be. But try to save wha lives you can, amigo. Give them a chance to surrende I believe, since you have his talking jar, Faustino himsel has no more wish to fight you. I hope the others will la down their arms. I hope they will."

200

"Can you tell me any more, Briones? With the picture to remind you?"

"The trail by which I arrived is over here. Outside the painting. There are more houses than this, I think. But I can tell you nothing more. My view of the valley was limited. And I will ask no questions of you, señor capitán. I do not wish to know when you go." He added hesitantly, "What will you do with this picture?"

"Destroy it."

"Then I am going to ask for it."

He insisted; and after Morrow had called Ramos to look at the pictured landmarks, Briones took the painting away with him.

9

MORROW and six men sailed in the *Obediente* down the estuary and westward on the bay. They left at noon. Ramos and six more men were to leave the cuartel as quietly as possible that night at high tide; they were to cross the estuary, wait until nearly dawn, and then take the trail behind the mangrove and nipa swamps following the coast. From this trail Ramos had found a branch leading inland, where he and his party were to turn off, on the assumption, which was hardly better than a guess, that this might be one path to the *pulajanes'* refuge. Morrow and his men were to go beyond Panglao, on the strait, leave the *Obediente* well concealed, and, also at dawn, take a mountain path that began behind that small barrio and might lead to the same mountain hiding-place. Morrow hoped the two parties would meet near a valley dominated by the peak resembling a head with hair on it.

Lying on a matting that had been arranged for him, and shielding his eyes from the painfully brilliant, quivering reflections of the sunlight on the water, Morrow considered his plans. There was much to be said against them, for they were based on surmises that in turn were based on second-hand information. A cautious man in his place might have pointed to various parts of Briones' story as perhaps deliberately misleading. Morrow was not unaware of the fact that Briones himself was the *ilustrado* most likely to be Faustino's spy in Magtalisay. Yet he trusted Briones.

And he trusted his men. He looked around at them. They were good men. Their confidence in him touched him warmly. He had noticed how each man's eyes had been glad of the sight of his locket at the open neck of his tunic. But what did it matter if part of their confidence was based on superstition? Perhaps there was always some element of superstition in the courage each man summoned when he knew he was going to face death. And they had courage, all of them, and endurance, and a willingness to suffer hardships. He thought again of their great superiority in these islands to American soldiers, their knowledge of the jungle and their skill at following a trail, their uncomplaining acceptance on these *patrullas* of whatever food could be supplied and of whatever miseries the weather thrust upon them.

If his own confidence in himself had equaled theirs, he would have been glad to see the land draw nearer when they approached the straits. But they were coming too swiftly for him to the end of their short voyage. Sails were lowered, oars were readied, and a man went to the bow to watch for the numerous banks and shoals that made the straits dangerous. Using the chart he had made a few days before, Morrow directed their course toward a small island on the Samar side, and then into a channel behind the islet. Here they would enter a narrow stream and conceal the parao.

The stream was just wide and deep enough. Between two walls of mangroves rising on stilt-like roots from the brackish water and mud, they moved slowly and silently forward on their twisting course. The water was black and opaque. Swarms of mosquitoes enveloped them. But they came at last to a fork, and in the side-stream they left the boat. By sunset they had covered the difficult though short distance through the swamp to solid land. Since a young moon promised light for a short time, Morrow decided to proceed at once. For they would have to circle Panglao sometime, and it might be safer in the evening than in the early morning.

The last of the moonlight saw them moving like dark specters around the village rice paddies. Dogs barked, perhaps at them, but no disturbance followed. They gained the cover of the forest with the certainty that their presence was unknown.

It was an uncomfortable night, made more wretched by a torrential rain that proved the wet jungle could get wetter still. Morrow slept hardly at all. This patrol weighed more heavily on him than any previous one had done. Doubts oppressed him. Where was Ramos now? He should have left Magtalisay by this time. Had he been followed? What if the *pulajanes* should meet him and cut him down with all his men? And suppose Ramos came through successfully and they all met as had been planned. Would there be another failure? Morrow, though impatient, dreaded the answer. Did he carry within himself the seeds of failure, and was he doomed to achieve nothing at the end of these long patrols?

The men were likewise wakeful. After the rain ended, the insects were more annoying than before, and the air was filled with the din made by all their various organs of sound. Louder than the rest, a click-beetle that had fallen on its back and was trying to right itself by snapping its brittle body into the air, made a sharp and regular sound that might have been the slow tick of an enormous clock. Some soldado muttered and tried to find the small creature in order to stop its gymnastics. He failed.

With the earliest morning twilight they were on their way, shivering in the chill air and slipping in the mud. The day began clear, but the trees continued to drip and there were only rare glimpses of sunshine. They climbed, they descended, they scrambled, they fell. Frequently a brook crossed their path; often the path itself seemed a brook.

They took every precaution to avoid being seen or heard. Once when they neared a cogonal, they sent a scout ahead, and on his report that a large family of mountain people were busy about the clearing, they made a wide detour. Another time, in crossing another open spot where cogon grass had grown tall over the abandoned ground, they almost met a man coming down the narrow path. But, hearing him in time, they dived into the high, coarse grass, which closed over them like a sea. When the man had passed, they went on, with hands and faces bleeding.

Approaching night stopped them in the jungle high on an unknown mountain. They camped away from the track near a ravine, where a swift stream, running over and among great stones, provided an accompaniment to the million humming and trilling insects which sang them to sleep. Under a shelter of palm fronds and on a leafy bed, even Morrow slept hard.

In the morning as they went on, he felt a stronger belief that they were traveling toward the *pulajanes'* stronghold. The trail remained open, with every evidence of constant use. Where could it go, if not to some secret settlement in the mountains? The few *montesinos*, with their little patches of sweet potatoes and rice, were not numerous enough to account for it.

After about two hours of traveling on that second morning, they heard voices ahead, and scattered on both sides among the trees. Two women, not of the pagan *montesino* type, passed by, unaware and unconcerned, talking and laughing, walking easily, each balancing a bundle on her head. Their complete carelessness of any possible danger was good proof that no warning of the Constabulary patrol had reached the end of the trail; and their presence at this point at this time was, Morrow reckoned, an indication that he and his soldados were some two hours from their destination, whatever it might be. For it was likely that the women, with the long trip to Panglao before them, had started at dawn, and it was logical to measure the journey left for the Constabulary by the length of time the women had probably been on their way.

The men went on with more caution but with more excitement. In less than an hour and a half after the

204

women had vanished behind them in the jungle, Morrow and his men came into thinner forest, through which they could see into the brilliant light of a large clearing. Morrow moved carefully forward into and through high cogon grass until he came to a place where the ground dropped away and he could look out and see what sort of country they were in.

He stood on the edge of a saucer-shaped valley, about which rose mountains covered with dark green forest, and there were equal heights behind him. One of the peaks behind him, he was certain, resembled a head of limestone hung with green hair.

For this had to be Faustino's stronghold; it could be nothing else. It was strangely like Morrow's painting. The brown thatched roofs of the houses, half-hidden among feathery clumps of bamboo, were dotted along the banks of the stream. There were a few patches of cultivated ground, though not enough to support as many people as could live in the houses; after all, these people were outlaws, who lived by stealing from their more industrious brothers and did not need to toil. Yet in spite of the signs of neglect and indolence, this was an idyllic scene.

Morrow brought his men to the saucer edge, and they settled down to wait for a signal from Ramos.

Ramos had been told that, if the trail he was following led to a place resembling Morrow's water color, he was to remain hidden, with his soldados, near enough to see what went on below. Beginning on the morning of the second day, or at any time after that when he might arrive, he was to signal, not too precisely on time but soon after each hour mark was passed. He knew how to crow like a jungle cock or scream like a calao in an imitation that was perfect, at least for human ears, and he had as well a trick of repetition that Morrow was certain to recognize. Ramos was to make no move down into the valley without Morrow, but was to wait through two days, and then return to Magtalisay if Morrow's party had not appeared. But if Morrow's party arrived and heard the signal and descended into the *pulajanes'* settlement, Ramos and his men were to join them.

Watch in hand, Morrow waited for the cockcrow or the cry of the hornbill that might come within the next few minutes. The monsoon blew steadily, not howling or shrieking, but rushing past his ears with a constancy of movement that washed him in a stream of air as mighty, as indefatigable, as unswerving, as an ocean current. It seemed that it must dull his hearing, yet he was not deafened. He heard a dog bark. He heard the thump, thump, of a woman he could see, insect-size, beating the dirt out of clothes on the bank of the stream. He heard once a screaming laugh. But no signal came, near eleven o'clock, from Ramos. No signal came at twelve, or at one.

There was time to think, too much time. This was the moment of low morale, when a man could wonder if this time he was going to be killed. Any action seemed better than waiting. Yet it was not impatience or recklessness that made Morrow tell his men they would start down the mountainside without waiting longer for a signal from Ramos. It was reason. This was the siesta hour, the hottest sleepiest part of the day, when men and animals dozed in the shade and expected all creatures to do the same. Over the valley there was an air of somnolence and of security. Now was the time to strike. Let Ramos come when he would. They could surprise as at night, if they moved now, and escape the night's confusion.

The houses stood quite near together, along the stream. Between them and the edge of the cogon grass directly below the soldados, there was a wide stretch of open ground offering no cover at all for an approach. But if they followed the rim of the saucer to the north and came back up the brook, bamboo would screen them almost the entire way after they left the tall grass. They started out then, moving cautiously to the north, around the great natural circle of the valley.

When they reached the valley floor and looked back, the landmark peak was visible, rising above the spot they had just left. It was nearing two o'clock, and they paused again to listen for Ramos' signal.

It was oppressively hot where they lay. The wind blew above the pocket in which they were hidden, but about them the air was motionless. Thunder sounded in the distance, and masses of cloud were beginning to climb the sky behind the ridges their eyes searched for some sign of Ramos and his men. They dripped with sweat, and they knew that in a short time they would probably be cold with rain. No cockcrow came, no calao screamed. Morrow murmured his orders to his men. There were a few yards of open ground to cross before they reached the edge of the stream. They were to follow him singly, creeping along, depending on distance and the trees around the houses to blind any watchful *pulaján*.

Quickly he reached the thicket of bamboo along the water, found a place where rocks made a natural opening in the thorny wall, and scrambled through. From here on the brook itself was to be their path, its own rippling chatter covering the noise of their wading, and the plumy bamboo forming a cool screen to protect them from men's eyes and the sun.

Morrow's hope was to reach the cluster of huts unseen; his plan then was to scatter his men behind the trees some distance from the houses, which, being raised on their stilts several feet above the ground, gave their occupants the advantage of being able to fire from above. Then a sudden shot in the air, a hint that the houses were surrounded, and a demand that Faustino and Ola surrender might be enough to end the fight before it was begun.

The water gurgled about Morrow's ankles, and his shoes were heavy and slippery on the stones. He wished, not for the first time, that he could go barefooted like his men. He stopped to glance back at the single file behind him, and one by one they stopped too, regarding him. Their uniforms were faded, stained, and torn, but there was nothing lackluster or drooping about their eyes and faces. Smiling, he made a quick gesture, the shadow of a salute, and turned again upstream.

They went slowly, able to see ahead for a number of yards at a time until they reached a place where the rivulet divided around a tiny island so overgrown with bamboo that both passages were nearly closed. Cautiously Morrow pushed his way between the giant canes, and came out unexpectedly in the open beside a muddy cleared bank, looking directly toward a house not more than thirty yards away. On the ground beneath the house, a woman squatted. She was ironing, facing Morrow, but looking down. Beside her a hen suddenly flapped its wings, squawked, and rushed at another hen. The woman raised her head and her eyes met Morrow's. For an instant she was completely motionless except for her mouth, and it seemed to open without her will or knowledge, while the scream that poured out seemed to have nothing to do with her at all.

Then the frozen moment was past, and she was on her feet, running in a demented way, looking back, zigzagging, shouting that she had seen an *asuang*, an evil spirit, rising out of the water.

Once the alarm was given, everything happened at once. From a window of the house a head stuck out; it was withdrawn; two men ran down the notched pole that served as a ladder and fled in the direction of the other houses, some of which Morrow could glimpse through trees and bushes. He shouted, "Surrender! Surrender and we won't shoot!" Another man, unarmed like the first two, leaped to the ground and rushed after them. "Faustino! Ola! Surrender!" Morrow called. Not one of them turned.

The *soldados* were hurrying through the bamboo-veiled passage around the island, and Morrow sent them to spread out and find shelter behind trees. All moved gradually forward. But their progress speeded up, for before they could come near a house its occupants had spilled from it and had run from them, the women screaming, a man occasionally swinging a bolo but otherwise unarmed, and all of them flying along a path beside the stream as fast as they could go. Morrow shouted to them again, and he fired once in the air, but most did not even glance behind, and none stopped.

The path curved around palms and clumps of bananas, and it was impossible to see where it was leading. The noisy flight was extremely puzzling to Morrow. Not a man hesitated, but all ran in the same direction as if they had prearranged such an action in case of a surprise visitor. The unanimity, the lack of any need for questions or orders, pointed to long preparation and a well-known destination. What could it be? A road of escape? A fortified house?

And then, leaving houses and bushes and trees and bananas behind, he was running in the open with the pulajanes before him, and he could see the place they wanted to reach. From the slope where he had first observed the valley, he had seen that the southern rim was rocky. Now he discovered extensive craggy heights that had been hidden from him; here he could see how part of this south wall formed a natural fortress. The hill rose in three steep and stony terraces, the first one reached by a grade not too difficult for climbing, but those above, such vertical ascents that they could be made only by ladder. Ladders were in place, waiting for the running pulajanes. The women must have hidden somewhere among the houses, for only men could be seen ahead now.

At this point everything became to Morrow unnaturally vivid to the smallest detail: the scene before him, the sound of running feet, the heat of the sun, a numbness in his legs, the dark smooth path, a sharp pain in his breathing, new cries of excitement from the outlaws. Very clear also was the simple fact that, once the pulajanes gained the hill and climbed the ladders and pulled the ladders up behind them, they would be out of reach. And there was another fact: the men ahead of him outnumbered his party by more than three to one. But he thought only of the necessity of stopping them before it was too late, the necessity of running. He ran, and near him his soldados ran, and before him bare brown feet struck the ground and never tripped or stumbled. It was impossible to gain on them, and he felt it was wrong to shoot first.

He could not run fast any longer. He had reached rising ground. Soon he was using his hands to pull himself over stones. Looking up, he saw that some of the pulajanes were already surmounting the highest ladders. His own men were ahead of him now, scrambling faster than he could go over the loose rocks, some of which, dislodged, were rolling back behind them.

But no. Those rocks were not rolling back from this slope ahead. They had been thrown from the top of Faustino's citadel, thrown wide of their mark because the outlaws had still to take care not to hit their own. This was the first warning of the battle to come.

If there had been fewer *pulajanes*, they would have won the race. But there were too many of them and there were only two ladders on each terrace. Before the last of the counterfeit pope's men had reached the second flight, the Constabulary soldiers had already anchored the first two ladders; and they succeeded again with the others. They were hesitating, waiting for his orders, when Morrow dragged himself up from the first terrace and paused a minute to ease his breathing.

He used no words, but started up the next ladder with his revolver ready. At the same moment a new shower of stones began. One grazed his shoulder. From behind him came a short cry of pain and anger, and from above another cry of pain as his shot shattered one of the hands that had dropped the rock. Stones first, he thought, and bolos terrible as a headsman's axe at the top of the ladder. But he kept on moving. He did not know that blood had dripped on his face, or that he scowled because the sun had come out again for a little and was shining into his eyes. He climbed, and was at the top. The ladder shook with the movements of the climber below him.

Before his fierce and haggard face as much as from fear of the revolver in his hand, the outlaws fell back briefly. He stepped over the low parapet, and stood there alone with the *pulajanes*. They might have killed him a dozen times over if they had moved on him; he would not have had a chance. But they were held by their awe of the legend about him, by his appearance, by his daring in facing them alone; and in the pause, short as it was, his men began to appear beside him, reducing the odds he faced.

He said, unable to raise his voice above its normal
210

volume, "Faustino! Ola! Surrender! There will be pardon for your men if you surrender now!"

The *pulajanes* nearest him drew away, turning to each other, and he saw reason to hope that his demand might be accepted. The hope, however, had no chance to live. From the outlaws at the back of the terrace came a shout of rage and triumph, and then their first shots, wild and foolish, since outlaws and *soldados* were too close together at the front of the ledge for any but a good marksman to be sure he would hit foe and not friend. A *pulaján* beside Morrow groaned as blood ran from his bare arm.

This was the last Morrow knew of the fight on the terrace as a whole, except that he grew more and more sure, because of the confusion and the ineffectiveness of the *pulajanes'* resistance, that Ola was not among them. He still hoped that Faustino, who was not a fighting man, might be concealed somewhere at the back of the ledge.

He fired in the direction from which the shots had come; beside him, he knew, his *soldados* were firing too. An outlaw swung a threatening bolo, and Morrow shot and jumped away from the falling arm and knife. Then, catching the man's uninjured arm, he turned him in his forward rush, and by a miracle of pressure forced the man to be a shield for him. Together, crabwise, they sidled to the back of the terrace. More outlaws came at him, and he fought them back. He wanted prisoners, not dead men, but he could not choose; he had to fight in this bloody, merciless combat, hand to hand. He emptied his revolver and used it as a club. He found himself swinging a bolo, and did not know how it had come to his hand. There was a circle of *pulajanes* around him, and his arm was tiring.

He thought: so this is the end. His arm dropped. He could not raise the bolo again.

But one of his soldiers was at his right, and another appeared at his left. The circle of *pulajanes* retreated; two of them fell. And then it was over. The others threw down their weapons.

Morrow sank down on the rock and sat with his knees up and his head hanging forward against them. He wanted only a few deep, restful breaths before he began to question the prisoners, but the groans of a wounded man interrupted that short rest, and he got up again. He noticed then that the attention of most of the uninjured men was centered down below, and he turned to look. Men in Constabulary uniform were running toward the slope leading to the terrace. He tried to shout to Ramos, but his voice failed him; he raised his arm and waved. Ramos shouted an answer.

Had the pulajanes seen Ramos and the rest coming, and had that hastened their surrender? Perhaps; it didn't seem to matter. What did matter was having Ramos there now to help with the prisoners. He set him to work, telling him to arrange a guard and then to count everyone in the valley, after rounding up the women, and check over the weapons and ammunition that could be found.

Morrow had done the best he could with the worst wounds and was beginning on the minor injuries when Ramos returned with his information. "Corporal Saavedra is dead, señor capitán."

Morrow nodded; he knew that fact too well. Saavedra had fallen defending him.

"Lim is dead also. You know Benito Pulay and Vicente Resurrección have bad bolo cuts. All the rest but the señor capitán have small cuts."

Morrow nodded again. He already had all the facts about his own men.

"Of the pulajanes, twelve of these lazy, big-snouted hogs over here with their teeth chattering are hardly scratched. Five of their brothers are dead, and their lice are looking for a new home. Nine more are lying here crying like—" At Morrow's angry exclamation he stopped and began again. "Twelve prisoners without bad wounds. Nine with bad wounds. Five dead. Fifteen bolos. Eleven Remington shotguns. Twelve Remington rifles. Three revolvers. Ammunition for all, not yet counted. These guns gracias á Díos, were hidden in a cave in the rock there at the back; they had been able to get out only four guns and get them loaded. Yet if they had had more, perhaps it would have been better, for they would have fired the guns instead

212

of using their bolos, and as you can see, a monkey with each hand caught in a coconut could shoot better. All of the soldados were wounded with bolos and not with shot, and one of the *pulajanes* was killed with one of their own shotguns."

"Have you learned anything about Ola and Faustino?"

"They say that both have gone away, with half the men who should have been here. They had no warning. It was chance. And I searched the houses. Only women and children are down there."

"Did you look at everyone's hands?"

"*Sí*, señor capitán. I looked among all for a right hand with a finger missing. One man has a bullet hole in his right hand, but all the fingers are there. And the rest—four fingers and a thumb like mine, but no use for shooting a gun."

"All right, Ramos. All right. Have the prisoners get the wounded down under cover before it starts to rain." He glanced at the sky, astonished that the gathering storm had not yet broken. "We'll have to see about burying the dead. Find out if you can where Faustino went and why." He returned to his bandaging.

It was raining before he started down to the lower part of the valley, and he was grateful for the hard shower. It would wash away the blood and the smell of blood and gunpowder, and the smell of sweat and fear. He was too tired to feel any further discomfort from being soaked through, but he knew enough to take care of himself. He went inside one of the houses, stripped, and rolled himself in a blanket. Later he could evaluate the day, and decide what had been achieved, and if it could balance what had been lost. He lay down on the floor and fell asleep.

10

THE victorious soldados found when they reached Panglao on their return journey that, although there was a shrewd appearance of support for them, feeling was secretly in sympathy with the *pulajanes*, who had used this barrio as a base for transferring stolen goods to Leyte. Their arrival in Magtalisay, in the twilight that same evening, was more to their taste. As they marched with their prisoners from the estuary, they drew an enthusiastic crowd who were no longer afraid to show their delight at a successful fight against the outlaws. Exaggerations flew from lip to lip as they went through the town, and Morrow heard his name repeated in wonder, "El Moro Blanco!" But they were less amazed than he at the fact that he was, as always, unharmed.

By the time they reached the steps to the Escarpa it was dark, but enough of the lively, noisy crowd had accompanied them to put the sentries on the alert. Lanterns appeared at the top of the height; the returning heroes shouted joyfully; and the handful of soldados who, to their regret, had been left behind on guard duty, shouted back in welcome. There was a little confusion, but the prisoners had shown no spirit since their defeat, and Morrow let his men enjoy this moment. It was short enough. Exuberance vanished when the loss of Lim and Saavedra was told. Soberly and sternly, then, the prisoners were conducted toward the cuartel.

Lloyd, at the door, offered Morrow his congratulations. "This is the biggest lot of *pulajanes* yet, sir."

"But Faustino and Ola got away again. What's the news here?"

"Well, sir, my replacement's due on the next call of the revenue cutter. And the Johnstones leave then. I'm supposed to—"

From inside the cuartel came a sudden commotion of cuffling and angry cries. Lloyd turned and darted through he door. Morrow, tired and a little slow, was behind him.

The lanterns cast towering and fantastic shadows, exggerating the turmoil, so that for one moment of nightmare Morrow wondered if the soldados had gone mad nd were trying to kill each other. Then eyes and reason ogether discovered what was happening: somehow the risoners had found the will to turn on their captors. There were a dozen fierce and confused contests before he doors to the cells, and apart from the rest in a separate attle of their own, two men, soldado and *pulaján*, rolled n the stone floor.

Yet, seeing the reality, Morrow remained unable to free imself of the illusion of unreality. His reactions and his novements seemed clogged and lethargic, while everyne else and every happening moved with swift and inedible ease.

Lloyd already struggled with a *pulaján*, caught in a dash r the entrance. Morrow helped to get him locked in a ell. Around him the soldados had subdued another, and nother, and another; and two and three at a time were ut behind bars. And then the whole brief, reckless, foolish bellion had ended.

Except for the fight on the floor. That went on, deserately, grimly, almost in silence, and alone, as if it had othing to do with the recent turmoil. Yet this, Morrow ow learned, was the clash that had begun the trouble. They recognized each other," Ramos said. "The soldado Pascual. A pity he did not go with us on the patrol, d get his fight finished outside the cuartel."

The two men were alike in build, and very evenly atched in temper and strength. Each kept trying for e other's throat or eyes, and defending his own. One ould win an advantage, only to lose it as, momentarily, e other seemed closer to victory, and then he in turn ould have his hold broken.

The concentration and ferocity of this fight made it private matter and yet gave it an epic quality. All the her soldados had become spectators. Morrow, too, with

Lloyd nervously taking the same attitude, waited, watch ing.

Then Pascual broke away for an instant and one of hi friends thrust a knife into his hand. Now, Morrow though sluggishly, was the time to stop this, before it becam murder; that prisoner must be locked up with the rest But before he could act, the *pulaján* in a sudden acces of furious strength had seized the knife from Pascual' hand, cut a long gash in Pascual's arm, and with wild eye with the bloody knife raised, was on his feet, his bac against the wall, facing his enemies.

Was it true that his glaring, darting glance came oftenes to Morrow?

"Watch out!" Lloyd cried, his voice shrill. "Tha knife!" He pulled Morrow back, and leaped.

Whether or not the man would have thrown the knife whether he would or could have hit Morrow with it, n one ever knew. He buried it in Lloyd's breast, and befor he had finished the blow, Ramos had shot him. But h had killed Lloyd as he himself died.

It seemed irrelevant to be told now that the man wa Pascual's brother, who had stolen Pascual's wife and joine Faustino's band, but it was, Morrow knew, a symbol the whole bitter, civil strife.

He went up the hill, through the darkness, to Lucy house, to tell her what had happened. Perhaps, dully, hoped for comfort. Lucy was not there. She had gor to Punta Arenas, where, as he knew, Palmer was.

Back on the Escarpa, he paced the rock a long tim thinking about Lloyd. His sacrifice meant somethin special to Morrow. That brave act said all the things th Lloyd might have been, and Morrow felt acutely the fa that he hadn't given him the chance.

The cold moonlight showed him a world devoid human warmth. Moving in their ordered, stately proce sion across the sky, only the brightest stars appeared, mo remote and disdainful than ever. Aldebaran, Rigel, Siri and Canopus traveled their constant paths; Alphard, th forever solitary, his own star, surrounded always by illim able and awful space, followed alone, burning fiercely a

216

icily. These were his old companions, whose chill comfort was the best he had known for many years, whose greater enigmas could sometimes make the questions of his own existence recede into unimportance.

Sometimes, but not tonight.

PART FIVE

1

LUCY came down the river from Punta Arenas the next morning. She was drowsy in the heat. Under the hood of matting that protected her from sunburn but not from sweltering, she kept falling into uncomfortable sleep. She was damp with sweat, heavy in mind and body in the oppressive atmosphere, and uneasy over her day in Punta Arenas.

Waking as the banca neared the Sogod-Magtalisay ferry landing, she shook off the fragments of an unpleasant dream and wished she could dismiss as well the recollection of the day before. For the first time she had seen the whole estate; Harry had taken her on ponyback from one end to the other. That was the reason she was so stiff this morning, but her chief discomfort came from other causes. It had not surprised her to find the place badly run down; she had expected that. What shocked her was Harry's attitude. A stranger would have thought the property his, not hers.

Yes, his proprietary air deeply disturbed her. "I am going to do this," he had said. "Here I'm going to do that." He told her, "I'm going to have a money-making estate here and not a money-loser." It seemed to her, too, that he ordered the servants and the laborers around with unnecessary curtness. When she made the beginning of a protest, he pointed out to her with satisfaction how they leaped to obey him.

218

Could it be that he was just what the plantation needed? A man, a bold man, Emerald had said.

Yet it was more than bold for him to have been living in Emerald's house, the owner's house. Lucy was sure he had been doing that. On her arrival he had been in the house she had told him he could use, but of course there had been ample warning. That razor strap she had seen, and that pair of shoes . . . They had vanished after her glimpse of them, but she was convinced they were already back in the big house again.

She was angry with herself, and ashamed because she had not dared to accuse him of this presumption. She had not even succeeded in telling him forcefully enough that she would never marry him. His last words had been that he would go on hoping. And he had not sounded hopeful; he had sounded sure.

She got out of the banca, and with old Engracia behind her, duenna-like, began to walk toward the town. They had gone about halfway when they heard the drum of the Constabulary band. Phrases of music reached them next, and at last a recognizable tune. Lucy idly followed the mournful words, ending with the final refrain: "Dying tonight, dying tonight, dying on the old camp ground." She knew so well that the band played with an innocent disregard for suitability that she was indifferent to the melancholy meaning of notes and tempo until she came in sight of the small American cemetery. A cluster of people stood there in the treeless, sun-flooded field, and an empty carabao cart moved away down the road.

She was stunned, half-suffocated with alarm. In the Constabulary there were only two Americans for death to strike, and Morrow had been on one of those dangerous patrols in the mountains. Surely, surely he had come back safe! Surely his luck, or whatever it was the Filipinos whispered about him, had not failed!

She lifted the hem of her dress and tried to run, unable to take her eyes from the people in the cemetery in order to watch the rough ground, stumbling and moving awkwardly, clumsy after the pony ride the day before and the numbing, cramping hours in the banca.

219

But she drew closer. Quite soon she could see they were grouped around what must be an open grave. And there at last, thank God, thank God, stood Morrow! He faced the others, with his back toward her. She slowed, and let her pounding heart ease.

Now she could think calmly about who lay in the grave. It had to be Lloyd. But what had happened to him? She stopped at the gate in the new hedge and waited. The murmur of Morrow's voice reached her, but none of the words.

Then the group around the grave broke up, and Morrow saw her and came toward her.

She had feared with almost intolerable pain that he was dead. Now she had a natural but illogical resentment for her needless anxiety. She felt, almost too obscurely to realize, and far too obscurely to understand why, that she had been tricked into ridiculous emotion—it was a fleeting reaction, but it lasted long enough to show in her face. And Morrow, very conscious that the last time they had met he had told her he loved her, sensed the momentary chill.

"Who is it?" she asked. "Jus Lloyd?"

He nodded. "You must have come down the river and found us here without warning. I'm sorry you had to learn like that. I went up to your house last night to tell you."

"What happened to him?"

Briefly he gave her the facts.

"Oh, poor Jus! Brave Jus!"

"It happened too fast, before I . . ." Morrow left the sentence unfinished. He was deeply depressed by Lloyd's death, and his hope of Lucy's sympathy had been ended by the cold look he had noticed on her face.

To his surprise, her response was warm and comforting. "I think Jus is proud of this. I suppose I knew him better than you did. He talked to me a lot. Somewhere he may be listening now. He isn't sorry. You shouldn't blame yourself."

The others had left the cemetery and were on their way toward the town. "Shall I call my sergeant," Morrow asked "before he gets too far away, and have him send a cales for you? There's a bench inside the hedge where you could sit and wait."

Again her friendly warmth astonished him. She said, "I'd rather walk with you."

They began to follow the hot, rough road in silence, while he wondered if he had heard those simple and amazing words. If he had, and of course he knew he had, he must make some response besides this dumb plodding in the direction of Magtalisay. He must say something; he must at least look at her again and discover what he could read in her face.

Lucy said, "I think those two girls must be waiting to see you"; and he saw ahead of them, in the shade of some palms, Encarnación, Lloyd's sweetheart, and her sister María. Encarnación stepped forward, and the other shrank back.

"Yes; she's waiting for me," he said. "Would you like to talk to her too?"

"Who is she?"

"Didn't Lloyd ever tell you about her? He'd made up his mind to marry her. He never mentioned her to you?"

Rather stiffly, Lucy said no, and Morrow thought for a moment the change in her voice had come because she had noticed the girl was pregnant. But Lucy had been thinking of the girl who had drawn back, and of what Johnstone had told her. That other girl looked pregnant too. It did not take any great leap of thought to associate her with Palmer. With an effort, Lucy turned her mind back to Lloyd's girl. "Poor Jus," she said, "and this poor girl. She looks very young. What's her name?"

"Encarnación, and she's barely sixteen. I've talked to her in Spanish—I saw her last night—but I think she understands a little English that she picked up from Lloyd."

"Then I can at least say a few words to her. But you tell her for me," she went on rapidly in a lower voice as they came closer to the girl, "that if she'll come to my house I'll give her some cloth for clothes for the baby—only their babies don't wear many clothes, do they? Tell her anyhow that I'll help her with the baby. She can count on me."

"Why not clothes?" Morrow asked. "She might like

221

some American-style clothes, even if the baby only wore them once. For a christening."

"But of course!" Moved by a quick impulse, Lucy slipped her hand through his arm, and smiled up at him. "I wish I'd thought of that!"

At her touch he stopped and half turned toward her, his eyes meeting and holding hers, and with his free hand he caught her fingers and pressed them tight against his arm. They were not standing very near together, but strangely and without warning, with no other contact between them than this strong clasp and the deep, searching, revealing look, both felt the intimacy of a close embrace, each knew the other trembled, thought he was deafened by the other's beating heart. Then it was over, but not finished. Neither could have said how long they had remained like that; it could not have been more than seconds, measured by anyone but themselves. Nothing outside had changed. The sun shone as hot from the same place in the sky and no shadows had altered. Engracia, who was following, had not overtaken them. Encarnación, who waited, was still motionless and patient. They walked toward her again, with Morrow holding Lucy's hand firmly where she had placed it on his arm.

There her hand remained until the end of the interview with Encarnación. Then she drew away and said, "Tell her to come to see me tomorrow, not today. I must go back to Punta Arenas. Now." She added, in explanation, "I must tell Harry about Jus Lloyd." This was not reason enough but Morrow did not question her, and when she refused his company back to the landing place, he said nothing but "Good-bye. Come back soon." The expression was worn but not meaningless in the tone he used and the look accompanying it. He saw the color in her cheeks deepen, and she felt her cheeks burn.

2

THE trip back to Punta Arenas was harder for every reason than the trip down. Lucy dreaded seeing Palmer, and she had regretted almost at once not explaining fully to Morrow why she was returning. But it would take a lifetime, forever, to say all she wanted to say to him. She had been too excited to talk; excitement made her breathless now each time she thought of the moment when she had put her hand on his arm.

How could she have wondered if she loved Harry Palmer? How could she have asked Morrow himself if love ought to be sure? Sure? She could not be more certain that it was day and not night, that she was alive and not dead. Why had she not seen from the beginning that her trust in him was more than trust? He was so lonely and alone, he was so little used to talking to his own people, that he found it hard to talk to her. She would change that. He was not used to asking anything for himself. She would change that, too. Only she would give without being asked. She was triumphant, and she was ashamed. How could she wait until she saw him again?

Yet she knew her impulse to return to Punta Arenas was right, and she made herself think ahead to Harry and to what she must say to him. She had been a coward to leave unfinished business between them. Now it must be settled, and it was for her to handle, not for Morrow, who had settled his own problems with Palmer. She must make the man understand that he was the manager of her plantation and nothing more, that for Emerald's sake he was on trial, and that this was his last chance. Any further presumption, like living in the big house, any mistake of any kind, would be the end.

She landed late in the afternoon, feeling, as Emerald would have said, that all the starch had been taken out of her. The day had already held so much that she could hardly believe it was only this morning that she had set out down the river. She would go back again by moonlight, she told the boatmen, and with all the resolution she could summon, started toward the big house.

It was about the time when Palmer would be coming in from whatever part of the estate his work had taken him to. As she had surmised, there were signs that he had returned to living in Emerald's house and that he was expected there for his supper, but the house was empty. She called him and called for a muchacho, but got no reply except the chirp of a small lizard on the ceiling, "Tsk, tsk, tsk, tsk."

With Engracia still following her, she set out for the bodega. She would perhaps find Harry there.

That was where he was, as she knew as soon as she reached the door, because she could hear his voice. It was dark under the corrugated iron roof, and she was unable to see him at first; she looked through the bodega as through a tunnel, seeing nothing but another open doorway at the opposite side of the building. And Harry did not see her, either, as she knew when his voice went right on without a change.

Her alarm began then, while she stood peering into the thick shadows. Probably, almost before she could distinguish the syllables, she had reacted to the fact that he was speaking English in a place where there was no one for him to be speaking English to. And the tone of his voice was different from any tone she had ever heard him use. It was soft, almost caressing. The words became clear. "Now are you ready to tell? Are you still full of the same lies? Now are you ready to tell the truth?"

Lucy's eyes were learning to pierce the darkness. She saw first a head looking around the edge of the far door and then ducking away; and then she saw another head at the other edge. Next, halfway down the long bodega, she made out a ghostly figure with arms upraised, a tall figure. That would have to be Harry. She heard a new question, "How much more of this do you want? Tell me, how much more?" This time there was an answering

224

sound, a gasp or a groan, quickly cut off. Lucy grew so cold she shivered. She stepped into the building, and her heel scraped loudly on the concrete floor.

She could not remember later what happened next. Perhaps she called to Harry, perhaps she started to walk toward him. Was it then that he shouted, "God damn you, I told you all to keep away!" or was it then that she saw he was pulling on a rope? Or was it only then that she called to him? And was it her presence that made him let the rope go?

But she saw much too clearly in her memory the rest of what came. She saw the rope fly from his hands, slip over a rafter, and follow a falling body to the floor. She heard the sound of the fall, and then Harry's cry, "Lucy!" She was terrified of everything, she wanted to run away, and she was made of lead and could not stir. As the figure on the floor began creeping in her direction, moving slowly on knees and one hand, the other hand fumbling at its throat, she felt she had known forever that the rope was around its neck.

She could have sworn that she didn't look at Harry again, yet afterward she recalled his face, his eyes brilliant, his cheeks flushed, his lips loose and no words coming from them. She was sure her gaze never left the figure creeping along the floor, moving faster, and reaching up at last to the long table against the wall. The groping hand hit something that fell with the crash of breaking glass.

Then the figure was upright, standing in the fading sunlight coming through the open door, and she recognized the overseer. The sun struck the piece of broken glass in his hand, and the reflection danced through the dark warehouse.

"He's a thief!" Palmer said, his voice harsh but not loud. "He's been cheating you, Lucy."

The man's empty hand continued to pull at the noose, while his staring eyes were fixed now on Lucy. Then Palmer had the rope again and was taking up the slack. The man felt the movement, and for one terrible moment was rigid. His next act was so fast that Lucy knew what it had been only by seeing what followed it. The hand holding the jagged glass flashed to his brown throat. Blood spurted. His hand dropped to his side, but for a long, long time he stood there, dying, before he fell to the floor. Engracia bleated and whimpered. Palmer came closer.

Lucy felt the threat of nausea and fought against it, forcing herself to stand straight and face Palmer.

He said, looking down at the man, "What a fool! Trying to cut himself loose! Cowards always run into worse than they leave behind. Good riddance!" He dropped his end of the rope. "The dirty thief was stealing from you. He stole from old Emerald for years. She was a fine judge of character!"

Lucy tried to speak, but made no sound.

"God, but you've got courage!" he said. "Not a scream or anything. You're like me. We belong together."

Lucy's voice was half hoarseness and half whisper, as if her own throat had been tortured and torn. "Get out. Get your things and get out of Punta Arenas."

"What's the matter with you?"

"Get out. Walk. Take my boat. I don't care how you go. But get out."

"But you saw what happened. Why do you want me to get out? I'm taking care of things for you here. It needs someone to straighten things out."

"Maybe he cut his throat by accident." Her voice was stronger. "Maybe he cut it to escape from you. Either way, you killed him."

"You're crazy."

"So get out. I'm giving you a chance, for Emerald's sake. Get out, or I'll swear that I saw you kill him."

He moved nearer, staring down at her.

She said, "Get out of here and get out of Magtalisay. You won't be safe in either place. And don't dare to touch me, or you won't be safe anywhere in the world. Captain Morrow . . ." She met his stare, opposing to his brutality a hardness she had just discovered. "Courage? I have enough to do what I said."

He turned suddenly and walked past her out the door.

3

AT the end of that same day, a message took Morrow to
Briones' house. Limping more than usual, Briones crossed
the sala to meet him. "I could not climb to the Escarpa
tonight, amigo. This old wound. And I have just come
from a very tiring trip." He sighed. "I have much to tell
you, but I cannot tell all. I must depend on your belief in
my sinceridad. I must count on the friendship between us.
And I must not have hair on my tongue. I must speak
out. Amigo, I have only now come from Faustino. That is
why I did not witness your return yesterday. But I had
already heard of your victory. Faustino sent for me when
he learned of it himself. Do not ask me where he is; that
is the one thing I must not tell you. For the rest, I will
tell you all.

"To begin, there are only sixteen outlaws left, and the
two leaders, or so they say. This I cannot prove. We both
know many outlaws lived in two worlds, theirs and ours,
passing from one to the other as they wished. Perhaps
these sixteen are the only survivors of those who were
never more than outlaws, who had no other trade but
thievery. I do not know. But I can swear the rest I have to
say is true. Faustino is afraid of the White Moro, who
has destroyed all his hiding places, who has killed and
captured so many of his followers almost, he says, single-
handed, who has carried away his talking jar, who even
sees what his stronghold is like though many miles away.
You will forgive me, I think, if I showed him your painting? And I told him his jar talked to you.

"Señor capitán, he is ready to surrender to you. I think
that will make you happy?"

Morrow felt stupefied by Briones' words. "Did I hear
you right?"

"I think you did."

"I was beginning to believe Faustino didn't exist. You say he's ready to surrender?"

"That is what I said. That is what he said, too. He said if the god has talked to you, that is a sign."

"Briones, I don't understand him."

"You will, amigo. It is very simple. But I have not finished yet. There is a condition that he has made. And I have still more than that to tell you. Faustino has been the leader of the *pulajanes* not because he is a bad man but because he is good. Ola has led the men to fight and to rob and to kill. He is evil. But Faustino is different. He has led because he has promised them a better life. He has promised them Independencia. You may say he does not know all that Independencia means; and I must agree. You and I are practical men; we see that Independencia must be built slowly and carefully. You have helped me see that. But he sees only the vision. He is wrong about much. Yet his vision is one that leads. You have felt yourself the power he has over some of his men."

"A lot of it is superstition."

"But not all superstition is bad. Señor capitán, you yourself have led by superstition. And do you yourself never feel superstition? Also, tell me, where does superstition end and love of a flag begin? They are close; they are brothers. Amigo, all things belong to each other; all men belong to each other; all men are brothers. You believe me?"

"I wish all men could be brothers."

"Amigo, Faustino is my brother."

"Go on, Briones," Morrow said when he paused. "I think you have more to tell me."

Slowly Briones continued. "He is my brother as you are my brother, because we are all kin. He is my brother because we are both Filipinos, because we both, he in his way and I in mine, wish to see our country take her place in the family of nations. And he is my brother because we had the same father and the same mother." He watched Morrow, waiting for him to speak.

Morrow began, "Briones—" and stopped.

"Thank you," Briones said. "Thank you for not asking

228

the question that is in your mind. You have trusted me, and you wish me to know you trust me still. But I will give you the answer. You want to know how long I have known that Faustino is in fact Andrés Briones. They had sent for me, as I told you, offering me a high place among them. I thought that was only because they knew I had fought against the Spaniards. I believed Andrés was dead, like my brother Ricardo. I did not go then; I did not see Faustino. I did not guess until the day you told me Faustino had lost the small finger of his right hand. Then I wondered, amigo; then for the first time I went to see him, hoping if it was Andrés to end the bloodshed. I wished to tell you then but—this is my shame—I was afraid it might spoil your trust in me."

Morrow looked into the proud and passionate eyes. "I believe you, amigo. I have trusted you from the first. I know this has not been simple for you."

"The rest," Briones said, "will not be simple and easy for you. We do understand each other, you and I. You see my problem. I see yours, which you do not yet know, which I am about to give you when I tell you Faustino's condition. You will want time to consider it, and you need not answer tonight. Only hear it."

Morrow prompted him. "Well? What is it? You understand I have no authority to offer immunity to the leaders. Or to anyone, perhaps, in a surrender like this. But I'll cable to headquarters—"

"No. It is nothing like that, which is what I myself would have expected, like you. This is for you alone to decide. Faustino asks that you be unarmed, that you receive his surrender with your arms laid down as a proof of brotherhood, of peace, and of good will. And that is all, amigo. I am not going to try to persuade you."

"This is unusual, Briones. From an outlaw it's . . ." He was going to say it was dangerous, but he did not finish.

Briones understood. "I know what you are thinking. I am not surprised. You will understand when you see my brother."

Morrow looked at him. Briones was an earnest and resolute man, wary at this moment because he was unsuited to the role of go-between. What could his brother be like? But that did not matter now. In the decision he must make, Morrow felt he had no choice. "I agree to his condition. How soon?"

"Do you wish it the soonest possible, señor capitán?"

"Before he changes his mind. Or makes another condition."

"Tomorrow?"

"Is he near enough to Magtalisay?" Briones nodded. "Then tomorrow afternoon in the plaza, where we can make a public ceremony of it. Will Faustino object to that?"

"He left such details to me. Anything more, señor capitán? I will get word to him tonight."

"Then if everything is all right, we'll tell Don Florencio in the morning, and he'll make the announcement. I want everyone to know what's happening. What about Ola, Briones? He is surrendering too?"

"Amigo, he is worse defeated than Faustino. Faustino sees you no more as an enemy, but Ola sees you as one always victorious."

4

"IN the afternoon, when the siesta hour is past," Don Florencio said, smiling in anticipation. "And all of Magtalisay will behold the ceremony, and then in the evening we shall have a *baile*, with the Constabulary band to play for the dancing, and perhaps the señor capitán himself will consent to lead the *rigodón* with the wife of my son. The dancing can be in the school, and others can stroll in the plaza in the moonlight—Ah, señores, it will be a happy ending to a happy day!"

His bed was pulled away from the closed windows, which seemed only a feeble barrier against the wind and rain beating on them. The sliding panels rattled. Water was driven between them in strong little jets and ran beneath them in a thin but persistent flood, spreading over the tile faster than the servants could mop it up. Don Florencio added, "If it stops raining."

Very little gray daylight penetrated the shell panes, and the room was quite dark. Morrow strained his eyes to look at the faces around him. The old presidente was smiling faintly; Morrow could believe in the simple sincerity of the pleasure with which he regarded this surrender. But what of the rest of these leading citizens? Morrow wondered. What were they thinking? They had offered him formal congratulations. Surely they must feel something more. Surely Faustino's activities had touched them all so intimately one way or another that the announcement of Faustino's identity and of the end of his raids must affect them more strongly than they had shown. Their white clothes stood out in the dimness, but their faces were hard to see.

"Hear the wind," Paterno said. "It sounds almost like a typhoon." His pince-nez, hanging from an invisible ribbon, glittered as he swung it back and forth.

"This is the wrong season," said the thickset, stolid Villamor.

Rufino Zúñiga was sitting with the blind side of his face toward Morrow, one arm moving monotonously as he lifted his cigarette to his lips and lowered it to knock off the ash, in a nervous gesture, when the ash had hardly formed. He said, "Typhoons come when they please. They don't follow laws. You lawyers are always thinking about laws."

Paterno turned on him quickly. "Laws are good to have."

The wind grumbled, whined, suddenly thundered, and then whined again.

Morrow tried to see Briones' face, but Soriano, who sat between them, was fidgeting, running a comb through his hair, and Morrow could not see past him without making an obvious effort. Briones had said nothing since entering the house; he had left all explanation to Morrow.

In English, without turning his eye to look in Morrow's

direction, Rufino asked, "If it rains for the grand ceremony, Captain Morrow, what will you do? What a pity to spoil the great scene of your triumph!"

Morrow put Rufino's words into Spanish for the others, and added his own comment. "It would take more than rain to spoil the day, I think. And it is not my triumph. It is a triumph for all law-abiding Magtalisayanos. Like the abogados, I too respect the law."

Now Rufino turned to look at Morrow. "And what would it take to spoil the day, Captain White Moro?"

"That should be obvious, I think. It would spoil the day if Faustino did not come."

"But you have the honorable Miguel Briones' word that his brother will come. Surely that is enough for you?"

"It is enough. Because my friend Briones is honorable, as you say, I do not expect the day to be spoiled. Señor, will you please speak in Spanish, as I do, or do you wish me to continue to translate what you say?"

"I should be glad never to hear your English language again." He changed to Spanish. "Here is something else to think about: There are other ways your day may be spoiled. Are you not exposing yourself to great danger? You say you will be unarmed when you meet Faustino."

"He made that condition."

"And you want us to think you will expose yourself like that?"

"I have been asked to do it to show my desire for peace. To show my belief in the brotherhood possible between Americans and Filipinos. Do you think I would refuse?"

"No, señor capitán Moro Blanco, of course you cannot refuse. Not in words. You must agree. In words. But you will carry concealed weapons, naturalmente. I am familiar with the legend about your invulnerability, señor capitán Moro Blanco. But you and I do not believe in legends, do we? We believe in guns. You will have your gun."

Old Don Florencio had been moving his hands in futile gestures and trying ineffectually in his soft voice to interrupt his grandson. It was Nicolás who stopped Rufino, putting a hand on his shoulder and saying firmly, "That

232

is too much! We know the captain well, and we know him as a man of his word."

"I understand how your son feels," Morrow said. "And he gives me a chance to tell all of you that I am not going to carry a concealed weapon. Do you think I would throw away this opportunity Faustino has given me? It is my chance to prove that I hope for friendship between your people and mine. I could not ask for anything better.

"So, señores, let Rufino speak. If he has more to say, let him say it. Now is the time. I have time now to answer or explain."

Rufino had shaken off his father's hand, and he was standing a little apart from the group, so that several had to turn around to watch him as he spoke. "I am sick of the pretense!" he cried to them. "It makes me want to vomit! The Americans are our enemies, they will make themselves our masters at any cost, there is no honor or brotherhood possible between us. Why do you keep saying there is? Even Morrow's own countrymen know better! But you all sit around, whatever you think, pretending you are friends. Friends! Friends with the americanos! There is the guilt of blood on their hands!"

Before anyone else could speak, Luís Soriano had Rufino by the arm and was pulling him toward the door, wiping his own forehead with a handkerchief, its strong scent heavy in the close air. "You are a fool, Rufino! I think you must be crazy. Every man with sense in Magtalisay is grateful to the señor capitán. We haven't had any money to live on, with those *pulajanes* stealing everything the *taos* can raise. My mother was afraid she would have to sell some of her diamonds soon if . . ." Still talking, he disappeared with Rufino.

Nicolás began another apology.

Morrow protested. "He had a right to speak. Everyone has a right to say what he believes. I wish the rest of you would say something. Haven't you any questions? Or any advice?"

"We do not doubt your word," Paterno hastened to assure him. "Nor the word of our old friend Miguel Briones."

233

"That is true," Villamor agreed. "You are both men of honor."

They were polite, but they seemed to stand a long way off. Morrow understood. It was his affair. They were leaving it to him. They would see how it turned out. He got up now, concealing his heaviness of spirit, and went to Don Florencio's side. "The rain has let up. I think I'll go."

But Don Florencio had something more to say. "About one thing Rufino was right. We know Miguel, but we do not any longer know his brother, who calls himself Faustino. And there is Ola, too. What man can foresee what may happen? It is hard to believe those two leaders will surrender and face their punishment. You are taking a dangerous risk, and surely it is not necessary."

"For once," Morrow said, "I cannot agree with you. I think it is very necessary." He shook hands with Zúñiga, and turned to say good-bye to the others.

From Villamor, to his surprise, he got a friendly comment spoken with deep sincerity. "I understand you, señor capitán."

The others preferred a lighter attitude. "Understand an American?" asked Nicolás. "I wonder!" There was a little laughter. "At least, I shall never understand an americana. Señor capitán, ask my father what he has promised to Señorita Leslie."

Don Florencio smiled, shaking his head in amazement at himself. "I cannot believe it myself. When the pulajanes are cleaned out, and people can again pay their taxes, and the municipality is rich, the first new thing we will buy will be a water-closet for the school. No. Two of them. One for the boys and one for the girls. And then she wants so many other things! And she has taught Elena to ask for things, too. Magtalisay will surely have the finest school in all the islands. We cannot help ourselves. And ask Señor Villamor what she has done to him."

Villamor shrugged. "I am her lawyer. So she manages my business. There is a small muchacho in my house. He is there, you understand, because of a debt. His father owes me money, so he places the boy in my house to work out

234

the payment. But the señorita americana says this is slavery."

Morrow nodded; he called it slavery, too. And Lucy with her simplicity and directness had seen it and named it. Lucy . . .

"So I have to let the boy go to school. So he eats and sleeps at my expense and does no work at all. I do not know what to do about it. Except perhaps I may tell her there are two such *muchachos* in my friend Paterno's house. Why should he escape trouble?"

There was more laughter, and at the same moment one of the servants slid open a window, letting in some gray light and a puff of air, fresh and cool. The tension in the room had eased. All the faces seemed friendly.

There was silence behind Morrow as he went down the stairs. He knew they would talk again after he was gone, and he wished he could hear what they would say. But he was somewhat cheered. If he had to be replaced soon, his successor would have a better start than he had had. Could a man do much more than that? It was an achievement, not great enough for pride, but not so poor as to be shameful.

He could be glad, too, that Lucy was in Punta Arenas, where she would be safe. And he had heard that Palmer was in Magtalisay, asking for a boat to take him to Tacloban or Catbalogan. Lucy was safe from Palmer, too. Thank God, there was no need to worry about her. He could not help regretting that he had said nothing to her the morning before, but perhaps it was just as well to let it stay in his heart. Time enough for that later, if there was time for anything.

5

THE rain had stopped, but it was chilly, almost raw. Underfoot, too, it was disagreeable, so wet and muddy that it seemed impossible the ground should ever dry out again. Yet the plaza held a crowd of people when the Constabulary marched in to the lively tune of *The Girl I Left Behind Me*, and more people kept coming.

The band was large in proportion to the number of soldados who followed it; the company was top-heavy with musical instruments. But no one could reproach them for that. Musician or not, there wasn't a man who didn't have a well-deserved reputation for bravery, and there wasn't a man who didn't know it. They carried themselves with pride as they marched to the center of the plaza, wheeled, and came to a halt. The music ended. They stood at ease and began to look about them.

Morrow, at one side, regarded them with pride even greater than their own. He knew what stuff they were made of, and he was grimly aware of the fact that on this dangerous and doubtful day, unarmed, they had followed him as unquestioningly as ever. The Pulay twin whose wound was not healing as it should had wanted to be brought down on a stretcher, and the soldados who had been chosen by lot to remain as sentries on the Escarpa were equally indignant about not being present. The rest, mud-spattered to the knees, clean and starched above, would rather have been where they were than in any other place in the world. Morrow's eyes lingered on their faces; he knew them all well and each man was dear to him.

Seeing Briones with Don Florencio and his family in the wide window of the Zúñiga house, Morrow crossed the plaza in their direction. Briones disappeared from above and met him as he approached the door. "We're here on the minute," Morrow said. "Faustino is on his way?"

"He should be. He understood the time. He was to be here almost simultaneously."

"You have talked to him again yourself?"

"I have. An hour ago. He had come as far as Sogod and was resting there. I have just returned, and he was to follow."

"Good. Then we shouldn't have long to wait."

He swung around to cross the plaza and rejoin his men, and to his astonishment saw Lucy come out of the door of the school, where a number of her pupils grouped themselves around her.

236

His delight at seeing her lasted for one unsteady breath, and then was lost in an agony of fear unlike anything he had ever felt for himself. Why hadn't she stayed in Punta Arenas? If the outlaws were planning treachery, anything might happen. Even this friendly crowd might change; who could foretell the temper of a mob? And she was here. She was looking at him with a smile. He had never seen her smile like that, and it was for him. He said, "Lucy, why did—how did—" and stopped, afraid he had shown his alarm. No one must know, she must not guess, what grave doubts he had.

"I just got back in time for this," she said. "Wasn't I lucky?" She looked tired; she looked older. She smiled at him, and he was warmed but not dazzled. Yet the radiance was there; it was all hers; she had borrowed none of it. "I can see you when this is over?"

"Watch from the window up there, Lucy."

"But I couldn't see enough up there. The trees hide so much of the plaza."

"If you're up there, I'll know exactly where to look for you." He saw her open her lips to question or protest, and he added a little desperately, "I think this is the first favor I ever asked of you."

"Yes, I noticed." She was not smiling now, and her eyes were startled and aware. "I'm beginning at last to understand you. Did you think that I could never learn?" With a gesture she gathered her pupils behind her and re-entered the school, but inside the door she turned and found him watching her. She wanted to run to him; she wanted to cry that wherever he was, she was too, that knowing he was in danger was the worst peril she could face. She dared say nothing. She pressed her hand to her breast as if to stifle the pain in her heart. He seemed to nod, and he motioned to her to close the door. She obeyed.

The crowd had grown larger. Morrow saw Palmer, lounging against a wall. There were the Johnstones, all dressed up; it was the only time Morrow had ever seen the sergeant in his complete uniform. But that was not for the ceremony of the surrender; it was because this day they expected to sail away forever from Magtalisay. There

237

was no sign yet of Faustino, and the people were growing restless. Morrow signaled and the band played again. An admiring group of boys approached the soldados, and a naked baby, just learning to walk, followed them. He stood up, staggered, fell, and crawled; stood up, staggered, fell, and crawled, in a rhythm that roughly matched the music. Everyone laughed. But eyes kept turning from one to another of the streets leading to the plaza. The sun came out, low in the sky, tinting the clouds above a soft coral, and giving to everything beneath, the church, the houses, the light clothes of the men and women, a glow of delicate green.

Again everyone was quiet as the band came to the end of its selection. The group of boys dissolved. A shrill whistle announced that the government cutter was about to drop anchor in the bay. There was a murmur of voices, but no one left the plaza. On ordinary days the whole town turned out to watch arrivals and departures, but on this day they had something better to hold their attention.

But Morrow began to wonder if the arrival of the small ship had been interpreted as bad faith on his part, and if, consequently, all the plans had fallen through. Everyone must know that a new Constabulary officer was expected. Faustino and Ola might believe that Morrow had arranged his arrival for this time, though Morrow had learned only at noon that the cutter would reach Magtalisay that day.

Then suddenly he knew that Faustino was near. The knowledge did not seem to originate in any one person who had seen or heard anything; it seemed to be the possession of everyone at once. All, Morrow included, found their attention centered on the street that reached the plaza at the corner of the church. Still some distance away, a group of men was slowly approaching.

The soldados, obedient to orders, came to attention behind their officers. Over the heads of the silent crowd, the wind swayed the branches and rustled the leaves of the great banyans. This wait seemed longer than the earlier one.

There was no band preceding Faustino and his men with music. They did not march in files but walked in a group. As they came nearer, Morrow saw nothing about them to indicate that they had ever been desperate and lawless. Except for the two leading figures, they might have mingled in the crowd and so have lost at once their identity as *pulajanes*. There were not sixteen of them, however, but only half that many.

The two who led might have hidden in a crowd, but could never have been absorbed by it; they were different. Morrow knew Ola from Briones' description. This most dreaded of the outlaws walked like a tiger, with controlled power and wariness in every step. But his pace was checked by that of the man beside him.

And this was Faustino, el papa Faustino. He was a small man, dressed in a sort of white robe that hung in loose folds yet did not conceal the emaciation of his body. Though he could not, as Briones' brother, have been very old, his hair was white and his face was deeply wrinkled; he might more easily have been thought El Cojo's grandfather. In his thin, mummy-like arms he carried a box of black wood, carved and polished; it was borne as an object of the utmost preciousness and veneration. His slow steps, Morrow thought, must be due to weakness rather than to deliberate design, for as he came close a restless brilliance could be seen in his eyes, and a feverish impatience in the frequent turns and nods of his head, proving an inner longing for haste and action.

"Americano!" he cried. "I have brought it, here in this arca, so that you and I and the god can guard it for the people." His thin voice, pitched high, rose shrilly. "Independencia! Independencia for all the people! I carry it here, safely closed in, waiting for the day when the people should have it. Is that day today, americano? Is this the day?"

Morrow knew then something that had never entered his mind before. Here was neither saint nor devil, neither pope nor bandit, but an inhabitant of an enchanted world, some of the spell of which he was able, by his own belief and devotion, to cast over others whose aspirations and ignorance had combined to make him their idol. He was a visionary who had crossed the line to madness. It was easy for Morrow to see why he had been powerful, why he had been called holy, and how he had been used. And now, too, Morrow could understand why he himself had almost doubted the man's existence. Faustino had seemed unreal because he had lost touch with reality; he was less a person than a symbol and a tool.

"Independencia is in this box," Faustino's voice went on. "And here are the names of our president and of our cabinet and of all our members, written in their own blood." From the folds of his robe over his heart he drew out a roll of heavy paper.

Morrow could feel the people all around the plaza as their suspense pressed in on him; yet they seemed to draw away, too, leaving him and Faustino and the mysterious box isolated by respect and fear.

"Captain White Moro," Faustino said, "you will put your name here too. You will help me guard Independencia for my people." He held box and paper out to Morrow.

With his hand outstretched, Morrow stepped forward to meet the small robed figure.

He heard the shot and saw the blood on his wrist at the same moment. In the long second before he felt any pain, in that space of time both brief and strangely protracted, thoughts and impressions assailed him rapidly, fleetingly, in no logical order. That cry was Lucy's. Who had fired the shot? Treachery! He had risked it, and it had come. No use reaching for a gun with a wrist like this. No use reaching for a gun that was not there. Why was Ola waving his arms and shouting? What were those answering shouts? Who were those men, armed with bolos, running toward his unarmed soldados? *Pulajanes?* Treachery! And young Rufino Zúñiga. What was he doing there, raised above the heads of the crowd? He must be on a window ledge. Was he aiming a rifle? Then it was he who had fired! Treachery!

As Morrow felt the pain from the first bullet, the second one came. He staggered as it hit his chest. With his good hand he touched the spot and incredulously felt the warm dampness of his tunic. He thought: So bullets have

240

reached me at last. He thought: So one eye was all Rufino needed, after all. He was not sure whether he heard or imagined a cry in Rufino's voice: "Sic semper tyrannis!"

The confusion about him increased, and he stopped trying to understand. Everywhere the people were moving; it was like the boiling over of a gigantic pot. He turned toward the school, toward Lucy. He took a step and another and another, a little closer, a very little closer to her. He heard two more shots. His soldiers were shouting, meeting the men who wielded the bolos. His soldados, brave, faithful, but, at his order, without a single weapon. And Lucy . . . He must get to her . . .

He took another step, and fell.

6

HE was not lying on the ground.

He knew that first. It was a solitary discovery, with a disturbing element of surprise. Slowly then, almost cautiously, his awareness spread. It was very quiet, another strangeness, as if his ears had expected clamor. Each breath was pain; but that, somehow, was a matter of course, as if he had never known anything else. His arms seemed useless, heavy, inert, weighed down.

Were they bound?

With that question, he awoke to full consciousness, trying to move his hands, and opening his eyes. The yellow flame of a lamp shone through a mosquito net that everywhere else closed his vision inside its soft white wall. He was in a bed. His arms were bound with bandages.

Recollection swept over him with an agony worse than the pain of any wound. Faustino, Ola, the one-eyed Zúñiga, treachery, his soldiers unarmed . . .

White fingers lifted the edge of the net, and he caught the scent of violets. He tried to turn, and then her face was close to his, her hand was a cool, light touch on his forehead. Even before she spoke, some of the agony had left him.

She murmured, "I saw your eyes open. I've been waiting. I wanted to tell you at once that everything is all right. There's nothing to trouble you. Nothing. Nothing for you to regret."

"When?" His voice was empty. He could hardly hear it.

"Don't try to talk. Just let me tell you." Her words flowed softly but eagerly. "You've been here in bed since yesterday afternoon. Now it's nearly morning, almost time for the first cockcrow. Do you remember being in the plaza? When I got to you, you . . ." At the thought of that moment, when she had believed him dead, she had to stop. "You know it was Rufino who shot you? He was the first to be killed by your friends."

"Ola?" he whispered.

She had been bending over him. Now she knelt, letting the net drop behind her, so that she was enclosed with him and still nearer than before. "Ola escaped. He was the only one who did. Your soldiers and the people made a wall around you, and they fought the *pulajanes*. The people . . . Oh, it was a miracle! I wish you could have seen it! You would be proud! You will be. Everyone will tell you."

"Faustino?"

"Faustino is dead. No one is sure who shot him, but I think it must have been Harry. Harry was in the plaza, and he always wore a gun. But I didn't see him again, and he's gone now. You remember the government cutter was to call here yesterday afternoon?"

Fearfully he asked about Ramos.

"Wounded, but he will recover. Please, think of yourself. Get well; that's all you must think of, and all you must do." She touched his forehead again, lingeringly. "Forget your worries. They are over. I've been waiting here for the very minute you opened your eyes so that I could tell you." She made her words more deliberate and emphatic. "No worries. No regrets. Only pride. Won't you believe me?" In silence she watched him a moment. "That's better. You

242

see I can read your face and your eyes. It's taken me a long time, but I know you now."

He tried to say, "Lucy," and heard no sound.

But as if it were true that she could read his thoughts, she responded by laying her face lovingly against his, and then kissing him, shyly and quickly, on the cheek and on the lips. "I love you, how I love you!"

With astonishment and wonder he felt her tears, and then from the wonder, elation grew, and gratitude. Out of all, slowly, came peace, and in peace this interval of clarity dissolved.

Yet it was not lost. Through the long days and nights that followed, though consciousness was never complete, neither was oblivion absolute. Among the specters that surrounded him, Lucy was always real. In the vast emptiness where he sometimes found himself, he felt her love beckoning him.

Very gradually he made his way back to life, and at last awoke again to the reality of the white walls of the mosquito net. This time it was day, and he saw Lucy silhouetted against the brilliant square of the open window. She was standing at a table, her hands busy with something there. He heard her murmur to someone he could not see, "I don't like to disturb him, but the bandage must be changed, of course." When she turned toward the bed, he noticed how her shoulders drooped, and he saw a new fragility in the hand and arm that lifted the net.

He said, "You're thin. You're tired." His voice was weak, but it was his own again.

With a little cry she dropped on her knees beside the bed. "Is it true? Are you really here? Do you know me?"

There were a thousand things he wanted to say, but they would have to wait. He repeated, "You're tired."

"I never felt better in my life! Don't you understand how strong I am? I can stand anything in the world, if only I have you."

"You must rest."

She laughed at him. "Rest? Hearing your voice rests me enough. And that's a lucky thing. Because when they learn you're getting better, everyone will want to see you at once, and I'll have to stand guard. Because everyone wants to tell the White Moro he is their hero and they are his friends. Everyone wants to join the Constabulary. Everyone has been praying for you. Tell me, do I look tired now?"

There were lines that he had never seen before in her face, but it was true that she no longer seemed tired. Instead, she was more radiant than ever, with that luminous quality that he knew would always tempt and escape his pencil and paintbrush, and yet—this was the marvel—was for him. He lay gazing at her without replying.

"Because you are going to get well, aren't you?" Her laughter was gone. "You are going to stay with me?"

He saw anxiety threatening to return to her, and he wanted to answer quickly and fully. But a lifetime would be too short for all he wished to say, and all the languages he knew were too poor. He could do no more than make a beginning.

He said one word only. "Always!"

It was enough. Like the deep look that bound them together, it was a promise; and he could see in her eyes that he had told her everything.

ABOUT ELINOR CHAMBERLAIN

The early part of this century saw a new consciousness enter into American life—a consciousness which is only coming to its fullest growth now. In the early 1900's, as a result of the Spanish-American War, the United States assumed duties and responsibilities overseas.

Up to that time America's interests had not ranged much farther than her borders. Today, of course, after two world wars, after UNRRA, the Point Four Program, and the Marshall Plan, the idea of large-scale American service overseas is a fixed part of our national thinking; but this is where it started—in the Philippines, over fifty years ago.

This novel takes place in those islands at that time when that idea was coming into being.

Elinor Chamberlain was born a long way from the Philippines, in Muskegon, Michigan, in 1901; she reached the islands at the age of twenty-one. This was about a year after she was graduated from the University of Michigan; and she became a teacher of English in the University of the Philippines.

"This was a peaceful period in the islands," she writes, "but nature in the Far Eastern tropics always has unusual diversions in store to keep life uncertain. I grew familiar with typhoons and earthquakes; I saw a cholera epidemic conquered by modern methods of prevention; I lived for a time only a few feet from the edge of the jungle in a house shared with two charming American women and a changing assortment of ants, cockroaches, spiders as big as saucers, house lizards of various sizes, and snakes. The snakes I met personally were said to be harmless, but a king cobra had been killed in the living room shortly before I lived there, and I came home one afternoon just too late to see an eighteen-foot python caught and carried away by eighteen men—one for each foot of its length—from the deep grass beside the veranda.

"I admit some of this frightened me a little, but in spite of such alarms I fell in love with the islands, and I had liked the Filipinos from the start. I wanted to put this feeling in a book, along with my pride in the ideals and the labor of the courageous Americans who saw a chance to make the Philippines the leader of the Orient, and the home of a healthy, happy, self-governed people."

This is the book, but it has taken a long time to get written. Other things have interfered. Miss Chamberlain traveled in China, Japan, and Korea, to Singapore, Java, Borneo, and the southern Philippines. Then she came back to the United States, where she spent a number of years as a dietitian, cook, gardener, chauffeur, valet, nurse, plumber, electrician, general handyman, upholsterer, dressmaker, purchasing agent, and entertainer, or, in a word, a housewife, and brought up two children, who are at present in college. She still goes to school herself now and then. This year she is enrolled at Columbia University, where she has studied before, and not long ago she was a graduate student at the University of Michigan, where an early version of this novel won a major Hopwood award for fiction.

Miss Chamberlain goes on to say, "In a sense this is a first novel, as my three previously published books were in the mystery field. Mystery novels preserve an old convention of novel writing. They tell a story. It is a convention I believe in strongly; I think a writer owes the reader a story. This novel tells a story, too. There are many more stories to be told about the Philippines, and I expect to tell some of them.

"I hope to be able to return to the Far East for two purposes, to see what it looks like there today and to satisfy some of my appetite for travel. But the journey may be delayed. I have just settled into an apartment in New York, and I'm considering the adoption of a cat. Cats and travel, both of which I love, don't really mix well. My life, I have learned, is made up of incompatible tastes like this. I am fascinated by science fiction, but it has to compete with Pilgrim's Progress or The Faerie Queene for my time. I claim that I enjoy solitude, but if there's a chance to go to the horse races, I am at the rail. I would like to live in the tropics, but I cannot get along without autumn, spring, and a snowfall or two. This confusion should probably be blamed on my combination of French, Irish, and Puritan ancestry, and I suppose the only way to straighten things out would be to exchange my grandparents for four of a kind."

BALLANTINE BOOKS · 404 Fifth Ave., New York 18, N.Y.

9. THE RED GATE by LaSelle Gilman

An illuminating suspense novel set in Korea and China *now*. "It rises as much above the usual suspense story as an Ambler novel does."—*New York Journal-American*

10. CONCANNON by Frank O'Rourke

A two-fisted action novel of a railroad detective in Dakota by the author of *Blackwater* and *Action at Three Peaks*. "Will delight every mystery and adventure fan."—*Wichita Eagle*

11. *WAR BONNET by Clay Fisher

Western historical of pioneers and Indians in Wyoming. Clay Fisher has also written *Red Blizzard* and *Santa Fe Passage*. "...a stirring tale of loyalty and courage, love and war...that will delight and entertain."—*Montgomery, Alabama, Advertiser*

12. HEYDAY by W. M. Spackman

The portrait of a desperate generation by a talented new novelist. "Exciting, sometimes brilliant."—*W. G. Rogers, Associated Press*

13. *FIRST BLOOD by Jack Schaefer

Superlative Western by the author of *Shane* in which a young deputy becomes a man. *"First Blood* confirms the promise of *Shane.* Mr. Schaefer has what it takes."—*Omaha World-Herald*

14. WHY DID THEY KILL? by John Bartlow Martin

The author of *Butcher's Dozen*, a great reporter, presents the grimly important case-history of three boys—outwardly just like the kids in your neighborhood—who committed a brutal murder. "Mr. Martin is a talented, thorough writer who brings total reality to his work."—*The New York Times*

15. THE WHEEL AND THE HEARTH by Lucia Moore

An epic of the daring women who helped to win the West. "She tells the story...tenderly and with skillful development." —*The New York Times*

16. STAR SCIENCE-FICTION STORIES
edited by Frederik Pohl

Fifteen fine short stories—never before published anywhere—by such masters as Ray Bradbury, Henry Kuttner and C. L. Moore, Murray Leinster, Lester del Rey, Judith Merril, and many others. "They are really exceptional stories, brilliantly written, and the best argument for the increase in science-fiction reading put out to date."—*Pensacola, Florida, News*

---

*A HOUGHTON MIFFLIN book, co-published with BALLANTINE BOOKS

Paperbound editions of these books are distributed by BALLANTINE BOOKS

BALLANTINE BOOKS · 404 Fifth Ave., New York 18, N.Y.

17. THE RACER by Hans Ruesch
A mature, sophisticated sports novel about European auto-race drivers by the author of *Top of the World*.

18. KINGDOM OF THE SPUR by Gene Markey
A large-scale Western historical of a Texan who rode south of the border to fight for a cattle empire.

19. STORIES OF SUDDEN TRUTH
edited by Joseph I. Greene and Elizabeth Abell
An anthology of fine modern short stories, all of which explore various aspects of self-realization and self-knowledge. Authors represented include John Hersey, Eudora Welty, Frank O'Connor, Arthur Miller, and sixteen others.

20. #I THOUGHT OF DAISY by Edmund Wilson
A vivid novel of the Twenties by one of America's great writers.

21. THE SPACE MERCHANTS
by Frederik Pohl and C. M. Kornbluth
A novel of the future—when the advertising agencies take over.

22. *THE BIG RANGE by Jack Schaefer
Ten magnificent stories of the western frontier by the author of *First Blood*.

23. *PATROL by Fred Majdalany
A truthful and memorable novel about the courage of ordinary soldiers.

24. DESERT PASSAGE by Richard Poole
Arizona—the fight for the stage-coach lines.

25. THE UNDYING FIRE by Fletcher Pratt
The story of a dramatic quest in outer space, by a master of science fiction.

26. THE CITY OF ANGER by William Manchester
A towering and intense novel of the warring worlds within an American city.

27. SUMMER STREET by Hal Ellson
The penetrating account of an adolescent's sudden maturing, by the author of *The Golden Spike*.

28. THE SECRET MASTERS by Gerald Kersh
This famous author tells a fine suspense story—of a few men who wanted the world for themselves.

---

*A. HOUGHTON MIFFLIN book, co-published with BALLANTINE BOOKS
#A FARRAR, STRAUS & YOUNG book, co-published with BALLANTINE BOOKS
Paperbound editions of these books are distributed by BALLANTINE BOOKS

ABOUT BALLANTINE BOOKS

This company publishes new books (not reprints)
of high quality—in two simultaneous editions:
paperbound and hardbound. The former are priced
at 35c or 50c, the latter at $1.50 to $3.00. Available
at all newsstands and bookstores.

"*. . . One thing is fairly sure; either this scheme,
or some other related to it, is going to revolutionize
the book trade. And 'revolutionize' is not too strong
a word in my opinion.*"
—Joseph Henry Jackson, *San Francisco Chronicle*

January 4, 1953

BALLANTINE BOOKS, INC.
404 Fifth Avenue • New York 18, N.Y.